The Unfinished Story

Caroline Greville

© 2021 Caroline Greville

Faithbuilders Publishing
12 Dukes Court, Bognor Road Chichester,
PO19 8FX, United Kingdom
www.faithbuilderspublishing.com

ISBN: 978-1-913181-67-3

All rights reserved. No Part of this Publication may be reproduced, stored in a retrieval system, or transmitted in any form or by any means without the prior permission of the publisher.

British Library Cataloguing in Publication Data. A catalogue record for this book is available from the British Library

Unless otherwise stated all scripture quotations are taken from the Holy Bible, New International Version® Anglicized, NIV® Copyright © 1979, 1984, 2011 by Biblica, Inc.® Used by permission. All rights reserved worldwide.

Scripture quotations marked NLT are taken from the *Holy Bible*, New Living Translation, copyright © 1996, 2004, 2015 by Tyndale House Foundation. Used by permission of Tyndale House Publishers, Inc., Carol Stream, Illinois 60188. All rights reserved.

Formatted by Faithbuilders Publishing
Cover by Esther Kotecha, EK Design
Printed in the United Kingdom

Contents

Four locations, each with their own unique challenges, that together demonstrate the unceasing mission of the church; our collective unfinished story, to be completed on the Lord's return.

Dedication 5
Acknowledgments 7
Endorsements 9
Preface 11

JOPPA

Chapter One 13
Chapter Two 19
Chapter Three 23
Chapter Four 29
Chapter Five 37
Chapter Six 47
Chapter Seven 57
Chapter Eight 65
Chapter Nine 73
Chapter Ten 77

JERUSALEM

Chapter One 83
Chapter Two 93
Chapter Three 101
Chapter Four 111

MACEDONIA

Chapter One 127

Chapter Two 135

Chapter Three 143

EPHESUS

Chapter One 195

Chapter Two 205

Chapter Three 213

Chapter Four 233

Resources 252

Dedication

For Christ followers, everywhere

Acknowledgments

Writing this book has been quite the journey, and thanks must go, first of all, to my family who've allowed me space to live and breathe these stories. Rupert, Annie, Maddy, Eliott and Jemima, you are an inspiration – as always – and you may just find elements of yourselves in some of my characters this time!

Thanks too to those we've been called to foster. Researching this book confirmed to me how welcoming others into our families is always on the heart of God.

Grateful thanks to my publisher, Faithbuilders. David, Laura and Joanna, you have been a pleasure to work with once again.

Thank you to my local ACW group for your feedback on selected stories, and especially to Bobbie Ann Cole, for her reading and endorsement of the book. You are a very special group of people! Thank you too to Grace Turner, for downing tools to read and endorse – your approval means so very much to me, and to Carolyn Oulton, for your sensitive reading and endorsement once again. Having such kind and incredible readers is a big help.

Finally, thank you to my wonderful readers of *Gospel Voices* who have encouraged me to write another volume. I really hope you enjoy this one!

Endorsements

Just as Gospel Voices brings fresh perspective and vibrancy to our reading of the Gospels, The Unfinished Story brings us right into the lives, the fresh faith, the challenges and sacrifices of the early Church in the days of the book of Acts.

I think this is a must-read for Christians in the 21st century church! We face different cultural and social standards, but new believers entering our churches (just like those in Joppa, Jerusalem, Macedonia & Ephesus) either come without previous Christian experience and background, or are often affected by other current religious or identity political issues.

There is much for us to learn from the early church in a now post-Christian society. Caroline Greville is that rare thing, a skilled story-teller and dynamic teacher. She challenges us through these glimpses of the early church, to live more bravely, to trust more deeply and to rescue the poor, the outcasts and the hurting. These stories could, and should, be our stories, because Jesus is the same today as he was then and will be forever.

-Grace Turner, Senior Pastor, RiverLife Church, Bern

Caroline Greville opens up the world of early Christianity, 2000 years ago, through relatable characters that we come to care about, and she does it with a delicate touch.

-Bobbie Ann Cole, Christian writer, speaker and writing teacher

In this companion volume to Gospel Voices, Caroline Greville introduces us to a new cast of characters – all of whom are struggling to make sense of the world they live in. In The Unfinished Story we meet a good man who just isn't very good at being a father as his children hit the teenage years, a woman struggling to come to terms with her husband's infidelity, and the less than sexy reality of coping with illness in old age. There are urgent questions and no easy answers. But this mosaic of stories assures us of one thing: 'We know how God feels about us – he's shown it.'

-Prof. Carolyn Oulton, Subject Lead Creative and Professional Writing, Canterbury Christ Church University

Preface

What did life in the Early Church look like, when Jesus's legacy was fresh, and his physical presence, for some, a living memory? The Book of Acts has been our go-to source as Christians – and rightly so – but we are not discrediting the Bible when we explore issues it doesn't mention. There are actions of the Early Church written widely of elsewhere, indisputable historical details that speak loudly to us today; the abandonment of babies and children is one such topic.

We have all heard sermons on how the believers 'met together in one place and shared everything they had' (Acts 2:42-47); *extreme*, we may think, and *irrelevant now*, and perhaps *a little off-putting*, so we don't stay with these characters long. But we are missing out on much if our understanding stops here. (Besides, this approach to life is only noted for the believers in Jerusalem.) So, what else were the believers doing? And how would that look today?

Please read the Bible passage listed for each location before you read its story. While Bible characters and events do feature in what I write, it's important to me that you see the given facts ahead of entering my imagined versions of these places. The stories have been researched to bring plausibility and genuine challenge to the reader. As with *Gospel Voices*, I hope what you read will take you deeper in your own study and enrich your understanding of God's character.

Pure and genuine religion in the sight of God the Father means caring for orphans and widows in their distress and refusing to let the world corrupt you.

James 1:27

Leader of the Early Church in Jerusalem

JOPPA
Acts 9:36-43

Chapter One

'Where am I?' you say, your hands searching the floor around you as you sit up on the divan. You rub your eyes with vigour, then open them wide, searching the room for a familiar face. You won't find one.

'Ah!' says my husband, dropping his wooden cup on the floor and turning to face you. 'You're in Joppa. You were shipwrecked, we think,' he tells you.

'Joppa?'

'You've been unconscious for days, you're lucky to be here,' he explains. 'Well! You're awake at last.'

You don't look as if you feel lucky and roll on your knees as if to stand. You wince with pain and sit back on your mattress, defeated. I pass my husband a bolster cushion which he puts behind your back, before lingering beside you. I am familiar with his awkward ways, as he runs his fingers through his untidy curls, then blows into his hands for warmth. He claps them together, crouches beside you, then stands up again. It's a wonder he's been able to cope with your coma, such is his boundless energy, coupled with his incessant need to communicate.

A baby cries from the basket on the other side of the room and I stoop to pick her up, placing her little body against my chest and feeling her small fists give me a pounding. You look startled, as if her presence triggers a remembrance in you.

'Where are you from?' I ask, raising the question that has long been on our lips.

You look disturbed by my asking and shake your head.

A long silence follows, during which your eyes fix on the cup that has rolled across the floor.

'Give him a chance!' says my husband at last.

'I don't know – I can't remember. Wish I could.'

He sits beside you now and puts a hand on your back. 'No one else was found that day. You were fortunate! And the memories will soon come back. Just don't put pressure on yourself. Give it time.'

'Fortunate?' you say, and reach for the blanket to cover your legs, but stop halfway, your hand retreating to your ribs that you now clutch, as if by holding them you can take away the pain. 'I don't call *this* fortunate. I don't know who I am, where I'm from – don't even know my name.'

'Ah! The Lord does and we'll pray to him,' rejoins my husband, taking the baby from me and jogging on the spot, in an attempt to lessen her tears. Her tiny head wobbles as she looks at me from over his shoulder. I reach for the cup on the floor so that he doesn't kick it, placing it on the shelf by the door.

'The Lord? You make no sense to me. But I'd like to know about *you* both. What keeps you here, what lives you lead. And tell me where you found me – in what state?'

'Of course,' I say. 'Let's get something inside you, and as you eat and drink, we'll talk.'

'The Lord,' you mutter under your breath. 'You're not from the *Way*, are you?'

'Well! What if we are?' my husband replies.

'Only I've heard things. Grim things,' you say, looking around you with a new nervousness.

'It's all gossip. Lies,' I say. 'Stay with us a while and you'll see.'

'Don't have much choice at the moment, do I?'

I pour you a cup of water from the stone pitcher and hold it to your lips. 'We have stew from earlier, and bread that's almost ready.'

'I'm not sure he'll be able to chew,' says my husband, and then to you, 'The bruising on your face is considerable. Take things slowly – we're in no hurry to see you go.'

You stare into our faces and I think you can see that we are trustworthy. All the gossip really gets me down. I have no idea why such terrible things are said about us, though it helps to know we're never alone. I couldn't live like this for a less noble cause.

'Don't know why you keep me here,' you say, and you sigh long and deep, hunching your shoulders and resting your head on your knees for a brief moment before staring at us again and going on. 'For what purpose? I cannot repay you, you know. It'll be weeks before I can even start to earn my keep.'

'We want nothing from you,' I tell you. 'Relax.'

I lift the old stone pot onto the fire that's burning and inhale its warm scent. Perhaps it will be too spicy for you, so I add more water to thin the broth as my husband begins.

'Well, you were found down on the rocks ten days ago. You were unconscious even then, your body covered in gashes, your scalp raw in places from where you'd been thrown against the crags by the strong waves.' You touch your head now to confirm that this is true. 'You were all but naked, though we know you wouldn't have set off that way. We've clothed you, even managed to get some water into you, with difficulty. To be honest, we didn't know if you'd pull through. Of course, we've been praying for you. All the believers have – you are very well-known in Joppa; news of your recovery will bring much rejoicing.'

You manage a weak smile and prop yourself up on one elbow. Crying is coming from the back room and I am feeling the pressure. 'Your meal is almost ready,' I say. 'John, can you stir this? I should go to them. Sounds like they've both woken.'

'No bread this time,' you say.

I return with a baby in each arm; the newest, youngest addition is back in her basket and kicking her legs with renewed energy. John tastes the broth and pours some into a clay bowl. 'It's good,' he announces to you, putting down the small jug on a stand by the fire, ready for the next serving. 'My wife is an excellent cook.'

'She's very young to be a mother of so many little ones,' you say, your voice raspy. 'Don't know how you manage it all,' you finish between coughs.

I laugh. 'Oh, they're not all mine – ours, I should say. Well, they are.'

You look confused and listen with wide eyes as John begins to feed you, the bowl of broth lifted slowly to your lips for you to sip. 'I mean, I didn't bear them.' You pull back from the broth, the sensation of food on your tongue a shock after so many days. 'They were abandoned,' I tell you. 'We are bringing them up as our own.'

'That's very noble,' you say, a shiver running through you as the broth warms you from the inside.

'Not really. John, there was talk of another dead infant found yesterday.'

'Ah! It doesn't surprise me,' says my husband. 'We should have a system going, a list of some sort where we all take turns. These unseasonably cold nights aren't helping. We must talk about it when we gather later. The Lord won't like it – it's his will that not one suffers.'

***

15

I am all too aware of the widows in our community and tell Tabitha to inform the others of this new development. By evening they all know, and a deputation arrives, keen to meet you. Unfortunately, you are asleep again, worn out by the effort of speaking to us for so long. I feel sure you will wake again, but for now we talk around you in hushed voices.

Penelope is pushed to the front of the group and we wait for her to speak. She is the only one with a missing husband, though we know the chances are very slim. She twists her plaited belt cord around her fingers repeatedly before speaking, and her fingertips start to turn red. 'It's not him,' she says, finally, and with great assurance.

'Look at him more closely,' I say. 'You can kneel in front of him. You won't disturb him, he's a deep sleeper,' I tell her with a smile. Instead, she backs off and Tabitha, our old friend, places an arm across her shoulder.

'His nails are beautiful,' I comment in the awkward silence.

'Such soft looking hands,' adds one of the older women. 'Like young girls' hands. Never done a hard day's work in his life, I'll say.' She glances at her own and I can see they are dry and cracked, like ancient leather left to disintegrate in the sun, all forgotten. 'What I'd give for his hands.'

'He looks a bit like your John,' says Xanthe. 'It's the hair I think, what's left of it – and the build. Looks like his body forgot to fill out and spent all its energy in growing up.' The resemblance hadn't gone unnoticed by me, but I simply nod in agreement. Seeing you lying as if dead on our floor has brought me up short once or twice.

'I'm surprised the babies didn't wake him from his coma much sooner,' says Tabitha, and we all laugh, glad of the mention of normality. Penelope is shedding quiet tears, though, and the comment causes her to sniff hard. 'Come on now, don't worry,' we tell her. I feel bad but we're just trying to lighten things. Life is always so intense around here.

'I don't know why I got my hopes up,' she says, her deep brown eyes all staring and vulnerable. She looks too young to bear such pain, though her beauty means she'll always be looked after in this life. 'Oh, this is just so awful. I don't think I'll ever see him again.'

'Come on now,' Tabitha replies. 'You mustn't think like that. You should come back with me this evening. I'll give you something to eat, then perhaps you'd like to stay the night.'

'What if he returns and Penelope isn't home?' asks Sarai.

'He'll have done well to find her in Joppa,' says one hardened by widowhood; not the most sensitive soul. 'But word will reach her soon enough,' she goes on. 'We have to think about her needs right now.'

'She came to the nearest port – it makes sense to wait at the place he departed from,' says Tabitha.

Penelope's tears have really taken hold and now she's sobbing.

'It's okay,' I tell her. 'It will be okay, just take one day at a time.'

'I've very little money left,' she whispers to me. 'I'm not sure how I'm going to make ends meet. It was hard enough when we were together, but now – I don't know what to do.' She's twisting her plaited belt cord again distractedly.

'Can you sew?' says Tabitha, hearing every word.

'Not very well.'

'Well, I can teach you,' she replies, taking her young hands into her own. 'I can provide you with some work, and the believers will support you where they can. You're really not alone, you know.'

'But I'm not one of you,' says Penelope, pulling back her hands. 'You have enough of your own to help.'

'You're in need, aren't you?'

Penelope nods.

'Then you're one of ours. It doesn't matter what you believe. I think you'll find our God is trustworthy, but our help isn't dependent on this. We just want to see things come right for you.'

'Tabitha, I hate to ask, but can you check on Talia on your way past this evening?' I say. 'We haven't heard from her in a while, we just need to know she's okay. I've had my hands full here.'

'Of course,' she says. 'She always thinks she's a bother, that one. Leave it with me.'

Soon the little deputation departs, and we are left to ourselves. The babies are taking it in turns to cry and I'm starting to question the wisdom of taking on so many. John seems to know what I'm thinking.

'Well, we don't have to keep them all,' he says. 'There are plenty of couples in Joppa who can help. And they don't all have to stay in this town, either.'

'I can't let any of them go,' I tell him.

'We haven't even started a family of our own,' he says.

I raise a questioning brow at him. 'You sure about that? What do you call this lot?'

17

I look at the newest baby who is now asleep on my lap, arms thrown above her head, her little fists relaxed in sleep. 'I'm thinking, it's about time we gave her a name.'

'You sure? When they've got a name there really is no going back. She is the one I would give up – not Ruth or Charis. And they are little *people* now, babbling, nearly walking, and this new one – she's… Well, you k-'

'How about Anastasia?' 'For new life, resurrection.'

'Sleep on it. If she'll let you!'

'I think our guest may be waking, you stay in here with the babies, I'll see to him.'

Soon I shut my eyes and hang up my hospitality for the night. Any guests around here, any needy folk or travellers, won't pass my threshold, unless John welcomes them in, of course. It's hard when no one grasps my need for just a little quiet, but John is getting better. How difficult it is to distinguish the Lord's will sometimes, too, and to know when we've taken on too much. Yet everyone needs uninterrupted rest, and for now any sojourners must roam.

Chapter Two

On the edge of Joppa's Kedumim Square stand two figures, a couple perhaps, for they are engaged in deep conversation. We will draw closer. The time is early, not much past dawn, and looking intently at the woman now, we see that she has barely slept. She clings tightly to a bundle that she holds, her arms wrapped around it so that it cannot be taken.

'Walk away from her. I mean it – you must choose between us, Elena. I can't keep you both.'

The woman appears not to have heard.

'Elena!' shouts the man, with what seems to be a hatred in his voice, and too loudly at such close range, yet still she hesitates – 'You have one more chance with me.'

Then, at once, she puts down the bundle, which lets out a shrill cry as the stone floor replaces the warm arm that had held her close. It seems to the woman that the child is aware of its peril, and the wrench brings physical pain to her temples, that begin to throb.

'This is a safe place. She'll be found here, of course she will.'

'What if she becomes a slave? Or a prostitute – think on that!'

'The followers of the Way will find her. It's what they *do*. It makes them feel good about themselves.'

The man turns to go but the woman lingers. 'Let me hold her just once more,' and she bends down to pick up the child. 'She's reaching out for me – look, she has a fistful of my hair. You can't do this to us – it's too cruel!'

'We can't afford to keep her – not another girl. And that mark on her cheek – no one'll marry her! She'll be a burden forever more.'

'Oh, I can't bear it. And the day is so gloomy – it's starting to rain,' she says, pulling her grey woollen tunic close about her.

'You know the choice, woman. It's her or me.'

And so, she steps backwards, every throb of maternal instinct commanding her to stay, every thought for her own survival telling her to follow her husband. She would never release the child from her heart, for a mother never really lets go. Perhaps she will find her again in time. With that birthmark on her cheek, there is every hope that she will.

The couple make their way across the square, the man commanding his wife that she does not look back. The baby's cry now mingles with the shriek of petrels, for a catch has come in at the shore.

***

Just down a flight of steps from here and along a narrow, cobbled side street is the house of Talia. Tabitha had forgotten to knock the previous night, such was her preoccupation with Penelope, but now that it's first light, she calls by, as she had promised.

'Oh, Talia! It's Tabitha. May I come in?'

There is no answer, so Tabitha calls again. Hearing no response, she pushes open the door, to find the old lady shivering in a corner, blankets wrapped around her, though her face is flushed and sweat gleams from her brow.

'Tali, it's Tabitha,' she says, crouching down beside her. 'You are quite unwell – you have a fever! You must let me look after you.'

She sets to work, enabling her friend to sip water, dabbing her brow with a wet cloth, removing bedding, washing dishes, sweeping the floor, until a couple of hours have passed.

At last, confident that she is comfortable and out of danger, Tabitha sets off for home, returning via the town square just in case another infant is in need of care.

It is the manner of things that the believers habitually keep an eye on the square, not always wanting to, for fear of what they might find, but taking it as their responsibility. It has become known in their circle as 'the place of wishes'[1], for it's understood that this abandonment is not the will of both parents in most cases, and, whatever the intentions of the parents, the children are loved by God and in need of care.

Here, as she had feared, lies another bundle on the low wall, wrapped with tight and neat precision, in a last moment of devotion.

---

[1] Place of Wishes, Joppa. The Zodiac Fountain in Joppa's Kedumim Square is said to be on the spot of an ancient wishing well. There is now also a 'Wishing Bridge' close to the square. In my story the location is the site of many women's wishings and longings, for the safety of the children they felt compelled to abandon. The well had not been built, but I have imagined its origins.

The covering is thick and the child's face is lost inside a deep hood, yet it offers her no protection, for it's saturated from the morning's early downpour. 'Shalom, little one,' she says in a quiet voice. It makes her feel cross, that children are deemed so worthless. Never having been a mother herself, she finds it hard to handle these small ones, to even know where to start – the widows are her concern, and that everyone has different roles within the church is understood. She would have to take the child to Mim and John's house, and they would look after her in the short term, or know where to send her.

As she bends over the child and peers at her, wondering how heavy she'll be and whether she'll be able to carry her all the way to Mim's, she finds herself somewhat startled. Two beautiful, dark liquid eyes look back at her, staring directly into her own as if imploring her to help. It is surprising she is not crying or showing any signs of distress, especially as she's wrapped in all this wet cloth, which Tabitha loosens gently. But this is not the reason why she reacts so. For the child has a large mark on her right cheek, so large that it reaches from beneath her eye all the way down to her jaw. It is raised and angry, the likes of which she's never seen before. Tabitha feels doubly sorry for the girl and determined that she will find her a good home herself, if she needs to. But what makes parents think they can pick and choose? Demand physical perfection, or reject a child because of a disability or simply its gender? Tabitha knows that while she's not articulate in expressing her faith, or convincing in debate, she can at least demonstrate God's love and mercy in the way she lives. In fact, she will keep hold of this little one for a while. Why should she say she can't deal with children? If she doesn't try, she'll never learn.

Tabitha picks up the child and tucks her under her cloak to keep her warm. Too many infants don't survive, even with the care they are given, due to their exposure to the elements. She feels quite weary after helping Talia and will be pleased to reach home, though now it won't be as restful as she was anticipating, and she sets herself a brisk pace, peeping inside her cloak at intervals and humming to the child her favourite hymn. 'O son of God, giver of life,'[2] she sings, when

---

[2] There are records of a few ancient hymns, thought to have been sung by the early church. The line 'O Son of God, Giver of Life' is from the lamp-lighting hymn 'O Gladsome Light'. We cannot be sure how early this was sung, but it

the content touches her spirit. Her God is the sustainer of all things – surely this one will be okay? The child quietens and she stops to check on her, such is her anxiety for her survival. But then she collides with something, someone – 'My goodness, I am sorry,' she says, looking up at the local tanner. To be honest, she had smelt him before she had seen him.

He gestures an apology by shrugging his shoulders and lifting his hands into the air. She is trying not to judge him – it's only fair that he comes into the town from time to time, though of course he wouldn't be allowed to live here. His is a filthy occupation, and no doubt he has come in early in the hope he won't encounter too many people; few would be as polite to him as she. 'Shalom,' she says, and he returns the greeting, smiling kindly before apparently remembering his position. His eyes are bright and there is a warmth about him, despite the shabbiness of his appearance. She wonders what the state of his faith must be, without the possibility of worshipping corporately. Could the men in her community show him some kindness, perhaps bend the usual rules a little? And whose rules are they, anyway? Is there ever an outcast with God? She must pray for him and ask God to reach him in whatever way he can.

She doesn't feel polluted by their collision, of this she is sure – she is confident that sin comes from the inside – from a person's heart. She's heard enough of Jesus's teachings to know this, and she suspects that, had he visited Joppa, the tanner would be one of the few people he'd have sought out.

is a beautiful thing that the content of the song resonates through the centuries to us today. See also the Oxyrhynchus hymn if you are interested in this topic. The song itself is found at end of this story.

Chapter Three

'I've just had the most awful dream.' The words break into my thoughts and I put down the woven dress that I'm sewing to look at you – the seam is all wonky anyway. You seem disorientated like before, your eyes wide and unblinking as in the earliest days of your stay. You are seriously troubled, and I can't help thinking again of how you're an intense, anguished version of John.

'No! What was that, my friend?' John says to you, putting Ruth down on the floor next to a bundle of empty shuttles, playthings from the weaving loom.

'All these women crowding round me,' you tell us, 'talking about me, wondering if I might be their husband. Ludicrous, wouldn't you say?'

Now my husband clears his throat and I shoot him a long look while I wind Anastasia on my shoulder. For once he seems lost for words. '*Tell him*,' I say.

'Well, you might have had a few visitors. It was a few days ago, mind – I'm surprised it should occur to you now.'

'What? Go on.'

Ruth stares up at you, the wooden shuttle in both hands that she sucks on and presses into her gums. You've reached for your stick and are attempting to stand, but give up and sit back down heavily, rubbing your sore leg with both hands.

'There are a number of widows in our community,' John explains, 'Or likely widows. You have to understand, one or two of them have missing husbands – they needed to be sure you're not their own. Some of these women have moved into Joppa. They'd heard of our friend Tabitha who'd help them, especially if they're without family.'

'Couldn't it have waited till I was awake?'

I can see how exasperated my husband looks, and, just for once, he's struggling for words. 'We've all been praying for you,' I say. 'That's the thing. Some of our group have lost sleep for you, even fasted. I think the suspense was too much for them and, to be fair, I did say they could come. It's just that you were asleep when they arrived.'

'Hardly makes me feel any better. So these women sat gazing at me in my sleep?' you say, staring back at Ruth who is refusing to blink.

'It's really not as it sounds,' I tell you.

Now you are on your feet and you don't look steady.

'Where are you going?' asks John.

'I don't know.'

You sit back down again with a heavy sigh and punch the floor a little too hard. You look shocked at yourself and I turn away to open the shutters, allowing the daylight to flood in.

'I could take you down to the harbour in a day or two, when your strength is back. See if it triggers a memory. Has *anything* come back yet?' says John, 'even the slightest thing?'

'Nothing. Nothing at all. I'm thinking, in the short term, could you give me a new name? Only a temporary one, mind. My lack of name makes me such a curiosity. It is terrible! And I'm fed up with you calling me "you".'

We nod in agreement.

'And it's hard to remember anything – life is too fervent here. I feel I might remember if you could do something –'

'Of course,' we say.

'Just pretend I'm not here.' We must look confused at this request, so you go on. 'Or at least take the focus off me, just get on with life; ignore me as much as possible. I'll let you know if I remember anything.'

'How about Zachary, or Zac?' says my husband. 'It means "the Lord has remembered".'

'It'll do.'

'I think it's a good choice,' I say. 'You might have forgotten who you are, where you're from, but he hasn't. Just give it time and the rest will follow.'

***

Zac seems to be settling in now, though I worry about his family – he must have one, and how are they surviving with him away so long? It's been a couple of weeks now at least. I can't imagine life without John, the prospect is just unbearable. The babies are all sleeping now, and the house is quiet. I woke to Ruth's tears a while ago and I'm *still* awake – I know I must get back to sleep or I will be tired tomorrow and struggle to cope, which makes it harder to drift off. In my mind I see a row of babies and they are all crying out for me; I wish a few others in the church would share the same calling, yet I do love it. Charis whimpers in her sleep and I lay a hand on her and whisper soothing words that calm her – soon she is breathing next to me, rhythmically and deep.

'Shalom,' comes a call from outside. 'Mim, are you in there?'

They are in the yard already! Is there any thought for the babies or our guest? The voice is accompanied by a gentle tapping on the door, and I rush through to open it before Zac is disturbed, for he sleeps with his head against the doorframe, his feet in the centre of the room. 'Shalom!'

I open the door to Tabitha, her eyes dashing, her spirit all of a fluster. 'So sorry Mim, I did try with this one, but I need your help.'

I usher her inside and she pulls back her striped cloak to reveal a tiny infant who is clammy and still. 'I just can't do anything for her – at first she wouldn't be consoled, once I'd got her home, but now she won't be roused!'

'Bring her up to the rooftop,' I say. 'It will be okay, of course it will.'

The moon is bright and casts enough silver light for me to see the child. I sit down on the floor and place her in the cradle made from crossing my legs. 'She has a fever,' I say, touching her cheeks, then her brow. 'We must unwrap her and remove all this clothing.'

'She's been shivering,' Tabitha tells me, 'and her cry, it's so weak now, so feeble. I'm worried she won't pull through – I just can't do it on my own – I did try. She's been with me for a couple of days, and I really did want to look after her. I'm sorry Mim, I'm just –'

'Shush now, you go home and get some rest. I can see how tired you are. Why not call by tomorrow and see how we're getting on?'

She takes no more encouraging, which is unlike her, and makes her own way down the steps and out onto the street. I hear her coughing as she goes – and I didn't even think to ask after her, or offer her a drink. Still, things with this little one are pressing.

I place her on a rush mat on the floor beside me and feel each of her limbs with my hands – she barely whimpers, though the desire to be held must be real in her. There are no broken bones that I can feel, she is perfectly intact; perfectly beautiful too, though a birthmark that covers her cheek means she wouldn't have met someone's standards, hence the abandonment, I can only assume. I place a finger in her mouth – there isn't even the desire to suck, and she is all but lifeless.

I lift her with both hands and, placing her across my shoulder, rush down the steps to wake John. 'We have another baby,' I tell him.

'What?' he says, blinking away the night. 'Since when?'

'Since Tabitha arrived with her. She's really poorly and I worry she won't survive until morning. Can you take her back to the rooftop while I find the things we need? We must isolate her for now. I fear her illness may be contagious.'

Soon we are back on the rooftop, sponging her little body with cold water and trying to get some goat's milk into her that I drip through a grass reed. She is sucking now, clearly hungry, and at last I feel her grip my finger in her tiny fist. 'She's fighting,' I say. 'I like to think she'll make it. But keeping her away from the others will be hard.'

'Well, we'll manage! You need to get some rest now – go and join the girls and I'll take over till morning. You're going to feel exhausted at this rate.'

So I leave him to it, and creep into our room to sleep between the babies. To my amazement they haven't even stirred, and at last tiredness overcomes me.

I awake to bright sunlight and a room absent of children. 'John?' I call. He appears through the doorway, a baby on each hip. 'Where's the new one?' I say.

'Zac is on the roof with her. He says he wants to make himself useful and will be the one to nurture her.'

'It's chilly up there at this hour – it was fine for her fever, but it won't do –'

'Ah, don't worry! It's warm enough, I think. I'd scythed the grass only yesterday, now that it's spring.'

I sigh at his endless optimism and pull the blanket over my shoulders.

'We've plans –'

'Of course you have!'

'No, listen. Plans to construct a shelter up there – we'll bring her down when the worst has passed. He's happy you know, and it seems like the perfect solution. He says to leave his meals on the stairs and he'll collect them. He seems determined that if anyone gets ill from this, it'll be him.'

'Does he even know how to feed her?'

'I've shown him. And, to be honest, he seemed a natural.'

I raise an eyebrow at him.

'Ah, trust us, Mim! She's taken some mushed beans this morning, you know. I really think she's going to be okay.'

Solid food already? I simply smile back. Babies are good at leading the way, after all.

Ruth reaches out a chubby arm for me and I take her, and so another day begins.

Chapter Four

Tabitha is feeling quite unwell – no doubt caring for a small child has taken it out of her. Still, she can rest now, the baby will be well taken care of and she can just sleep herself into good health. If only she could have nurtured her and not given Mim and John yet another job... though you just can't risk it with young lives, and they always know what to do.

The journey home had taken a while and she'd needed to stop at regular intervals. She even thinks she might have slept. For was it not nighttime when she left them?

The exertion has made her cough worse and she pours herself a cup of water, then slumps against the wall to regain some strength. Perhaps she should sit on the roof – the sun is shining in Joppa today and it seems winter has well and truly passed – yet this isn't Joppa, is it? For it seems to be where she grew up, and her mother's voice is calling to her.

She makes for the stairs – crawling mind, for suddenly her room seems very dark, as if her sight is failing her. She needs air, fresh air, and a burst of sunshine. Then she will start to feel okay. She feels pain when she drops her head and her neck is very stiff. In fact, she really isn't well, and has never felt this way before. Her head is hurting now, and it means her very house seems unfamiliar – but is this the stairs? She just doesn't know any more. She feels so hot and there is pain every time she inhales... breathing feels very difficult – no matter how hard she tries, the breaths do not satisfy. She has found the bottom step though! That feels so familiar, and she smooths it with her hands, then crawls onto it, repeating the motion until at last she is on the top stair.

Her upper room is within reach ... once she finds her mattress on the floor in there she can just sleep. She has no responsibilities now today, no commitments. No one needs her. She can feel the threshold with her hands... it is hard to stay awake, but she is nearly there. The smell of incense that she placed on the side just a couple of days ago reassures her that this is indeed her special room. She knows her wicker sewing basket is behind the door, and can feel the edge of her quilt now, the one she'd spent months embroidering. She had prepared the room for Penelope recently, but she had refused to stay. But who is Penelope? And why can she not stop this cough? It's difficult to catch your breath when a cough takes hold as badly as this. Oh, she could sleep now. Oh, she could sleep. Dear Jesus, let her sleep.

***

It can be hard to know how to handle all the good will when you are grieving. People can seem so genuine, but in the midst of sorrow, just sometimes you want to be left alone. The most well-meaning people can be those we shun, and we may find ourselves drawn to those of our own choosing, when we feel ready to talk. So it is with Penelope, who appreciates the help of Tabitha and the other widows, but considers them too old to understand her, or really relate to her properly. Mim, on the other hand, isn't too intense. She has her house full of babies and that shipwrecked fellow, and just perhaps they could be useful to each other.

And so, we find her knocking on Mim's inner gate a few days after the widows' visit to the house. She waits in the cold, pulling her green cloak about herself, studying the knots and the swerves of grain in the door, when at last it opens to reveal Mim, one baby in hand, and another attempting to stand by grasping tight the drapes of her skirt.

'Penelope, oh shalom,' she says to her. 'It's so good to see you! I would invite you in, but we're nursing a very sick infant.'

Penn looks at the baby she is holding, who looks fine to her.

'Oh, no, not this one,' says Mim. 'We have her up on the roof, out of the way of the others.'

'Can I help? I have some experience with babies. I'm the oldest child from a very large family. I know h-'

'I would love you to, but I'm not sure it's wise. Would you mind checking on Tabitha though? She brought the infant to us a few days ago, and I remember her coughing as she left. It would put my mind at rest. Then come and tell me how she is – if you don't mind that is?'

'Of course, Mim, I'm happy to help.'

She doesn't think it was a brush off – not really. And it included an invitation to return. She does struggle with Tabitha though… She seems so intense; she has this ability to see right into her, and she empathizes just a little too much. Penn doubts she ever felt the anger that has been her experience since her husband disappeared. This one woman, the other widows claimed, had clothed them all in their hour of need. To be so perfect... It's not exactly human and well – it just makes her hard to relate to. And that's the other thing – labelling them all as 'the widows' as everyone does... from the moment she met them, it was this group identity. It's as if they're not individuals at all. That could be a self-fulfilling prophecy, if she joined them and become a part of their band. She would prefer to think that her husband is coming back.

Penn has spent the night at the lodging she'd been in for the last couple of weeks and, to be honest, perhaps if she had been with Tabitha she would have been a lot happier. The thing is, if they all turn out to be weird, these people of the Way, if it's some kind of extreme cult, as people claim, then she really could find herself stuck. From what she's seen of them, their faith plays out as a kind of lifestyle – you're all in, no half measures. And her husband may hate them all... it could cause such problems for them if he returns. The joy though – she's witnessed that... the more committed the person, the happier they seem. Illogical joy, when they are living in such challenging circumstances. Early days, to be making her mind up.

Joppa then ... What an intricate maze of little side streets and alleyways. Twelve paths leading off from the town square, and they all look alike. It could be beautiful, yet she'd rather not be here – she should be home with her husband, not roaming this place like some eternal nomad. They hadn't been married long when he disappeared, and this was the last soil he had trodden before his voyage. His family had begged her not to leave, but the waiting with nothing to do was killing her. She's decided now that if he doesn't return neither will she. In truth she was an inconvenience there on her own, and her brother-in-law had made it clear that they owed her nothing. Should she go back to her home village – and tell them what? She actually liked her husband, anyway...*likes* him. He is coming back, isn't he? Her parents wouldn't choose so well a second time, and who would have her? Damaged goods, and 'unlucky' now for any household. So Joppa it is, and to Tabitha's now... Surely her best hope for comfort and sustenance, after a little swallowed pride.

On reaching the square Penelope looks about her for the correct path – she has before found herself in the money changer's alley, quite by accident. A sailor looked her up and down like she was one of the prostitutes he was there to buy currency for, to pay for his 'visit'. She had turned and run then, as fast as she could without looking back. These narrow, crowded streets always make her feel so very far from home. The thing about Joppa is so many people are passing through – they say it's 'cosmopolitan' like that's a good thing. She isn't so sure.

Penn looks forward to the city walls closing them in at night, but of course those kept at bay could include her husband, if a ship were to bring him in late. But now the steepest cobbled slope seems to lead off in the right direction and she follows a couple of lively boys who are hitting each other with sticks. Tabitha's door is ajar and Penn pushes it gently before stepping inside.

An unpleasant smell is filling the downstairs room and the shutters are drawn. 'Tabitha! Tabitha!' she calls.

No response.

Her absence creates an uneasy feeling and the prospect of heading up the stairs alone is worrisome.

'Shalom!' calls a voice from the street and a woman follows her inside.

'I'm Penelope,' our friend explains. 'Tabitha has been looking out for me whi-'

'I've heard of you,' interrupts the woman. She doesn't look surprised. 'I'm just dropping off a donation of heavy shawls to be distributed – where is she?'

'She hasn't appeared yet,' Penn says.

'She must be up on the roof, getting some peace and quiet. She *is* hard of hearing. I can't stop, the family are waiting,' and with that she's out of the door and halfway down the hill.

'Stop, come back!' Penn calls, but it seems someone else is hard of hearing too.

There is nothing else for it, and Penn gathers her tunic folds in one hand and makes for the stairs, steadying herself with the other hand on the lime-painted wall as she climbs. She knows what she's going to find and the putrid smell intensifies as she reaches the top, as if to confirm what she's already grasped.

***

Penn is out the door and running up to the nearby square in the hope she'll find someone she recognizes. Why did she have to be the one who found her? She's had enough trauma just lately, and even that hangs over her, for hope battles with fear moment by moment inside her. Is that the state her husband is in right now? Has anyone found him, or is he floating on the sea, or submerged by it, oblivious to it all? But he's alive, of course he is, and she needs to think of Tabitha now.

To her relief she finds a couple of the women sitting and chatting on a low wall and she interrupts their conversation. 'It's Tabitha,' she says. 'You must come. She's passed away – cold as the winter sea, she is. I was the first to find her – shivered to touch her, I did. You need to come, *now*.'

***

The extent of the community's grief is shocking to her, and now she understands what a wonderful woman Tabitha was. Penn feels bad that she was so critical of her. If she had accepted her invitation, perhaps she could have saved her. The tales of her kindness just haven't stopped, and there has been much wailing. Some of their words have been incomprehensible, as inconsolable, tear-burdened women have uttered their longings and praise for this kind old woman. Penn feels that she really shouldn't be here – it wasn't her desire to visit the corpse either – and she descends the stairs in Tabitha's house to hear the men talking.

'Cephas is just a few miles away, I've heard,' says Ezra, a large, outspoken man she's slightly afraid of.

'He's in Lydda, isn't he?' says another.

'He is. I heard him speak once. The man is awesome,' he replies.

'It has to be worth it,' says John. 'He was *with* Jesus. We'll get him to instruct the women as some of them are hysterical.'

'I agree,' replies Ezra. 'Tabitha led the widows in a way we men cannot. In fact, she led all the women. It's like our community has had its heart ripped out. Very few of them will be able to hold things together as she did.'

'Perhaps Cephas will bring her back,' says John.

'What, really? I'm not expecting that of him,' adds a man Penn doesn't know.

'Of God, not of *him*, you idiot!' says Ezra. 'And he was around Jesus, and *he* was good at it.'

'They say some fellow is walking there now – he was paralyzed,' comes a voice from the back. 'The whole community is coming to faith. Cephas will probably move on pretty quickly from there now; his job is done.'

'I'll go,' says Ezra. 'John, you come, too.'

'Tell Mim what's happened, someone. I hope we'll come straight back with him, no point staying the night as we won't sleep.'

***

For once Penn feels useful, needed almost, and this is an opportunity to take her mind off her own woes. She opens the shutters and heads upstairs again to join the group. Mim isn't among them, though perhaps that is best, or the rest of the infants could be exposed to this illness. Surely it lurks still in the building, and they are endangering their own lives by staying here.

'We must prepare her for burial,' says one of the old women, no doubt treating her with the dignity that she herself would like to be treated, in just a short time.

'They've gone for Cephas,' Penn blurts out. 'There is some hope that he will come and heal her.'

The women stop what they are doing to look at her, then shrug their shoulders and carry on, as if she hasn't spoken.

'It's a very slim hope,' utters the first old woman who seems to be taking charge. 'We're not considered an important community in believing circles – a little backwater, that's what we are. None of us had even met Jesus, even *seen* him. I'm told we're forever doing things wrong, too, by the visitors we have had.'

'Don't worry about that,' Penn says. 'What are you doing this for, living this life for, if you don't expect his intervention every once in a while? Is your God dead like *this*?' she asks them, waving an arm down the length of Tabitha as if to present them to her. 'And what would Tabitha want? I think she'd want you to be faith-filled…'

'New believers. They're all the same,' says a voice at the back of the group. 'They have no idea of the realities, the ongoing struggles…'

'Who said I'm a believer?' she retorts, though the accusation does make her wonder, and even feel a little proud of herself. 'You say your God answers prayer. Well, I think you should be praying to him right now, not giving up so quickly. The men have already set out to find Cephas. Perhaps this is your chance not to be the little backwater but an example to the believers.'

A few assenting nods and a little nervous laughter is heard as the women look from Penn to Tabitha and back. The older women ignore her and get on with preparing the body, but a small group take Penn onto the rooftop and start to pray. Penn holds back at the top of the steps and watches the small huddle that has formed in the far corner. She looks beyond them, across the town and out to the little peninsula that is surrounded by sea.

'You know, you can't test God,' says Sarai to Penn in a hushed voice, having followed her up the stairs. 'Sometimes he answers our prayers. Other times it's a 'no' or a 'not yet'. We don't always understand his timing, but our faith shouldn't be dependent on what he does or doesn't do. Do you get that?'

'I think so.' Penn moves one of Tabitha's half-finished sewing projects out of the way so that she has somewhere to sit down at the back of the group, yet she hesitates and cannot settle. 'But then why *do* you pray?'

'It's a chance to be with God,' continues Sarai in a loud whisper. She walks towards the huddle and Penn follows. 'To dwell on him, wait in his presence. I mean, he's always around us but it's a deliberate drawing close. We come away from a time of prayer feeling invigorated, at peace, ready to face life's challenges. It's *always* a good thing, never time wasted, you see.'

Penn notices that the women have stopped praying as Sarai explains to her this mystery that has baffled her since she first met them. They are smiling broad, well-meaning smiles at her and she smiles back, a little lost for words. She sits with her back against the wall, brings her knees up to her chest and bows her head. As the tears start to flow she feels each of her hands taken in someone else's, and now they are praying for her. 'Dear Lord, help Penn to understand you, to love you, to believe in you.' 'And keep her husband safe,' says another voice. 'May they be reunited.' The tears really flow now, and Penn wishes the attention be directed away from herself. 'Dear Lord, if you are there, would you heal Tabitha,' she says. 'I want to know that you are real, and I want you to bless this woman who has blessed so many.'

She runs out of words and thinks what a rubbish prayer that must have sounded, but as the silence beats away in her ears she hears the women say 'Amen' in turn, then 'Please Father,' 'Please Jesus,' and other affirming utterances that make her feel that perhaps what she said wasn't really so bad. Now they are all praying for Tabitha, and she sits quietly and waits to say 'Amen' when the opportunity comes. She would far rather dally with this faith-fuelled bunch than the wailing women who have taken it upon themselves to prepare Tabitha for burial already. That does seem a little premature to her, especially without having prayed as they had here.

***

Chapter Five

'Mim, Mim, it's Amalia, you home?'
She's rattling the gate and now I hear it open. Just sometimes I would rather not respond. Is that wrong of me? Dear Jesus, give me strength –
'She's inside,' I hear, as Zac calls down from the roof. Calista, the new baby Tabitha brought us, starts to cry, her wail even louder as I remove the plank and open the door to Amalia, the thirteen-year-old daughter of Sarai. 'Imma sent me,' she tells me. 'She's at Tabitha's. She wants you to know John's gone to Lydda with Ezra to find Cephas.' The girl stops to catch her breath and lifts her hair off her face with one hand, leaving her arm extended mid-air while she clutches her locks, as if full of care. Clearly she's been running and the steep hill was too much for her.
'Why?' I ask her.
She looks confused and pauses until Calista stops her latest outcry. 'Because of Tabitha.'
'Is she that poorly? I was worried about her, come to think of it. I sent Penn –'
Now the girl lets go of her hair and it falls in front of her face; she pushes it to one side, like a heavy drape.
'Haven't you heard? Has nobody told you?'
I beckon her inside now, yet she lingers on the path, transferring her weight from foot to foot in quick succession.
'Told me what?'
'She died, Mim. Penn found her this morning.' Amalia stands still as she tells me this. 'The women are all there now – I'm sorry to be the one to tell you.'
Amalia is suddenly very grown up and she is the one to be comforting me. I feel stunned and start to lose my balance, putting out a hand on the doorframe, then leaning against it before knowing I just can't stand and sinking to the floor. 'It will be okay,' the girl tells me. 'The men know that Cephas is in Lydda and they've sent for him. John's gone, like I told you.'
That's so like him, I think, to take action as a way of solving a problem. Always hopeful, always believing the best is possible.

Amalia crouches down and takes my arm, leading me into my own home, where I settle in the middle of the floor. 'And what do you think, Ammie,' I say, 'are they crazy to hope? Do we take things too far sometimes?'

I can never speak like this with John, and probably shouldn't air my doubts to one so young.

'I think we have every reason to hope,' she says, pulling the door gently behind her as Ruth emerges and begins to crawl towards it. Ammie sits beside me and places an arm around me. 'You've always inspired me, the way you live like Jesus, always giving out so much. You're not allowed to doubt – you're my hope, the one I look to.' She squeezes my hand and I pull it back, ashamed.

'Don't look to me – to any woman or man for your best example,' I say as Charis leans on my knees that I lower into a lap for her to climb into. I ignore the child just for a moment as I speak to my friend's lovely girl. 'People are always going to let you down and are not always what they seem. Look to Jesus – he's the only one who can truly help you.'

She looks confused.

'If you expect perfection in anyone else, you'll be disappointed,' I say. 'They told us when we got married and it *is* true – those we most respect show themselves to be human at times, fallible. We need each other, but even that's not enough.'

'I should get back,' she says to me, smiling with a wrinkled brow that hides beneath her hair. 'You going to be okay?'

'I'll come with you. Let me just tell Za-'

'No, stay. You've got the little ones to think of. We don't want them getting sick. I'll let you know when there's any news.'

'It will be a long wait,' I say to her. 'Nine miles there, nine miles back. We'll be lucky if they're home by nightfall. I really should come. But Tabitha! Of all peop-'

'Mim, stay here. The children need you.'

She pulls the door gently behind her and I listen to her light footsteps heading down the hill. The toddlers are both with me and concern is written into their sweet pouty faces, as if they might cry because *I* am upset, their little worlds now unsteady. I get to my feet and feel a baby hand in each of my own, and we peep in at Anastasia before going out into the courtyard to play. It's hard sometimes to be everyone else's security... But I do love these small people, and even if God isn't real, I won't regret what we are doing. Not one bit.

It's windy outside and I stop to reach into a basket by the door to find what the girls need. I pop over their heads small woollen blankets that have a hole in the middle – a design of Tabitha's – 'blankets they can play in' she told me when she presented me with them. They are beautiful, exquisite even, and I wouldn't even begin to know how to make them. Why Tabitha, of all people? Why did God allow it? Oh, is he even there? It's times like this that I really wonder. So many depend on her – she not only clothes them but she teaches them skills, finds them work, generally loves them like they are her own daughters tossed on the waves of misfortune. She brings them all into harbour and makes their lives sure again, rebuilds them when they are broken to pieces like the most storm-battered boats ever to make it back to shore.

Poor Tabitha.

At least the baby she brought here seems to have turned a corner. *Most beautiful* Calista, and she is. But perhaps we should have named her Tabitha.

Charis brings me a green leaf that she's picked from the vine that grows at the centre of the yard. I smile at her. 'No more,' I say as she turns and runs away. 'The plant needs its leaves to stay healthy.'

Oh, Tabitha! God wanted you for himself – how selfish of him!

Tabitha was ready for heaven – yes, out of all of us I can see why God took her – she was ready. But did he not have a thought for the rest of us? I struggle with my own commitments and taking on Tabitha's will be too much. Is there *anyone* able to do what she has done?

'Zac!' I call up to the roof, from where I'm sitting. 'How's she doing?'

'She seems fine,' he says in his deep, rich voice.

I get to my feet at the news. 'I'm wondering about heading out for a bit – on my own,' I tell him. Ruth slaps her hands on the bottom step and starts to climb; I lift her and place her back on the matting with some grain to grind and crouch beside her. I pick up my favourite egg-shaped stone and start to work it into the quern stone. Sure enough she grabs it and tries to copy me. I have always found this therapeutic and the girls are no different; Charis is now sitting on the mat beside her and I hold out to her the large hand stone that she wraps her chubby arms around. Well, that's them settled until I'm at the bottom of the hill at least.

Zac's face appears now over the parapet. He is still quite slow at processing when we tell him things. 'Why? What for?' he says.

'It's Tabitha. You must have heard us speak of her. She's died, Zac. John and Ezra have left Joppa in search of Cephas, to bring him back and pray for her.'

'What exactly do you think your presence will do to help matters?'

'Well, thanks. I thought you might be able to look after the girls, just for a little while. I think the women need me.'

'Think about it, Mim. All crammed into a little room, looking at a body. How exactly *is* that going to help? I can't think of anything worse.'

At this Zac visibly shivers, yet the sun is shining down on him, weak though it is. 'Everyone surrounding her, not wanting to catch each other's eye –'. Zac stops again and once more he shivers, and I feel sure this time that it's less about physical discomfort than mental unease. 'Mim, I wouldn't go if I were you. There could still be illness hanging on in there.' He pauses. 'By the way, there's something I want to chat with John about when he's home.'

***

I say nothing more and am persuaded to stay. John will be famished once he's back, and there is comfort in the routine of preparing a meal, even if *I* have little appetite. I peel and crush onions, which allow my tears to fall without upsetting Ruth and Charis, for they are used to this. I fry them for the base of my stew, then begin on the beans, all the while the toddlers taking off whatever vegetables they can find, rolling them across the floor, or biting into them raw, and Anastasia and Cali taking it in turns to wake and cry. I even make small cakes of crushed lentils, John's favourite, such is my nervous energy, for I am beginning to entertain the thought of Tabitha being prayed over and coming back to life. To think that Cephas will be visiting our believing community – I hope that he will be persuaded, for if Tabitha remains dead, we will need some instruction and encouragement. Perhaps he will eat my cooking – I take the pot of honey out from the store and the best olive oil in which to fry my cakes. More to the point, perhaps he will encourage a little more participation in this necessary work. But he is still a man – will he see the value in what I do?

I notice an added feeling of unease come over me and wonder what else could possibly be the matter – for our situation cannot get any more challenging. But then I realize what it is: silence. I check inside and see that Charis and Ruth have fallen asleep together, cuddled up beneath our heaviest blanket, and the babies are quiet too. I lift my skirts off the ground and take the most direct way up to the roof – via the ladder rather than the stairs – that brings me to the side of the wooden hut.

'How's she doing?' I ask John in a whisper.

He's muttering to himself, perhaps reciting something, and is pacing the length of the rooftop. His back is to me, though Cali is sound asleep.

He looks startled when he turns and sees me. 'She's fine,' he tells me. 'Don't worry.'

'I'm going to Tabitha's,' I tell him. 'I can't hold off any longer. Send for me if I'm needed.'

'You mean bring the baby downstairs now?'

'Of course. It looks to me like she's going to be okay.'

***

The door to Tabitha's house is open and I take myself to the upper room where I know everyone will be. I can hear crying as I make my way up the stairs – if they've been doing this all day, they must be exhausted.

As I enter the room the crying stops and my friends embrace me. We exchange sad smiles and I take my place at the foot of the bed by the flickering candle. It seems my presence has at least brought an end to their tears, for now, anyway.

'Leave her hair alone, Xanthe' says Thea to her sister.

'I always did it for her when she was with us, so I know how to do it just right.'

'What does it matter now?' Thea asks her. 'Look at her – she's not coming back.'

'We should cover her face, too,' I say, taking in the picture of my friend in wrappings from the neck down.

'Then she'll never be able to breathe,' says Penn. 'At least now there's a chance.'

A silence follows, punctuated by the occasional sob that is swallowed or choked on.

'She's very pale,' says Tansy.

'I think she looks better than ever,' adds Xanthe. What a ridiculous comment. We all stare at her. 'Her wrinkles have all but gone,' she explains. Am I hearing her correctly? But she always was vacuous. 'Her eyes are bulging though,' she continues. 'I think we should put heavier weights on them.'

Yet no one moves and the attention of everyone is caught by a fly that circles the candle at the top-end of the bed, before it heads my way to visit the candle at her feet. It seems early for insects – I wonder where they go when it's cold.

'Well, she smells beautiful,' says Xanthe. 'I love that oil.'

'What, really? You're in denial. She's emptied her bowels, or haven't you noticed?' says Thea to her. 'That's why we're getting flies.'

Someone will suggest we clean her up in a moment, but the prospect is very off-putting. The room grows quiet again, except for the fly that is joined by a second. I'd rather not talk anyway, for I need time to understand this – if I ever will. Sometimes it's hard to know what God is doing, what he's even about. But then I remember Jesus and how he's demonstrated all the Father's goodness, all his love. The cross speaks so powerfully whenever our human error begins to whisper louder to us than our faith. We *know* how God feels about us – he's shown it. And if we suffer, or if others do – does he love us any the less? Of course not. Jesus didn't exactly have it easy, but he didn't give in and walk away, complaining it was too hard, that it wasn't for him. Just imagine if he had.

So here lies Tabitha. The women start to clean her, silently, and with respect. No one looks at anyone else, and soon the soiled items are discarded. We are back to where we were, surrounding her, each lost in their own thoughts and knowing not what to say.

What does God expect of us here? Is he disappointed if we don't have the faith to bring her back, as we know Jesus did with others? Does he smile – or even frown – that we've had to send for Cephas? Or does that demonstrate faith in itself? In actual fact, I don't think he minds. I think he loves us so overwhelmingly. I think of the joy I've felt watching Charis and Ruth take their first faltering steps, and perhaps this is no different. I don't get cross with them when they fall, or when they reach out for a hand belonging to someone who already walks. And just look at Tabitha anyway – this is no tragedy for her – she's gone somewhere, and I feel sure it's straight to her

Saviour. She lived for him, and now she's died in him. Ultimately our every breath belongs to him, and when he calls us home – well, it isn't for us to question. But I look forward to asking him about why he allowed this one day – what good he felt would come of Tabitha no longer being among us, when she was so used by him.

I can't stop the tears from coming now, though I'm not sure why I'm crying. I miss the Tabitha that was – I think that's it.

Soon the others are bawling around me.

Penn sighs from the head-end of the bed and the candleflame flickers with her breath – I am impressed by this young woman; she seems to have more faith than many in our crowd. 'Keep it together,' she says to Sarai in a whisper loud enough for me to hear. 'Some of us have to believe in this – it's what you had said to *me*.'

The sound of someone running outside and Ammie is in the room, having taken the stairs several at a time. 'They're coming,' she says, pushing her heavy fringe back with both hands, then smoothing her tunic. 'They are in the square now – I saw them! John and Ezra with another man – he looks quite old with a big chest and this grey be-'

'Oh, Cephas is here!'

'We must tell him what she means to us.'

'Don't let him give up – he must pray hard!' says Penn.

Now the wailing picks up again with renewed energy, as if this will make him really appreciate what she meant to us. I know they are genuine, but if I were Cephas I'd find this off-putting.

Heavy footsteps on the stairs – laughter even, you do have to wonder at men sometimes – and they appear in the doorway.

Everyone is keen to talk to Cephas. 'Shalom,' we all say, before the women interrupt each other – 'Oh, look at what she made for me! I was destitute, I had nothing – she gave me a home, clothes –'

'Look, Cephas, look! We cannot be without her! We depend on her. This coat – she made it just for me. I have no one else. I cannot imagine –'

'Dear friends,' Cephas says, seizing a momentary break while several women stop talking to sniff and sob. 'Dear friends,' he repeats, louder than before. 'I need you women out of the room now. Go and take a little air. I need the room completely quiet. Just me, these two men and my Lord.'

The older women are first out of the door and make their way downstairs. 'Well!' I hear one of them say, 'well indeed. Is the man shy? I would like very much to witness it.' I wait and let them all pass and John reaches for my hand, which he squeezes before giving me a knowing nod. His fingers feel hot and swollen – it's clear they have been rushing to get back, despite Cephas' relaxed manner when they arrived. My husband is crying now as Cephas kneels beside Tabitha. I leave them to it, as requested, and place a hand on Penn's shoulder, who is waiting for me at the top of the stairs.

We gather in Tabitha's large courtyard and all link hands. Without being asked we shut our eyes and begin to pray, just quietly to ourselves. The Lord's presence is here – I can feel it. Oh, the Lord is near, and he has calmed these women for sure. I can feel his energy in my hands, and they even begin to shake a little. It's as if his Spirit is pulsing through all of us. Whatever the outcome of this, I feel sure that our Lord is in control.

Someone starts to hum the line, 'O Son of God, Giver of Life,' and others join in. The words are uttered now, and short bursts of prayer spoken out. 'Dear Jesus, heal her we pray,' 'Heal her, Lord,' 'Heavenly father, be at work. Use your servant we pray. May we see her alive again, bring her back to us.'

Silent tears fall and yet his presence comforts. There is a sense of completeness here, of being whole. What would life be without him? Why did I ever doubt his existence? He is more real to me in moments like this than I could ever explain. And it's not a 'take-over' as someone once said to me as I told of God-with-us, Immanuel. I feel more 'me' than ever, more whole. Yet I should be praying for Tabitha now, shouldn't I?

Just then a shout from upstairs – 'She's alive!' It is Cephas. 'An orderly line please, come and greet your old friend.'

This joy – I cannot contain it! It overwhelms me, God is just so good!

As I reach the upper room, I can see Tabitha's head bobbing through the crowd. She's here – she's there – full of her old energy. I hear her sweet laugh as I make my way inside. John stands by the window, so much taller than everyone else – he's just looking on, and for once he has no words – just the biggest grin, the most astonished wide eyes, the happiest expression I have ever seen him wear. I feel someone take my hand, and as I turn I am face to face with Tabitha. 'Dear Tabitha!' I say. 'You're back!'

'I know,' she says. 'That I am, dear. That I am.'

I embrace her with slow and steady hands, expecting her to feel fragile, anticipating that she might crumple if I hold onto her too tightly. I needn't have worried – she holds onto *me* like she's protecting me from the most giant wave.

'How's the little baby?' she asks me. 'I hope she has survived.'

'The one you brought us? She seems fine,' I tell her.

'What have you called her?'

'Calista. Most beautiful.'

'Well done, dear,' she says. 'Well done.'

'Tabitha needs something to eat and drink now,' Cephas calls out. 'It's one of the many things the Lord Jesus taught me about times like this. Please make a way for her to go downstairs.'

'You must all stay,' Tabitha calls out to the assembled. 'It's a celebration. I want you all to eat with me.'

'In good time,' says Sarai, taking her arm. 'Let's get something inside you quickly, then we can think about feeding the rest. How are you feeling?'

'Never been better,' I hear her say as she leads the way down the stairs. 'Never been better. God be praised.'

***

Chapter Six

'John, I need to stay away from the crowd. Down by the water if possible. For if I'm to keep my sanity I need some distance from your womenfolk, truth be told.' He looks down the narrow street at a glimpse of blue, just visible where the path runs out. 'I always feel at home by the water, no matter how far away I am. It always was my Ursa Minor[3], my signpost for home, before I met *him* of course.'

John smiles his broad grin at Cephas. 'We should go back inside; I'm surprised they've coped without you in there for this long.'

'Give it a bit longer. The food can't be ready yet. Tabitha is the one they want to talk to now. And that's how it should be. I do get so tired of all the questions.'

'You have a famous shadow, mate,' says John. 'It will take a lot for you to have a quiet stay around here. We do need you though – it would be a shame if you were to move on too quickly.'

'Can we wander down in the right direction, just to get the lie of the land? It's getting dark already and I need somewhere sorted out.'

'Of course – though you're always welcome to stay with us.'

'No offence but I don't think so.'

'You don't need to worry about my wife – she's lovely!'

'It's not your wife that bothers me. It's the talk of all those children. What a nightmare! I couldn't do it.'

'Well, I couldn't do what you do.'

'It comes with time, my friend. God allows you to see one miracle and your faith grows. It builds that way.'

'There has to be more to it.'

'Well, I have been forgiven much, for sure. I know what he's saved me from, how gracious he's been. I let Jesus down in a very big way – I can't even begin to tell you. Not now anyway – that's for another day.'

'Don't you need to get back home?'

'What? To Jerusalem? I've been away a while and I prefer it that way. It's dangerous for my wife, such is the persecution there.

---

[3] The star Ursa Minor (The Little Bear) was used for navigation purposes.

47

There's not many of us left in Jerusalem now – just us apostles and some of our loved ones. My wife will follow on from Lydda shortly. She wouldn't have kept up with us today, and she always smooths things over for me when I have to leave in a hurry.'

'How does she cope? We turn here,' says John, gesturing towards a narrow, cobbled path, flanked by houses that seem to grow towards each other overhead. 'It leads out of town eventually.'

'She's used to it,' says Cephas, 'and she's good at making friends. Sometimes our wives will hold back, and we'll send word that it's safe for them to travel. They always want to join us but on occasions it's risky. To be honest, whenever we part I wonder if we'll see each other again.'

'That's tough.'

'It's amazing what you can grow used to, with his help. All those widows though – they just remind me of what we are risking, almost every day. It's too close for comfort.'

'I'm sorry, mate.'

'Really, no. Don't be. And besides, how long do any of us have? For Jesus could return tomorrow. We have to give him our best and trust him with those we love.'

'You're right, Cephas. It's the only way.'

'There's a tanner's house here? That's where I'm to stay. I feel sure of it.'

'You wouldn't want to stay there, brother. No one will talk to you.'

'Could be worse!'

John stops walking to look him in the face, as if to read sarcasm in its lines and candid expression. 'I don't think you get it – no one will take you seriously. You want to be left alone, completely?'

'I'm only joking. But I think I'll enjoy the peace. Just the urgent cases will come to me, those who really want Jesus' help, who aren't motivated by self-interest – just think…And if the 'religious elite' choose to track me down from Jerusalem – ha! They'd run a mile rather than cross his threshold. You know, the more I think about it, the better it sounds.'

'Will your wife join you there? She'll be mortified. It's usually best to wait and hear their opinion if you're thinking of doing something as drastic as that.'

'As a fisherman I've smelt pretty bad. It can't get much worse.'

'Oh, it can, believe me.'

The pair walk on in the increasing darkness, John asking about Cephas' time in jail, about his choice to defy the command never to speak in Jesus's name again, enthralled by his devotion that has proven itself even stronger than his own. Being around someone this radical…it's exactly what he needs; it's so easy to settle into slovenly ways. And then, 'There it is, the last house,' he tells him, sorry that this time of asking his most searching questions has to come to an end.

'You don't need to tell me – I can smell it from here,' says Cephas.

'Have you changed your mind then?'

'Not at all.'

'You really don't have to stay here. My offer still stands – there are plenty of believers who'd jump at the chance of having you to stay.'

'That's what I'm worried about. And besides, I think the Lord wants me here. To be honest, I wouldn't be that willing otherwise.'

Cephas strides through the gate and hollers a greeting. 'He certainly has plenty of space,' he says to John while they wait. And the breeze is coming in off the sea. The smell really isn't *so* bad.'

'We're closed,' comes the reply through an unshuttered window. John gives him a nudge, encouraging him to walk away, but Cephas walks up to the doorway and pokes his head around the corner.

'Oh, shalom,' comes the reply. 'My deepest apologies but I'm up to my elbows in – well, take a guess. I'm afraid this is the reality of producing the leather everyone's so keen to wear. I'll be open for business tomorrow and early –'

'It's not your leather I'm after,' says Cephas.

'No one comes here for anything else,' comes the reply. 'You not from round here, then?'

'No, that's the thing. I need somewhere to lay my head for a night or two. Perhaps longer, depending on how I'm received around these parts.' The tanner waves them inside, just to hear their story out, it seems. 'My wife's coming on too, she'll be setting off from Lydda when it's light.'

'No one ever wants to stay with me.' The tanner's face is caught in the lamplight that flickers from the wall beside his shoulder. It seems he is actually crying now but can't wipe his eyes for the faeces that cover his hands – he brings a finger up to his face but stops himself short. 'Come in – just let me go and clean myself up before I

49

join you. I'm in no fit state for company fellows. I can't do this to you.'

And so, they enter into the tannery properly and find their way into the central courtyard where they sit themselves down on a low bench on the floor. It is cold now to be sitting in the open air, but they are glad of it. The stars are bright already and it seems lighter outside the house than in. 'He seems like a nice enough chap,' says John. 'I feel somewhat ashamed that I don't really know him. I mean, he lives so out of the way that our paths don't cross.'

Cephas is silent for a while. Then, 'He's very young to be living alone,' he says. 'I wonder if he has any help here.'

'I know the poorest families send their children to gather excrement for him. It's a grim old job. The worst,' replies John.

'I don't mean that kind of help. I mean, does he have no human contact except his business dealings? Is he really as isolated as he seems?'

The tanner is back and clears his throat as he walks in behind Cephas. 'Now, how can I help you?' he says. 'What's brought you to Joppa and why have you sought me out?'

It is apparent here just how young the fellow is, though he was unable to wash off all the mire – he seems somewhat stained. He has an honest face though – bright, darting eyes that reside under a heavy brow, that he wrinkles when he is brave enough to look his guests in the eye. He sits on the floor beside them and stokes the open fire with a long stick.

'What is your name, lad?' asks Cephas.

'I'm just the tanner, like I said. No one bothers with me. I'm polluted, as you can probably imagine so I'm left to get on with things.'

'*What's your name?*' Cephas says again. That seems a little harsh, but it has been a long day for them.

'Well, I'm Simon, but no one ever calls me that.'

'Simon,' says Cephas, with a smile on his face that seems inappropriate. 'Simon,' he says again, which is very awkward. He really isn't known for his ineptitude. But then, 'Simon. Yes, that was my name too, before the Lord took an interest in me.'

The lad looks Cephas in the face and wrinkles his brow again. 'I don't understand,' he says.

'I'm Cephas, friend of Jesus. I was called Simon by my parents, but Jesus changed it to Cephas, meaning *rock*.'

'Have you heard of Jesus?' John asks him.

'Have I? How could I not,' he says, stoking the fire again. He turns to Cephas. 'I've heard of you, too, more to the point.'

'Ah, that's where you are wrong. My life is meaningless without Jesus and he's far greater than me. So I'm just the messenger. And *that's* the point... That's the reason why we're here. I think the Lord Jesus wants you to know you are valuable to him. That he loves you.'

'The last I heard of him he'd died on a cross.'

'It didn't end there, lad. That's the thing. He came back from the dead and he's changed me from a quivering wreck to a leader of his church.'

'That sounds lovely, but, well, I don't know how you can be so sure.'

'I've met him, the risen Lord. Eaten fish he'd cooked me on the beach. And this very day a woman in your community is back from the dead. She'd died – her friends were wailing – you probably heard them from here.'

'There's always the sound of wailing carried on the wind – that, mingled with the cry of the birds, especially after a catch.'

'Anyway, I prayed for her and now she's alive again. I'm tired, having walked all the way from Lydda, and I need somewhere to stay; I really felt the Lord wanted me to be staying here with you.'

'I don't know what to say,' he says, poking the fire again, his gaze held as he looks on the stick that's come to rest. 'I can't offer you much comfort. I'm not poor – it's not that. It's just, well – smelly around here. If it's not the dung containers it's the glue water that's festering, and the smell of decomposing flesh isn't very pleasant, while we're on the subject.' He turns to look Cephas in the eye. 'You really don't have to stay here – no one's asking it of you.'

'I think *he* is. Tell me, Simon, are you happy? Don't you wish for some company?'

'I haven't bothered to dwell on it often – well, I try not to. It's not helpful to me, though now that I am, I realize that I'm far from happy. When something's your lot, you just have to get on with it. I should be glad that my father left me his business – that I didn't have to share it with anyone. Life could be a lot worse.'

'It could be better.'

'Yes, well.'

'Will you have me then?'

'Stay for a night if you're sure. It's getting very dark out here, anyway,' he says, looking away from the fire and up into the night sky. 'Who was the woman – are you sure she was really dead?'

'It was Tabitha.'

'Oh, I've heard of her.' He looks at Cephas. 'She was a kind one, from what people say. I expect she'd have been missed. Her friends were probably over-reacting – panicked at the thought of life without her.'

'She was dead alright. Her room smelt pretty similar to this, truth be told. There's only so much masking that can be done with herbs and spices. Why don't you come back with us and meet her friends – that might convince you.'

'They won't want me there. I'm an outsider – ritually unclean. You forget.'

'Oh, the believers in Jesus are different. Or they should be. They've been preparing a meal – a celebration feast. Please come back with us for the evening. I think you'll be pleasantly surprised. And when they hear I'm staying with you, they'll welcome you with open arms. You see if they don't.'

'I really don't know,' he says. 'I'll pollute the lot of them – it's just not done.'

'Do come back with us, Simon. I know you'll be welcome at Tabitha's,' says John.

'I've never felt welcome around here before. It's not a problem. I'm used to my own company.'

'Now we all know that's not true,' Cephas tells him.

***

Is that the believers' partying they can hear above the harbour noise? It certainly sounds like it. A ship has recently arrived, and its crew are busy transferring containers and baskets onto camels, to reach their destination before the Sabbath. There is a full day ahead before tomorrow's sunset, but this caravan is taking no chances. No doubt strict instructions have been given.

'I prefer walking out at night. Few people stop to stare at me,' says Simon. 'Too busy trying to get home before the moon hides behind a cloud. Or working like this lot. I don't stand out now – no one can see the colour of my skin, though of course they may smell me coming!'

'It is an outrage,' says Cephas. 'How backward our society is! When you know the heart of God, you know he excludes no one.'

John hums in agreement but something causes Simon to stop in his tracks and glance over his shoulder in the direction of the tannery. 'Listen, I just don't know about this. You go in without me – I think I should head home.'

'Oh no you don't,' says Cephas.

'I'd never have thought of doing this before you came along. I was pretty content really. Society doesn't change that quickly.'

'God's people are different.'

'Well, I've not noticed it so far.' He pauses to look at John. 'No offence to my new friend here. But rules don't change that quickly. Nor do people.'

'The church should be different. We are trying to be like Jesus, and he showed us complete disregard for so-called 'ritual purity'.

'That's nice.'

'*Nice*? It was never *nice* or easy to be around when he was at work. It was outrageous, but we loved it. I saw him touch a corpse on a funeral byre and bring the lad back to life – it's why I reached out to Tabitha as I did.' Cephas is sounding out of breath and stops walking for a moment so that he can finish. 'He called out Lazarus, but he actually *touched* this dead boy. We saw him touch lepers too and heal them, make friends with the Gentiles, break the Sabbath rules whenever he needed – it was always with good reason.'

'Sounds like he was a complete rebel.'

'Oh, he was more than a rebel,' says Cephas. 'How do we even begin to explain?'

'Your friends will struggle to accept me though. Most view my premises as like a public urinal. Rules aren't changed that easily.'

'We'll see, shall we? It's not far now.'

'You know, it was them we were hearing from the harbour – I've recognized Tabitha's laugh from the opposite end of a pilgrimage crowd,' says John. 'Sounds like they're worshipping now.'

They make their way up the cobbled street, passing a prostitute making her way towards the newly arrived sailors. 'Shalom,' says Cephas to her. She stops in her tracks and looks disorientated for a moment, but it's rude to stare.

'Really?' says John when she is out of earshot. 'A fallen woman?'

'Jesus spoke to everyone, gave them all a welcome. No one is completely what they seem – they all deserve respect. Not that they

53

could continue in their way of life if they were to join us, but they wouldn't need to. The church here is looking great, but it'll look even better when it's including more of the broken.'

'Cephas, we're mocked enough as it is. I'm not sure we're quite ready for the prostitutes just yet.'

'And when will you be? Why wait? For God gives you the wisdom and insight as you need it. He rarely equips ahead of time. He never fails to step in though when you make yourself available. I'm yet to be disappointed, anyway.'

'That's my favourite song,' says John. 'You hear it?'

'Restoring the broken – that's true worship,' Cephas tells him. 'Nothing warms his heart like the extension of his mercy, done by *us*. We can sing all we like, but it's when we demonstrate his love that we put a smile on the Father's face.'

'We are trying,' says John.

'I can see that. You're doing well with the infants and the widows. Now try and reach the unlovely ones. Those who seem far from God.'

'We might need your help in this,' says John.

'For sure. I'm prepared to stay around – particularly if this good man will have me.'

'Of course. I'd be delighted.'

Cephas steps inside first, followed by John, and then Simon, who puts a foot over the threshold, then withdraws it to wait in the doorway. The believers stop singing and some exchange glances with each other. The ones who'd been worshipping with their eyes closed have missed seeing Simon's face – he is now standing outside the house where no one can see him and wondering what to do. One or two point in his direction, but thankfully he misses this. Nonetheless, their silence is telling.

'Brothers, sisters, I would like you to meet a friend of mine. This is Simon, the tanner from the eastern side of town. I will be staying with him. I request that you make him very welcome.'

Still no one else speaks, or even moves. That is, not after more reticent stances have been adopted. For hands that moments before had been raised in worship now hang limp by their sides, or rest inside folded arms across their chests. Where is the presence of God now? Has this been a bad idea after all?

Cephas sighs and looks around for Simon. But then, 'You're very welcome,' comes a voice from the back of the room. 'Any friend of Cephas is a friend of mine. Please do come in.' The crowd make a way for Tabitha to come forward, and in a moment the bustle resumes. John steps outside and puts his arm through Simon's, and the two of them walk into the centre of the room, to be greeted with shaloms, pats on the back and the warmest of greetings. For the second time this day, Simon begins to cry.

Chapter Seven

'Ah, Mim, you sure you're okay going back on your own? I promised Simon I'd stay with him.'

'Of course,' I say. 'I can't leave the girls any longer. I must get home.'

He kisses me on the cheek as I make a hood out of my woollen scarf, and I pull my cloak tightly about myself as I step out into the night. My mind had been elsewhere when I set out, and now a new version of reality is returning – Tabitha back from the dead! How astounding and how the Lord will use it! It's been a strange kind of day all round; it's the first time in months – no, years – that children have been far from my mind, but now the anxieties are cascading down – but will Zac have coped? And will they have screamed when they realized I wasn't there? Was it wise to leave Calista? …the child *is* better now, isn't she? How quickly time has passed since Tabitha's return! This sleeping town will be very different tomorrow – nobody else is out tonight, but I think many will be drawn here when word gets out. The odd light flickers through the windows, but all is very quiet right now… if Joppa is transformed into an excited, faith-filled place, how much easier life will be. No longer a struggling minority without enough people sharing the load. No longer a community that looks down on us, excludes us from business deals, whispers when we pass them, and gives us half-measures. Most importantly, enough homes to share out these little ones… and homes that won't give them up in the first place. My cheeks are starting to ache from smiling so much. Oh, this is just too incredible! And how could anyone fail to believe in our Saviour now? Zac will be the first to hear it – he's had his doubts, but this changes everything…

'You've been gone a long time,' he says as I put my hand out for the door to prevent its bang as it falls into place behind me. Zac has lit all the oil lamps and has set a meal on the table – a round of olive bread, grapes and a green salad, like he's had time on his hands.

'I'm so sorry, such a lot has happened, and it was just hard to get away.'

'Don't apologize.' Well this is unlike him! 'I've enjoyed looking after the girls on my own. Once they settled, I was able to do all this,' he says, and he gestures at the room that I couldn't fail to notice. He's even tidied the clutter from the loom, untangled the piles of wool the girls had made a mess of and swept the floor. But he does look like they've been giving him a hard time. His hair is all over the place and I even wonder if he's been crying. We mustn't do this to him again. 'Getting them all to sleep was very satisfying,' he goes on, but I'm not convinced. 'Where's John?'

'Oh, he won't be long. He's been looking after Cephas – Tabitha is back with us, and you wouldn't know she'd been dead! I hardly dared hope this would happen, though we *had* prayed. Cephas is really stirring things up – he and John turned up with the tanner and told us he should be included in our community. The man is ritually unclean – I mean, wh-'

'Mim, now you're back I'm going to turn in. Forgive me but I'm very tired. Boundless energy doesn't last long; now the need to sleep has overcome me. When John returns please could you ask him to wake me?'

***

John certainly is taking his time, and after the long day he's had, ministering to Zac will be the last thing he needs. But this has been an age in coming... I really think he's remembered something at last. Zac didn't even ask about Tabitha! Did he not believe me, or did he not register what I was saying? He certainly seemed preoccupied. I know that I clean and cook with renewed vigour when I'm anxious, as far as the girls will let me, and I don't doubt that's what was happening here tonight. I think his old life has come back to him, for sure.

It's always impossible to sleep when you know discussions are to be had – whether you will be a part of them or not. Would it be wrong to listen in? He must still be awake... besides me and the children, no one else is in the house, and he's pacing with his stick that he taps on the floor as he walks. No need to wake him, despite his request. Whether or not to listen in then... They would assume everyone's asleep anyway, that's the thing, though they'll talk in hushed voices for fear of waking the babies, and me, no doubt. What could he possibly have to say that means secrecy is required?

Sounds like there won't be long to wait anyway – I can hear the door in the gate. John's quick, purposeful footsteps are unmistakable.

Now he's opening the front door, slowly as I do, to control its swing and creak. Zac doesn't need to explain his need of company – he's normally out cold by this time of night, and we whisper over him as he sleeps in our communal room, while the babies slumber here.

They exchange greetings and seem to have forgotten me, for John doesn't wander through to kiss me as he usually does – I nearly always go to bed before him, and it's been a part of our routine since we first married. Still, there is a positive to this – I pose no threat to their conversation, and I cannot help but listen now.

'Well, you're up late!' says John. 'I thought the little ones would have you exhausted.'

Gentle laughter which they catch and suppress, no doubt pointing in the direction of me and the girls.

'Have you heard the news? Astonishing, I can't get ov-'

'Mim told me.'

'Ah, of course. How could she not?'

'Listen, John, I've remembered something. In fact, more than something,' says Zac. 'I think my brain has probably been blocking it out. It's not going to be comfortable listening.'

'We're pretty unshockable around here,' John tells him.

'Don't joke,' Zac tells him. 'Don't joke at all.'

They seem to have wandered into the courtyard as I can no longer hear them, but soon they are back, complaining of the cold. I hope they settle where I can catch every word.

'Look, I can see you are tired,' says Zac. 'This can wait until tomorrow. Forget I said anything.'

'What? Really? No chance. You clearly need to get this off your chest. Come on now, out with it. We're brothers now – well, I like to think so, don't you?'

'John, I've no right to be here. I think I should set out tomorrow. It's ironic I've ended up here, at the very place Jonah fled from; I've shirked *my* responsibilities, too.'

'Hardly, you were washed up here, remember? With Jonah it was deliberate, escaping to our town to set sail. Now, slow down and tell me what it is that's come to mind.'

Charis whimpers in her sleep and I hope I don't have to get up to settle her.

'I'm responsible for a man's death. At least one. To be fair, if I'm guilty of this, which I am, I'm guilty of several. I don't even know where to begin, how to start...'

'Start with what you remembered, Zac. Come on, deep breath in.'

'It was the talk of people exchanging glances over Tabitha's dead body. We were sitting round one of my dead workers and I knew they were looking at each other; catching each other's eye. There was such anger there – I could see it build. Fingers clenched in palms; faces turning red; sweat on men's brows.' Zac stops talking here and I wait for John to prompt him.

'Your workers?'

'I own a company that produces dye – expensive dye.'

But his hands look so perfect – we'd all noticed that. They look as if they've never done a day's work.

'Go on.'

'I have men gather the murex shells. I pay them well, but the thing is, we need a lot. About 8000 snails for a single gram of dye. I've had targets for them. I'd get them to take risks – go a bit further out, dive deeper, stay under water for as long as needed. I've not been a very kind boss. Don't get me wrong, they want the employment, but I know I've been too pushy. Far too pushy. Looking after these little ones today, the memories have returned. I've been thinking of how some children are now fatherless, and all because of me.'

'Well, Zac! They didn't have to take the work. They didn't have to dive.'

'That's not how they saw it. I would make it worth their while, financially that is, if they could bring back enough. This lad I remember – the recent death. I'd had words with him. I had told him that I would have to let him go – that he was taking up valuable space on the boat, only to bring back nothing. They all got quite competitive with each other. It wasn't a healthy environment. My team were stressed out, always unhappy. The thing is, I owned much of the place; it wasn't worth them diving for shells on their own. I was the local who would sell on the dye. Business was done with me, mine was the name everyone knew. I seemed to have the best links, the regular deals.'

'You're talking in the past tense now.'

'Yes, well, I can't go back to it. That part of my life is over. But I need to go *back*. Sell up, make amends as best I can. Though there's no telling how I'll be received – what will happen to me. I don't think they'll be very pleased to see me.'

'You might be surprised.'

'I doubt it. Even their babies look at me accusingly. I've seen their heads, bobbing over their mothers' shoulders, crying inconsolably. There was one who stopped wailing to stare at me! I'll never forget it. Anger burning in her cheeks. Rage th-'

'You're paranoid, my friend.'

'No. Realistic.'

'Well, we know where you're from now – Tyre or Sidon.'

'I'm from Tyre. Sidon were not in our league. I believe that I hold most of the important contracts in the region. Mine is the best recipe, I am told. I do wonder what's been happening there without me.'

'So why did we find you washed up at Joppa?'

'I felt I had to get away. I'm not sure what I was intending, but I knew I had to escape from the locals, at least for a while. Never did I expect to nearly lose my life – it was just an ill-thought through voyage, at a dangerous time of year. Though I've been in charge of boats, my own competence on the water was always questionable.'

He sighs loudly enough for me to hear.

'Things have come to a head now. Since I've been here, I've seen there's a better way to live. I would like to set up home here in Joppa – start again. But first, I need to return.'

There is a long pause here and I keep waiting for one of them to fill it. I can imagine what's going through John's mind... though surely he won't shirk his responsibilities here? Then at last he speaks – 'Well, I'll come with you!' he says.

Whatever next! Does he forget me and the children sometimes? Is that what happens after a few years of marriage? I don't think the Lord would ask it of him – or would he?

'You don't have to do that,' Zac says. Well at least *he's* being considerate.

'Your leg still isn't right, and I think you're going to need someone to talk to. Someone who's on your side, that is.'

'What about Mim?'

'Ah, she won't mind,' he says.

***

The next morning, I find them discussing how they will travel, not if they should. I can hear them on the rooftop and make my way up the stairs with a child on each hip. 'Not by sea,' Zac is saying, as I near the top. 'I don't care if the route is mountainous – we'll manage.' I have to sound surprised when they explained the situation. 'Ah, Mim! Zac has some news,' John tells me as he brushes Ruth's chubby hand away from a map of the coastline chalked out on the floor. The towns on route are marked with stones, the obstacles drawn on with thick lines.

'What news?' I say.

'He's from Tyre, Mim,' says John. He pauses for once. 'Ah, it's complicated. I need to go back with him to help him clear up a few things.'

'Perhaps we should all go,' I tell them.

John raises his eyebrows at me. 'That's a ridiculous idea – take the children? It'll take days to get there. And where will we sleep? It's not going to work Mim. I think you know that.'

'Well, how long will you be gone?'

'I really can't say. Like I said, it's… complicated.' He shakes his crazy curls at me and is struggling as he wonders how to explain the situation.

'It's alright, John. I'll explain,' says Zac. He's on his feet and walking round the perimeter of the rooftop. John's gaze is instead on Ruth – he's given up on keeping her from their visual plan. 'Mim,' Zac says with an unusual intensity. 'The thing is this. I've wronged some people – badly wronged them, and I need to go back – make amends. I want to wrap up my life there. I won't need John with me more than a few days – he'll come back to Joppa ahead of me. But I really don't know how I can do this without him.'

I can see how broken Zac is looking and I can't stay cross with the pair of them for long.

'You do what you need to do,' I tell them. 'I can manage here.'

'Ah, I wish we could keep in contact in some way,' says John to me, putting an arm across my shoulder. 'Perhaps in future centuries there'll be a way, but I'm afraid you just need to trust the Lord on this one. I should only be gone a couple of weeks anyway, like Zac said. You should ask for some help here – see if a couple of the younger women will come and stay to make things a bit easier for you.' He takes my hand and squeezes it, and he looks from me out to the mournful sea beyond, still wondering if that would be the best way to travel, his journey already underway in his mind.

'We'll be okay,' I tell him. 'I think you should set off as soon as you can. I don't look forward to you being away, and the sooner you're gone, the sooner you'll be home.'

Well, what else could I say? I can't stop them, and I know that I shouldn't anyway. Sometimes you just have to take what life throws at you and walk even more closely with Him. How do we grow, otherwise? We have to trust that all things are in God's plan, and He unites us all, even when we are apart.

Chapter Eight

'Not another bag, Mim. What's in this one?'

'Enough provisions to keep you going – some extra parched grain, and some dried olives I'd put away in the store. I've wrapped the rest of the bread I'd made this morning in a piece of cloth. It should last you both a couple of days.'

'More like a week,' says John, landing the bag over the back of the family donkey. 'We won't have to stop to buy anything. Don't forget Nir has to carry Zac some of the way, too – his leg's not going to hold out.'

'She'll manage,' says Mim.

'Come here,' John tells her, pulling her into a close embrace. 'I'll be back as soon as I can. And do make sure you get some help here. I think you're going to need it.'

'I can hear Cali crying,' she says, letting go of his hand. 'I'd better head inside.'

And so the journey begins, Zac walking at this stage with an arm resting on Nir's back to steady him. John feels Mim is looking happier today – she seems to have accepted that they need to do this, even without being told all the details. That's just as well. Zac obviously finds this latest display of self-sacrifice hard to handle. 'Mim's a bit more cheerful now,' he says. 'She did look troubled yesterday. I feel bad about taking you from her, John.'

'You don't need to,' he replies, placing his hand on the weathered saddle as he looks at Zac. 'I'm well aware that plaintive, intense look of hers is enough to make anyone feel bad.' Zac smiles – he knows the expression, all right. 'People apologize to her all the time but she's not judging them – it's just her resting expression. And there's always plenty of thought, and prayer, going on inside her. She observes twice as much as she speaks. You must never feel uncomfortable around her – people have read into her silences, her ponderous stares, for as long as I've known her.'

'All the same, just stay in Tyre a short while. I won't keep you from your family for long.'

'I'll be with you for as long as it takes.' John hesitates for a moment, but then, if he doesn't ask now, when will he? 'You ever had a family of your own, Zac?'

'I've been too busy. It never interested me, not until recently.'

They walk on in silence for a time now, John looking out at the boats just off shore, feeling convinced it would have been quicker that way. 'Are you frightened of the sea after what happened?' he asks Zac after a few minutes. 'Is that it? I feel sure this would have been far quicker by boat, and it's not too late to change our plans.'

'Your black north wind here is worrying. It can whip up at any time.'

'Not on a day like today – it looks good for sailing; the conditions are perfect. I don't often have a chance to get out on the water and there *is* something about it.'

'I'd rather walk, John. I can send you back to Joppa with a horse and a stable lad. Ride the whole way back and he'll lead your donkey for you on foot. You'll be back in half the time. Then you can keep the animal.'

'What do I want with a horse? We have to try to live humbly here, to be accessible, though I appreciate the offer. You are a bit troubled by the sea now, aren't you? We should pray over you about it.'

'That's part of my old life now,' he says and then he's silent for a while. 'To be honest, I don't have the confidence on the water that I once did. I had felt protected – untouchable.'

'Well, you're now more protected than you ever were – as believers in Jesus we've nothing to fear. God spreads his protection over us – it's in the psalms[4]. We take refuge under the shadow of his wings – that's in the psalms too[5]. He's always right there for his people, and if disaster comes, he's somehow in it and beyond it. Ultimately *he* is our destination anyway – we lose sight of that sometimes.' John looks over his shoulder at Joppa, now high above them and to be visible for much of their journey. Getting away from the old town can be helpful for perspective sometimes – their lives are not about Joppa – they are about Jesus and whatever he calls them to.

'You forget, I'm new to all this,' says Zac, and he too looks back at the town perched upon that towering hill. 'If I hadn't seen your

---

[4] Psalm 5: 11.
[5] Psalm 57:1.

faith in action, I wouldn't be drawn to it. For you all, your faith is your way of life. It's the kindness aspect I want – the community that supports. Even aside from the fact that, I admit, your God does have power.'

'Ha, you couldn't have failed to have noticed that, Zac!' He manages to catch his eye now. 'I'm so glad that you've seen his powerful love at work. So why are you still afraid of water?'

'Perhaps I have trust issues.' He's looking at his feet as he walks.

'Why?'

'I know I'm not as worthy of protection as the rest of you.'

'Now come on –'. John stops walking and halts the donkey so that Zac has to engage with him.

'We'll never get there if we stop.'

'Just tell me what you mean then and I'll start walking.'

'As I've said, it's not so much about the protection for me.'

'Go on.'

'It will take a while for me to believe that I'm covered in that way. You know, I've followed a few gods in my time. I'm sure you've heard of Melqart – our most important god at home. God of business enterprise, and of commerce. More than anything, he's linked with the sea. Naturally, I made an offering to him before I set out all those weeks ago, before you found me. I still wonder if he looked after me in part –'

'Meaning?'

'If he ensured that you found me and revived me. I'd like to show you his temple – you'll love the entrance, with its two tall columns; one of gold, one of emerald. I really should return there as I'd like to ask of Melqart a few questions.'

'Your god is dead, Zac. There's no power in his name.' Zac starts walking and John has no choice but to join him. 'Can't you see it?'

'You are a bit blunt, friend. You can't rule out completely that there are other gods, too.'

'I think I can, because of what Jesus said about them.' Zac looks thoughtful and watches John as he talks. 'They might be worshipped, they might even appear to be active, but that's only the evil power they have about them, posing as something positive. Jesus said, "I am the way, the truth, and the life. No one comes to the Father except through me."[6] What evidence of goodness comes from your temple, then? What fruits by which we may know your god?'

Zac thinks for a moment. 'Well, none that I can think of.'

'Is there anything you dislike about the place?'

'Well, there is the thing of human sacrifices,' he says, looking away from John at this point, 'and it's usually children.' His voice is suddenly very quiet. 'Not everyone knows what goes on behind the scenes, but I do. It doesn't happen all the time – it's usually when there's some awful disaster and the people think Melqart needs pacifying. I mean, I'm sure he doesn't. People invent these things.'

There is a long silence for a while – John doesn't really need to say anything, after all. But then, 'I know. The irony isn't lost on me,' Zac continues. 'Your religion is all about life, about restoration, and your God is good and knowable.'

'Well. Well, indeed. I really think you need to leave the old stuff behind,' says John. 'Lay it down and move on. You can't encounter the living God as powerfully as you have and still hanker for the old beliefs, even if you are fond of them, in part. Ours is a jealous God and he has every right to be.'

'I know, I know. It's part of my purpose in returning, other than righting wrongs. But the anticipation is bringing back the old life; it's confusing to say the least.'

And so the journey continues, and after seven days of walking the costal route, Tyre comes into view. Zac sits on the donkey now, and it's much harder to engage with him. John notices that he's grown increasingly quiet, but at last he breaks the silence that's of his making. 'We should arrive when it's dark,' he says. 'I don't want everyone to know that I'm back – word will travel more quickly than I'm ready for.'

'Well, we're here now and we just need to get on with it, brother. Your reception really won't be as bad as you are expecting.'

'Perhaps not. There are those of the Way living in Tyre, though I don't know them personally. You know that Jesus came here? There were plenty of crowds, but I just left them to it – I thought I had everything I needed. What I'd give to relive those days. Go and listen to him. Perhaps I could have avoided these last few months – become a better person there and then. The church came about after his visit;

---

[6] John 14:6 (NLT.)

most of them live at the northern harbour, down the small alleyways that remind me of your streets in Joppa.'

'But you were not much more than a boy then?'

'I suppose that's true. My parents were not interested either. Now they're dead, and my sisters have moved away.'

They walk on in silence again for a while, Nir much slower than she was at first and braying on the steep inclines. Within half-an-hour they are on the final stretch of their journey.

'Ah, this causeway is very beautiful,' says John. 'It makes for a very dramatic approach.'

'It doesn't have a very pretty history. Much death went into the making of this idyllic setting, John. Anyway, stop the donkey – I want to get off and walk. Despite our long trek I need to slow things down now. I need more time to focus. Relocate my mind through my feet touching the slabs of the old stone Peninsula road.'

John halts the donkey, then pauses to remove his sandals, that he loops onto the belt around his waist.

'I don't mean with bare feet, though whatever you wish!'

'My feet are just a bit sore,' he replies. 'I haven't had these sandals long and they're rubbing. Barefoot is always best.'

'Fair enough.'

'So what's the route from here?'

'We walk straight through the centre – just keep your head down and walk with me. Don't stop to talk to anyone – not today.'

John would like at least a little eye contact to be able to read how Zac is feeling, but he's completely shut himself off. Being asked to say nothing is always hard when you are one for speaking your mind. Still, he must oblige – they'll be at the house in no time and then he'll ask all his questions. The breeze has really picked up and the sun is already beginning to set. The sea seems so much closer than it does in Joppa, where the community is huddled together in too little space on the hill that goes up and up. Here you can see the sea on all sides, and so much is jostling for John's attention – the shops selling glass, woven rugs and bags, carvings, the impromptu market stalls with fish that's just come in from the busy harbours; but it is the people who are distracting John from all this, for they have stopped their conversations and their purchasing to stare at Zac. He isn't looking at anyone but has picked up speed, walking Nir at a pace that she doesn't seem comfortable with. John feels he shouldn't be looking at them either as it's impolite not to share a greeting, so he keeps step with Zac, finding himself all but out of breath.

After a few minutes Zac takes a hard turning to the left and heads for a house set back on a small hillock that overlooks the rest. It is a narrow path and John allows Zac to walk ahead.

'It's very overgrown,' says Zac, pausing to observe a scratch on his forearm that starts to bleed. 'What a thorny mess, I'll have words about this.' He's walking now with a renewed purpose.

To *have words* – is that really necessary? John hums an agreement, just to fill the silence that comes, as much as anything, while Nir stumbles for a couple of strides –

'See what I mean?' says Zac, turning to watch her right herself. But soon the path is coming to a close.

'This is it, John,' he's told.

It is a welcome sight, though he'd much rather be looking at his own humble home. He'll linger over tying Nir up in the yard, he thinks, and fills an old stone trough for her from a jar of water that's standing by. Would Mim be thinking of them? If only he could let her know they'd arrived safely. Still, loitering out here isn't going to help Zac, he decides. 'Well done, old girl,' he says to the donkey. 'Now I'd better go and see to the master of this place.' For a moment he stops though to observe the beauty that surrounds him – there's an established grapevine in the courtyard and a gallery running around the edges, with pillars at regular intervals. The vine has wrapped itself around one of the pillars, though the leaves have dropped as it's received no water. How he could make use of a house like this in Joppa! How many rooms must it contain? There are two staircases that he can see, and two separate roof areas on different levels. How the other half live, he thinks to himself. But then Zac has talked of giving all this up – no wonder he went quiet on their return. John removes the bags from across Nir's back and heads inside.

'Zac, I'm here,' he calls out, his voice echoing in the large open space that greets him. 'Where are you?'

This is perhaps the most exquisite building he's ever been into. The sun shines in through a lattice window in a low ceiling above the door. Ahead of him the ceiling is very high, with exposed beams that run the length of the room. A wide wooden staircase leads up to the roof, while several arched doorways lead off in different directions on this lower level.

'Zac? Where are you?'

No answer.

John decides to explore, and takes the staircase two stairs at a time, only to see Zac on his knees in a room just off to the side, almost at the top.

'Ah, Zac, what's the matter?' he asks, stopping in the doorway to watch his visibly broken friend.

'It's been looted. Most all my things have gone – furniture, wall hangings, rugs. The cupboards are empty, and there's not a sign of anyone; I think my servants have all left me.'

'Well, you've not been here to pay them,' says John. Zac looks at him now and John can see that he's shaking, unable to control a tremble that's going right through him. He's sweating profusely, though the temperature is cool. 'They probably thought you were gone for good and took your property in lieu of what you owed them. I expect you'll get it all back though, once they know you've returned. Keep in mind why you've come back – it was only temporary, from what you've told me. That's right, isn't it?'

'I don't know any more. How can I set up home again when this one needs so much repair? What am I to do?'

'We can find the believers tomorrow. I'm sure they'll help us. Once word gets around that you're back everything will come right. Besides, they're only *things*. You could've been dead after what happened to you. Think on that, Zac. Think on that.'

Zac only sighs and ruffles his crazy hair before standing up.

'Right, we need something to eat. It's so cold in here, too. Let's light a fire in the courtyard and see if there's anything left to cook with. Have you any extra blankets, any spare clothing?'

'Nothing. All that's left is my cloak with the blue edging. That's deliberate, John. It's like the colour pronounces my crime. I can't bear to see it again.' He takes it from the hook on the door and holds it at arm's length, as if ready to dispose of it.

'It's a good cloak, and a whole lot warmer than the one I'm wearing.'

'Have it, though I suggest you only wear it in the house.'

John nods his gratitude before he speaks. 'Well, let's make a plan for tomorrow – who do you want to speak to first?'

'No idea, no idea.' He shakes his head. 'Oh, I'm going to wrap this place up quickly. Don't care if I make a massive loss. I'm simply reminded of so much here – of all my failings. I've decided something,' he says and pauses –

'What's that, Zac?'

'My fleet of boats – I'm passing them on – if they haven't already been taken, that is. I'm also setting up a fund.' He pauses again and John raises his eyebrows and shoulders in succession – 'Go on.'

'Obvious, I'd have thought. For the widows of my making – your Joppa widows always were a reminder for me. That's all for the morning. We'll find the believers and leave the details with them.'

***

Chapter Nine

'Penn, it's so good of you to come – had you heard I'm on my own with the girls?'

Mim's brightness looks like it's going to be a problem – she can see it now. 'Oh, Mim, I think it's *you* that hasn't heard.'

'Hasn't heard what?'

'Look, can I come in?'

Mim shuts the courtyard gate firmly for the toddlers' safety and Penn waits until she has turned to face her. 'I've left him,' she tells her. Well, there's no point working up to this...

'Who? Not your husband? I thought he was away.'

'Oh, he's back – well, it *appears* to be him, but he's not the husband I remember.'

'Go on.' Mim is sitting on the floor now, apparently having grasped this is not going to be a quick visit and will take some explaining. How easy it all is for her – Mim with her perfect ideals, but a husband who poses no threat, who makes her life a dream. Has she ever been challenged by life's circumstances? Has she ever even felt unloved? Her two smallest rest into her lap, each reaching up and grabbing her hair, her cheek, any part of her they can hold onto.

'He's a changed man, Mim.' Penn sits beside her and now the eldest enters the courtyard from the house and runs towards her, every step suggesting she'll fall, but in a moment she launches herself at Penn and clasps her hands around her neck.

'You can't just *leave* him,' Mim says, with that grave look of hers.

As she'd feared then – why did she think coming here would be a good idea?

'Changed how?'

'I saw him flirting in the prostitutes' alley,' she says, pulling the child's hand from her hair and encouraging her to sit beside her as she pats the floor. 'And I think he felt my eyes on him because he turned in the crowd and looked straight at me –'

'Any one of us can walk through there. It doesn't make us guilty.'

'Yes, but he was more than flirting. He was with one, Mim. I could tell – he'd just picked her up, of that I'm certain.'

'Certain how?'

'She held a fistful of his tunic, like he was some great catch even.'
'Ah. Go on.'
'He pretended not to know who I was at first. But I strode up to him and said, 'It's your *wife*, remember?' Still he looked at me blankly, until I said in a loud voice, "I know what'll identify you – I know exactly where you have –". At that he grabbed my wrist and marched me off rather forcibly, before I could even say. He kept me walking and I wondered where we'd stop. He walked me through the town and to the cliff edge – I even wondered if he'd push me off!'
'Oh, I don't think you're in any danger, Penn!'
'I think I was. He was so rough with me.'
'So what did he say?'
'"Penn," he said, with laughter in his voice. "A woman is pregnant because of me!"'
'I don't understand,' says Mim.
'Just listen. "That's nothing to be proud of," I told him. "But *you're* the problem," he said, "Don't you see!"'
'Mim, he blamed the fact we haven't been able to have any children on me.' She looks at the children all around her and shrugs her shoulders, raises her hands in the air with expression – oh how to explain? 'He said he's waited long enough, that he's had time to think and he's decided we're not a good fit. That he needs a son. I think it's just an excuse…'
'So when was this?'
'It's days ago now.'
'Oh Penn, that's no time at all. He'll be back, just you wait and see. In the meantime, you can stay here. Of course you can. Just so long as he knows where you are.'
'He doesn't want to know, but I'll be easy enough to find. It's over, Mim. It really is.'
'How can you be so sure? You need to give it time, see if you can work things through. Perhaps he has a head injury too.'
'We've talked at length. I don't think he was expecting me to see him in Joppa, but it was dangerously close to home. He says that he's been enjoying the temple prostitutes. He says I'm hung up, too. That, just possibly, I might have conceived if I'd let him hold me several times a day, as he'd wanted to. You know, I've seen his outline down there before but I told myself I was being silly, and I was seeing him everywhere, in all sorts of people, if you know what I mean. But I feel sure it *was* him now – the shadowy figure that so reminded me

of him *was* him, and it happened more than once. I just couldn't believe it, it seemed so irrational.'

'It makes no sense. If he wants to be a father, he needs to settle down. There's no shortage of children in our community – if you want to be parents, we could sort that tomorrow.'

'I don't believe he does, not now, not ever.'

'Well, you must stay here, at least until John is back. But then what? I mean, what of the future?'

'I'm not going back to him, not to that house either. He's dead to me, Mim.'

'Back to Tabitha?'

'Oh Mim, she's a different generation. She doesn't get me.'

'You should give her a chance.'

'I've always felt uncomfortable there. I worried I was going to catch her illness when I stayed in the room where she died. I know it's silly – illogical really. But I did fear it.'

'That's not going to happen, Penn. She's fine now anyway.'

'Oh, all that worrying after him. All for what?'

'Like I've said, you can still have children – look, there's plenty to go around!'

'Sorry Mim, but I'm not like you. It's so easy for you – life is easy. You could be happy if you were me – you'd find the good in it. I can't – it would have been better to have remained in my assumed widowhood.'

'That's not true, Penn. We'll get you through this. And that husband of yours – he still might prove you wrong.'

Chapter Ten

'You really are back quickly, Zac,' Mim calls from the roof, landing her basket of washing on the floor. What've you done with John? And where's the donkey?'

Zac says nothing for a moment and ties up the horse he's been riding. She's down the stairs and in the yard already. 'You could have waited for him – there's no way Nir would've kept up with you on *that*.' She's laughing now, whilst standing on tip toes to look between the houses and along the path. 'Why, you've been gone less than a fortnight. You were at least true to your word.'

She stoops to scoop up Charis who'd toddled outside and had begun pulling on her apron. 'Can I not spread out the washing, Charis? It needs the sunshine, look here – you messed this up this morning and I've washed it already! Isn't Imma fast?'

She's laughing again, no doubt relieved he's back, always so cheerful and buoyant.

'Mim, I don't know how to tell you this. I am so, so sorry.'

'Tell me what? You're starting to bother me now.'

Zac walks into the house, his head down and crouches in a dark corner, for the shutters are still closed. Now he is crying, his big shoulders shaking, rubbing the heels of his hands into his eyes.

'Zac – where's John? *Tell* me.'

'He's not coming back.'

'What? What do you mean?'

'There's been a tragedy,' he says between sobs. 'You know people always said we're alike, don't you? Well, he went to sleep in my chamber, wearing my best robe. I was asleep on the roof; I couldn't bear to be in the house. It was a case of mistaken identity, Mim.'

She is silent. Has she got it? 'I'm so, so sorry. Someone came in the night – they must have seen us arrive, or had heard I was home. I didn't imagine *he'd* be in danger! Of course I didn't! I'd never have agreed to his coming back with me. I've brought you nothing but trouble.'

'Perhaps we should send for Cephas. He should bring him back, like he did Tabitha. Oh, this can't be happening! What were you thinking? I need you to leave, Zac.'

'Mim, I never intended this to happen. You know I didn't.'

'This really shouldn't be! I need John – we're good together. And we've got all *this* going on – how can I possibly do it without him?'

'I know, I know! Oh, that you'd never taken me in the first time. I will supply all your needs here – I will fund these children, this home. I will try to do everything for you that John did.'

'I want you to leave! But where is he now? How are you going to bring him home? Can you send for Tabitha immediately – she'll know what to do. This was never meant to happen, Zac. Never!'

***

Tabitha arrives in a great rush of warmth and reassurance, but she isn't exactly helpful. 'Mim, it is as he said. You need to let him go now – leave him with the Lord. I know this is terrible, but there *is* no other way.' Tabitha is a blur of noise and colour, but some of her words reach Mim's understanding. For herself, she has articulate moments, but mostly she knows not what to say. 'The believers are seeing to his burial in Tyre,' continues Tabitha, 'and Zac is heading back there now, even though he'll clearly be in considerable danger.'

'But God brought *you* back, Tabitha! Where's Cephas? Shouldn't we at least try?'

'We don't know where Cephas is this week. But a group of them have prayed for John. They sent messengers and called a large number together. You know, I really don't think it's down to who's praying. It's the Lord who brings healing anyway. The ultimate healing is to be *with* him – and, oh, I know where he's gone, Mim. If you could only see it – and the tangible, closeness of the Lord! To be with him – Mim, you need to –'

'That's all very well for you to say, but we're young. Our lives were ahead of us, and we've taken on so much together.'

Why hadn't the Lord kept Tabitha but allowed John to come back? Wouldn't that make more sense, surely? Oh, why did he even have to go in the first place? They didn't think to ask, did they? If only they could go back in time, stop that conversation from ever happening.

What was the point in all this? To be with Jesus? That's years away... years! How hard it is to breathe – perhaps that's the answer anyway; to just go with it. But all these little ones... they need parenting, of course they do. Oh, how to move forward from here?

***

It seems that every day Tabitha is present, and today's most recent conversation now plays on Mim's mind. 'Has Zac gone?' she'd asked her. 'Where is he?'
'He's staying with Simon, the tanner.'
'What, Tabitha? Would no one else have him? I'm really not surprised.'
'No, Mim. He went straight there on the day he returned from Tyre. He hadn't asked anyone else.'
It's hard to keep track of the days now, the weeks. Occasionally it feels to her as if her consciousness comes up for air. There is always someone here when she does – Penn, most often, it seems. The children are being cared for, there is company in the house, the place is swept. But she's not easy to be around, and she is hard to know. They tell her she's been ill – delirious, all brought on by stress and a yearning heart. Her mind is a blank space, and she really is not good company. 'You would do well to leave me,' she tells her visitors – 'return to pay me a visit a long time from here.'

***

And so, the months turn into years, the believing community continuing to grow in number, the tale of Tabitha's return reaching new people daily, neighbour telling neighbour, friend telling friend. The hard work is still done by the few, but there is much love amongst them all, and in one corner in particular a rather special love has begun to grow.

The tanner will live on his own again now, though not through any falling out or ill-will, for Mim had begun to soften towards Zac a while ago, and at last a day of celebration has come. Sometimes she has to remind herself of his name, such is the resemblance. But it is his constancy and his tenderness, in the face of her hostility, that mean she trusts him now, and knows his love to be as steady and sure as John's. At times, she asks herself, *Why did God allow it? For what purpose?* It will make sense one day, but for now she mustn't overthink it – she simply puts her hand in his and in God's.

'I trust you,' she tells him today. 'I am yours, for as long as God allows it.'

The young girls look on and smile, for they love him and remember his fatherly kindness from when they were small. A stranger in the crowd observes the young girls in their beautiful tunics with wildflowers in their hair; perhaps she feels a pain in her chest, for her hand shoots to cover it when she sees the smallest turn to face her. A red birthmark covers much of the girl's face, though the woman's reaction isn't in horror or disgust. 'I'm from a neighbouring town,' the woman tells the person standing next to her. 'What a beautiful scene. Can you tell the family that a distant relative has witnessed them today and would like to visit them? I've had my own change in circumstances, you see.' She explains that they are imitating well the kind man Christ who she has heard so much of around these parts. Would it be possible to know more, she asks? How might she become more a part of things, and what must she do to show that she believes?

'Stay on for the celebrations,' she is told. 'Knowing the couple, it's certain that you will be very welcome. After the feast there will be dancing long into the night under the stars.'

The Bible story for Tabitha can be found in Acts, chapter 9, verses 36-42. For Simon the Tanner, visit Acts, chapters 9 and 10.

Note to the reader: While only Tabitha, Simon the tanner and Peter are found in the Bible, I have brought in some imagined characters to explore other aspects of life in Joppa. I have used details from the real Joppa and Tyre in the creation of this story. I hope I have been faithful to the life of the early church; their care for widows, the shipwrecked, the multitude of abandoned babies and anyone in need is well known, and so these aspects of their witness are elaborated on and explored.

The outcast is my main theme in this story, and I'm sure Peter chose to stay with Simon the Tanner to reach out to him, and bring him into the body of the church. A challenge for us is to consider who the outcasts are in our own communities. Who do we exclude, unintentionally or otherwise? Would a first century believer recognize us as one of their own by the outward kindness that we show?

'O Gladsome Light'
O gladsome Light, O Grace
of God the Father's face,
th'eternal splendor wearing;
celestial, holy, blest,
our Savior Jesus Christ,
joyful in Thine appearing.

Now, as day fadeth quite
we see the evening light,
our wonted hymn outpouring;
Father of might unknown,
Thee, His incarnate Son,
And Holy Ghost adoring.

To Thee of right belongs
All praise of holy songs,
O Son of God, Life-giver;
Thee, therefore, O Most High,
The world does glorify
And shall exalt forever.

JERUSALEM
Acts 12:1-19

Chapter One
Rhoda's story

'Rhoda, have you wondered why I haven't been talking to you lately?'

Rhoda stopped her sweeping just for a moment and turned to face the girl, so as to be respectful, of course. Squinting into the sun, she couldn't help noticing that she was now a little taller, though they were the same age. 'No, Miss, I can't say I have,' she replied.

'It's because I don't like you.'

'Oh,' said Rhoda, and she lifted her brush to resume the task she'd been given.

'Oh?' The girl stepped up closer to her and looked hard into her eyes, just to drive her message home. 'Is that all you have to say? Aren't you just a little bit upset?'

'You're free to like and dislike whoever you please.' Rhoda blinked away the glare of the sun and swallowed hard.

'You're right there – and you used an important word: *free*. That's something you'll never be. No one will ever notice you, remember you. They won't even know your name. Isn't that an interesting thought?'

'I'm not here to be remembered. I'm here to serve and I'm fine with that.' Again, Rhoda tried to go on with her work, but still the girl continued –

'*Fine with that.* Fine? You're so ditsy, so forgetful that you're lucky to still be here. Anyway, I have some jobs for you to do, some tidying, some sorting out, so come to my chamber when you've finished sweeping the yard. And I need someone to hang out with when you're done. In the absence of proper company, you will have to do.'

***

As it turned out, there was no time to 'hang out' together – thank goodness – for things were intensifying again. If it wasn't over someone she loved it would be quite exciting – why were all these things happening to those who were on God's side, anyway? She needed some answers on that one. 'Cephas has been arrested!' they said – it was whispered around the house at first, but soon confirmed by the believers who started to appear in the courtyard, in ones and twos and then more, until the yard was full and the house thronging. Rhoda had been down in the cool, vaulted cellar when the gossip started. She had to stop her singing to catch all of it, just to be sure. Then she was collecting washing on the roof and heard it there, and on every floor in between.

And now, as expected, her house was the place for the believing community to congregate. How flustered they all were, talking too quickly, wondering who would be next, what they should do. Grown-ups always needed more faith, in her experience. *But was anyone there with Cephas*? they said. *Well, the soldiers certainly were – four squads*, rumour had it, *to watch him through the night – can't take any chances with believers of Jesus, they stopped at nothing*, that's what people were saying outside, and *look how Jesus even defied the grave – dangerous, that's what they were*. What misunderstanding, and the frustration was so real! *Herod's going to bring him before the crowd after Passover*, that was the present rumour being shared – making a spectacle of him, just as they did with Jesus! Was it becoming a time of year when they liked to punish the believers the most, as if to make a point? Were they really such a threat? And Herod was just evil, everyone said it. Some people play board games with knucklebones, which Rhoda had always found creepy, but *he* preferred to do it with people – real, living, whole people, tossing them around like counters.

'How could he?' they'd said recently, when they heard of how he'd murdered James, John's brother – the house had filled up with believers on that day, too. Disbelief quickly turned to anger, and then increased fear. 'He'd met his match,' some said – 'James the son of thunder was more of a threat than most of us,' 'His temper always was a problem,' others said of him. 'None of us are safe,' they all concluded. John was stunned and walked around in a daze for days, uttering 'But how could he?' and 'How does our God of love manage to love even him?'. 'Dear James, how is it?' he'd wonder aloud. 'With Jesus already.' John seemed oblivious to the fact he was still in Mary's house, and Rhoda would find him stock-still in his trance-like state, sitting in a window seat recess, or gazing from the fortress-like parapet on the roof. She felt glad he was unable to fall with that low ornamental wall hemming him in.

Now Mary, Rhoda's mistress, called them all to order, clapping her hands and asking for peace while she spoke. 'Everyone in the courtyard, please make your way into the reception hall.' They did as she asked and seated themselves on the floor, that fear really taking over now as reality made itself at home. Rhoda stood to one side as everyone filed in, before taking her place at the back of the room, nearest the door. Cephas would usually speak to the assembled group like this, and his absence was made all the more poignant when the mistress of the house stood at the front and began to speak. 'Will we be led by fear, good people?' she said, for clearly, she was sensing it, too. 'What does the Lord require of us? To voice our fears or our requests to him? Hasn't Jesus instructed us to pray on these occasions? Hasn't our Father stepped into this situation already? He calls us to join him in this – he wants our effort, our engagement, not our panicked protestations.'

Then a holy silence ensued, before the Lord's name was spoken, praises uttered, and the imploring began. It was a radical time, where all human boundaries were forgotten, where men and women joined their voices, where free stood beside slave and agreed together in prayer. The household slaves were only distinguishable from the others by their matching light brown over-tunics[7], and their prayers and fervour matched those whom they served. It was the unity Jesus had prayed for in his church: "I pray also for those who will believe in me through their message, that all of them may be one, Father, just as you are in me and I am in you."[8] His disciples quoted him often.

'Lord, be not displeased with us, your church,' prayed an old believer. They said he was once a cripple who was healed when Cephas and John spoke to him in Jesus' name years ago, outside the temple. He's refused to leave Jerusalem, even though he knew the danger he was in. Rhoda admired his spirit. 'Don't punish us for whatever wrong you see in us,' he went on. 'First James – now this. We can't lose our leader, Lord. We need Cephas, we're not ready to do this without him.'

'Lord, we *know* you,' added Nathaniel in a voice loud enough for most of Jerusalem to hear. 'Oh, that we could *see* you again! We want you close like you were before. It's like when you were asleep on the

---

[7] See article, 'The Slave's Dress' by M. Maclaren:
https://biblehub.com/sermons/auth/maclaren/the_slave's_dress.htm
[8] (John 17, 20-21).

boat, Jesus. Please can you understand how urgent this is. Would you act, Lord? We need you to hear us. Don't give up on us now.'

'Lord, I don't think things are going as you'd want,' said Andrew. Well, that was an understatement. 'Please would you step in, before it's too late...'

'Lord, you were here among us,' said Rhoda's father, and suddenly she felt very proud. She opened her eyes to enjoy the moment – he was standing next to Nathaniel and had just as much right to pray as him; he mattered to Jesus just as much. 'Some of us met you – don't abandon us now!' he went on. 'Yet we all meet you daily, we know your presence here with us. Lord, please do your miraculous work again. Don't let Cephas die. Would you be at work, even now, on his behalf.' The believers agreed with him in 'Amens', emphatic hums and utterances of praise.

Cephas' wife was at the front of the group near Rhoda's mistress, and she could see her shoulders shake, as if she was sobbing. The mistress had placed an arm around her shoulder and looked as if she was trying to reassure her. Being married to one of Jesus' disciples couldn't be easy – had they known what they were getting into? Rhoda was a little in awe of her. Yet once you know how good the Lord is, how worthy of everything, there really is no other way. What choice did they have? Anything less would be unsatisfying for all of them – she felt sure of that.

The praying was getting louder now, as if to drown out the sobbing that seems to be catching on among some of the women folk. Rhoda wanted to give them a talking to – tell them to pull themselves together, that their crying wasn't helping anyone, but they wouldn't listen to her, and besides, she was meant to be praying, like the rest of them.

'Jesus, would you be with Cephas. Would you see to it that he is released!' Well, he didn't need to shout. The voice belonged to Thaddaeus – the mistress said they barely knew who he was when Jesus was alive but now he was radical – even more so than the others at times. They would all be far less effective on their own, Rhoda thought. They were greater, stronger versions of themselves when working together – that was something she'd noticed. She tried not to be fearful herself, but sometimes things got to her too. She couldn't help thinking of what they were meant to be commemorating, when God delivered their people out of Egypt, and she watched Thaddaeus just for a minute, worrying a thread on the sleeve of his tunic as he prayed. The man was practically jogging on the spot, but at least he channelled his surplus energy towards a worthy cause.

Thaddaeus would have been good on that exodus out of Egypt long ago, when there wasn't enough time to eat bread that had risen, and they ate it as it was.[9] He'd have got them all moving and would have run with his great long strides. They served the same God, and he had accomplished so much since those days of old. Weren't they simply part of a continuing story – hadn't Jesus overcome so much more since then? He hadn't changed, nor had his power... 'Oh, Lord, we're remembering how you delivered your people out of Egypt these days,' Rhoda found herself praying, 'and we know you deliver still. Father, would you please deliver Cephas safely to us? ...Amen.'

The praying went on as the day darkened, visible through the lattice windows in the reception hall. No one would be wanting a meal tonight, and so Rhoda enjoyed being a part of the prayer meeting that was going on around her, her official duties done for the day. The stars that flickered outside looked to her like the smallest of flames in the sky, blazing where no one could put them out. She had watched them come out one by one, as those around her uttered their prayers. The message of Jesus was exactly like this – unquenchable and breaking out wherever he pleased. Stamp out one believer, smother his flame, and another would appear somewhere else – God would get his message out there, come what may, and he would even use Rhoda in some small way, she felt sure. She loved to think of the flame her mother told her of, from that first moment the Holy Spirit fell on their believing community on the day of Pentecost. She was very small on that occasion, with no faith of her own to speak of, but amazingly a flame was on her then too. 'You always did have a mighty flame,' her mother would remind her. 'See, I remember you at that astonishing day of Pentecost... too little to know what was going on, you were, but the Holy Spirit didn't exclude you. I think you were only three. You did believe in him though, in your own way – how could you not?'

How Rhoda cherished that story. 'Tell me again,' she'd say. 'Tell me more,' she'd plead whenever her mother raised it, and it was often. Her mother spoke it to settle her to sleep when she was tiny, and now the conversation ran on in her head.

---

[9] Exodus 12:39

'See, the flames were on everyone's heads, Rhoda – male, female, slave and free, old and young. He made no distinction then, nor does he now. But I remember *your* flame, Rhoda. It seemed disproportionate for the size of you. That flame burns within you now.'

Her mother loved that story almost as much as she did, she felt sure, though they had no cause for complaint. It was strange to think of themselves as owned. *Slavery* didn't really explain their existence in this widow's house, though it was true – they were not free to leave Jerusalem at will. They had never wanted to leave the community here, and, if they did, she doubted the mistress would object. The reality was they were in the thick of things, where all the action was taking place, and it was exciting. God was using her. Her little friends, whom she could just about recall, left only a year after that special day, from what her mother had told her. The believers were scattered in a wave of persecution, and now there were few of her age around. She was told they would all have loved to stay round the apostles, but Jerusalem was just too dangerous – the 'slavery' of her family meant they would always be here, and her own mother and father would no doubt have taken them away from the horrors at the first opportunity, should they have been free to do so.

Sitting still in prayer meetings was always hard, but it did give Rhoda time to think. So she didn't have many of her own age to be friends with, and Chana was okay really. She was just one frustrated girl, and she'd be much better company if she could truly believe. It was hard to understand how she could be so apathetic in the light of what they were living and experiencing daily, and Rhoda knew she had a special responsibility here, though she would never say it to her face – she would really be in for it if she did. This was one area in which she was her superior, which was funny to think on. The grown-ups were much better – they really did live out the equality in Christ idea that they'd heard so much about. There was so much Rhoda would like to be able to say to Chana, but she had to stop herself. She knew that Jesus spoke about the last being first,[10] and that had often brought a smile to Rhoda's face that Chana had rebuked her for – 'Stop grinning, would you? I don't know what you've got to look so pleased about.' She'd be better off in heaven, she knew that. But then she reminded herself that she was way more like Chana than she was

---

[10] Matthew 20:16.

Jesus, and her character had a very long way to go. She and Chana might be together in heaven, at the very end of the queue. Yet to be there! To be serving Jesus – that would be something. But of course, they were serving him, in the here and now. "What you do for the least of these, you do for me."[11] Those words of Jesus were a help too. Perhaps the opportunities to serve him on earth would never be matched, and she would pray in her mind now that he would use her boldness, allow her to make a difference for him on earth. For that was what it all was really about – one hopeless wanderer telling the next hopeless wanderer where to find a home.

It was getting very late, and it looked like they would be up all night praying, though Rhoda didn't mind. Her community was at its best at moments like this and she loved it. But, oh! There was someone at the gate – Rhoda could hear knocking and it was her job to answer. It sounded insistent – urgent. Could it be that Herod was rounding them all up now so he could do away with the lot of them? She was determined not to be frightened. No one else seemed to have heard and she could just ignore it, but Jesus wouldn't be pleased with that. No – he wanted a bold courageous Rhoda, and she scrambled to her feet and slipped out of the door. The night air was cold, and she was glad to be outside, running with exuberance towards the gate. She stopped herself before opening it, her hand pressed against it in a momentary pause – 'Who is it?' she said, her voice croaking, the fear now taking over as she did what was required of her. 'What do you want?'

'It's Cephas,' came the reply. He spoke quietly but it certainly sounded like him. She knew his voice well; she had stood next to him, prayed with him, even poured a drink for him and taken his cloak. He was as familiar to her as her own family, and in importance second only to Jesus himself. Cephas – it was Cephas! Was he back from the dead like Jesus, or could it even be his ghost? That's what they said happened, didn't they?[12]

Rhoda found herself back inside the gathering, declaring what they had been praying for, longing for, since the moment of his arrest. 'Cephas is outside! Come and see! I went to the gate and his voice

---

[11] Matthew 25:35-36
[12] It was a commonly held belief that 'a guardian angel would sometimes appear shortly after death.' This explains the believers' response, "It is his angel." See Holman Study Bible, NKJV Edition, Holman, Tennessee, 1982. P.1854.

was as clear as mine, speaking to you right now. Our God answers prayer! Oh, I always knew he did!'

'Rhoda, go and sit down,' they said.

'Rhoda, it is his angel.'

'You're out of your mind.'

'It's late, you're tired, see,' her mother said, but then, with a glint in her eye, 'Who ever it is, they're still knocking.'

Why they bothered to pause to listen was baffling, and Rhoda had had enough. 'I'm coming!' she shouted, running across the courtyard to the gate. She flung it open wide and there stood Cephas, his face shining, the broadest smile on his face that matched Rhoda's own. How good was their God! Rhoda was practically jumping on the spot and flapping her hand, like she was a bird about to take off. But how incredible!

Some of the other believers had gathered behind Rhoda. Cephas suddenly looked very serious, and he put a finger to his lips to make them listen. Finally Nathaniel thought to usher him in through the gate and he closed it behind him, but still Cephas didn't head for the house – he seemed agitated, but then they began to realize that the soldiers were probably following him! They would be banging on the gate any minute, they knew where to find the believers, Rhoda felt sure – or they'd find them easy enough.

Cephas walked into the house now and quietened them down a second time. 'I have to be brief – there is no time to lose.' He really was radiant, there was no doubting it. 'An angel came to me in prison,' he said. Didymus touched his cloak very gently now from behind, just to make sure it really was him – the talk of angels seems to have prompted him, though Cephas didn't notice. 'It was the Lord's doing. Glory be to him! "Quick! Get up!" the angel said. My chains literally dropped to the floor, like they were nothing. For it was as if they'd been made of reeds, the lack of strength there was in them to restrain me. "Get dressed and put on your sandals," he said. I could have left them behind for the soldiers – a keepsake!' and he was laughing with tears. 'I don't think they saw me leave. But I don't know, for I was bewildered for a time – I barely knew what was happening. The gates opened for us – more readily than this gate here,' he said, again with laughter in his voice.

His wife stood by his side and he was holding her hand. He looked at her now, an apology in his eyes that were suddenly large and doleful. 'I cannot stay,' he said, 'for it's dangerous. They will be following me, as soon as they realize. Perhaps they already are. Tell James and the other brothers what happened,' he said to all of us. Turning to face his wife, 'You'll know where to find me. Just don't come yet, for they will follow you. Know that I love you,' and with that he was gone.

***

'See, I knew God had singled you out for important things,' Rhoda's mother told her on the staircase to the second storey, her face somehow glowing in the darkness. 'Right from when you were small, when the Holy Spirit came, I knew.'

'Yes mother, I know!' Rhoda whispered her reply, at the level she wished her mother would use. 'But keep your voice down. I was only doing my duty, and I didn't do that very well, by all accounts.'

'I don't see why?'

'Leaving him on the street like that! Imagine if he'd been caught by them, waiting there at the gate when he was in such danger. I'll never live it down!'

'Well I think you were very brave. I don't think it's right really that you should be the one to open the gate to strangers – it puts you in the path of trouble.'

'I like it, Imma. It gives me a chance to show my devotion to God. And if they take me, they've come for us all. It makes no difference – please don't say anything, will you?'

'Well, not tonight. There's enough going on anyway. I'll see everyone has what they need in the women's quarter. You get some sleep now, it's well past your bedtime, I think you'll find.'

The house was certainly full that night and not much sleeping would be going on, Rhoda felt, at least for a while. She didn't mind, though she was used to having plenty of space in what was, in a strange way, her house, as much as her mistress'. She lived here just as the mistress did – she knew it better perhaps, for she polished the mosaics, got on her hands and knees to clean each corner, to sweep every floor. It was her privilege. And to be born into this believing community – it was the best thing in the world. There was just one little sticking point – Chana was going to be insufferable in the morning, though perhaps the events of tonight might help her believe. Imma knew what the girl was like but tried to make light of it. 'See, she doesn't have anyone else her age in the house – you're the closest thing she has to a sister, and siblings always fight.' Rhoda knew that they might well be around each other into old age, when the parents, slave and free, had all passed away. That was fair enough. She didn't mean to antagonize the girl – but it wasn't just Chana, actually, who commented on her 'incessant enthusiasm'. 'Would you stop your singing?' she'd be told. 'Not everyone has your energy, or shares your joy at this hour.' Well, hopefully they'd all share her joy now, and would have a little less fear. God was on their side – how on earth could you keep a lid on that? Yes, God was in charge of the danger – oh, the joy when he overcame! It was harder to contain than ever! Jesus was with them and could bring them through *anything*. And the day he didn't they'd be with him. It really was as simple as that.

Note to the reader:
Some question whether Rhoda was actually a slave, but I think she was. The Greek words given indicate this, and suggest she opened the door as a slave would: *Paidske* meaning 'a maid-servant, a young female slave' and/or 'a maid servant who has charge of the door'. (From BibleStudyTools.com)

As she answers the door, we learn that 'the word used here, *hypakouo*, meaning "obey, listen, or answer," is often used in association with slaves, specifically doorkeepers in ancient literature', according to Christy Cobb (Slavery, Gender, Truth and Power in Luke-Acts and Other Ancient Narratives, Palgrave Macmillan, 2019. p.142.)

We don't know that Rhoda had a family serving in the house of Mary, John Mark's mother, but this is possible. It is also not known if they would all have been there on the day of Pentecost in AD30, but I like to think so. It is thought Acts 12 takes place around the year AD42, so any children who were present then would now be growing up.

By this time in the Acts sequence the believers had been scattered due to persecution. We read in chapter 8 that only the apostles remained. I expect this would have included their wider households.

To me, Rhoda demonstrates contentment in circumstance and a cheerful buoyancy, as she went about her task with acceptance and great enthusiasm.

Chapter Two
The night-watch

The night-watch then, at the Lord's behest. After years of service – centuries even – this didn't get any better, for silence never comes easy to an elated messenger of God. And the Lord was so worthy! What he had done this time! Sometimes, a finely-tuned human ear might hear their worship, and so it was advisable to utter nothing and simply observe. There were many of them surrounding God's people that night – every single believer they had covered, and it was their joy to serve in this way. It was such important work to the Lord, and their faces were so familiar to these heavenly hosts, their voices very dear, for they had heard their first whimpers, their first questions about who God was, their first declarations of faith – all of it. The Lord be praised! It was a miracle that each one believed – the most precious thing to their Lord – and protected they must be.

They had always done this and always would – to think of all the generations of believers to come that they'd protect and serve in exactly this way – the day this finished would be the day *he* had them in heaven for good, for the Lord's constancy never wavered. When each believer was escorted in turn to heaven, new souls would be theirs to watch over, from the first moment in the womb, the appearance of the single cell, dividing into two thirty hours later, and beyond – it's no wonder they grew attached to them, for they saw *everything*. The angelic forces were his feet on the ground, an army that together brought something of his presence. It was their duty to watch over them with great attentiveness, not missing a thing – and there went another one, cares cast aside and dreaming already!

The house was certainly quieting down and most of the believers were now sleeping, which made for an easier few hours in some ways. At last! For a change is as good as a rest – but it was another day well done on their part. Not that they could lower their swords, or let their guard down, as the people would say. If only they knew the provision God had made for them! Never were they alone, not even when, quite frankly, they'd rather leave them... they had learnt to avert their eyes whilst still remaining alert. Seeing their faith grow – yes, that was always a remarkable thing, and so often they wanted to congratulate them, tell them the Father was pleased with this deed or that, but to do so would be breaking the contract. Humans were always fickle, quick to transfer their devotion to something or someone unworthy, and the purpose was simply to protect them and point them to God, who was worthy of all praise. Glory be to him! How embarrassing it was when the people showed them gratitude, or spoke highly of them, or even tried to *pray* to them, speak with them – it didn't touch them – only mortified them. There had to be scope for faith to grow, and if they could see the spiritual realm there would be no achievement on their part, no depth of relationship with the Father.

Only occasionally would a believer see them, usually when they were in grave danger, or when they just couldn't grasp something. Oh, the frustration! The Lord enabled them to look like men when they'd had to instruct the disciples to stop gawping at the sky and get on with life: "Men of Galilee," they told them, "why do you stand here looking into the sky? This same Jesus, who has been taken from you into heaven, will come back in the same way you have seen him go into heaven."[13] He could only imagine how distracted they'd have been if God had shown them in their full regalia. 'Will I blend in?' he had asked a leading angel before the appearance. 'You're not glowing now, remarkably – dare I say it, but don't concentrate on the Lord too hard, just for a short while, or you'll radiate his goodness again, which will defeat the object.'

'Sir.'

'But blend in you will – everything about you looks average: height – neither tall nor short, by human standards; colouring – again, like the locals; hair – just mid-length, nothing noticeable. You're a bit ageless though – not a wrinkle in sight, on your face or your clothing. But no one would guess just how many eras you've lived through. The important thing is you're 'normal', which is very necessary in the circumstances – as soon as you've told them he's ascended they might just fix their fitful attentions on you otherwise, which is not what we want. Just act natural. As soon as Jesus ascends, you appear,' he was told. 'It has to be immediate. Then it's back to winged duty.'

All that aside, the ranks had thought then that life would be quieter with Jesus back in heaven – but no, that was just the beginning

---

[13] Acts 1: 10-11.

of things, and the angelic routine had not been the same since. In fact, they had never been so busy! Cephas had always been one of the worst, of course – the believer you always knew that you had. Some parents spoke of their children like that! The fellow kept them fully occupied when Jesus was living with them – always the impetuous one, you never did know quite how he'd react, and several of them had to be close by at all times. They did question why he'd been called at all, though of course it wasn't their place to. Not that Jesus couldn't sort him out, but he'd made them gasp a few times – they still talked about his stepping out of the boat onto those choppy waves, when the wind was at its strongest, as Jesus called him on – that was with the best of intentions, of course. They always reminded each other that he dearly wanted to follow, and the Lord hadn't finished with him yet. For it wasn't all good – far from it. As angels they had stood by him when he'd sliced off Malchus' ear, and even protected him when he denied his Lord – the silly fool.

But he'd pulled himself together lately and was living the life God had intended for him; the party-inducing sort that caused trumpet-blasting and cheering in the ranks, though thankfully the people had no idea of this either, or the tremendous family of brother-warriors all around them, so united in purpose with them. How satisfying it was!

Cephas never was quick to catch on, and tonight his slowness was astonishing! He'd had to strike Cephas on the side – he could sleep through anything, now, that one. The temptation was there to kick him – even the bright light that accompanied the draught of sweeping wings didn't wake him. As angels they were used to making a controlled entrance, but for once the instruction was to be attention seeking and not hold back on the glory, but still Cephas needed more! That said, he was very obedient and did exactly as asked, though it was doubtful he was taking it all in. Of course, it wasn't the first time… could he even be growing used to the Lord's ways? The angels all knew about the occasion when the apostles were set free from jail before, with angelic intervention, of course, and sent to the temple courts to testify – how awesome was their God![14] That had been the talk of heaven, so it was phenomenal, being given the task of leading Cephas out this time.

---

[14] Acts 5:17-41

Tonight had been such an enjoyable evening – being able to put into practice the training he'd received. They'd all been shown what to do, of course, and could be called on at any moment, but then they could be waiting for hundreds of years, as he himself had been. The wait was often about finding a group of believers who were passionate about the Lord's business – even just one individual – and willing to put themselves in danger for heaven's sake. For a significant stretch there had not been enough to go around. But there were a good few of them about at the moment – long may that last! Watching those soldiers fall asleep was entertaining – they thought they were *so* powerful, *so* in control, but even the greatest warrior is puny when the Lord wills something. Nothing can stand up to his might. Those locks and chains were *nothing*. Making Cephas invisible like himself – that was satisfying too. Causing those gates to open… it was the stuff angels dreamt of, and they liked to practice together when a house was unoccupied that they'd been asked to watch over. Nonetheless, there was a danger in thinking he'd made it. All this was the Lord's power, not his own, and he was simply in the right place at the right time, carrying out orders. Pride was a very ugly thing – always had been – and he must guard against it. It made him shudder to think the enemy was once one of them but had plummeted to the depths of the underworld because he'd claimed God's glory. 'The shining one', the head of all heaven's armies, second only to the Lord himself. Well, he *was* – not now. Back then he would ascend the holy mountain and speak with the Lord. That he was once blameless! How busy they had been ever since, but it would not go on forever. Jesus had defeated hell with his death and glorious resurrection. Only a matter of time until he would return, and they said not even he knew the day or the hour – the Father alone held that knowledge. How profound a thought!

And so, they surrounded this little body of believers, for their allegiance was beyond value to the Father. It was all part of his salvation narrative and it would be remembered forever. His people would be so glad they'd been included in his story one day, despite their fear in recent times – it's amazing how the centuries bring perspective. Many of them were not there yet, but the boldness was creeping in, and Cephas was a good example to them. As heavenly hosts they were guarding the believers from danger daily – if only they knew the times they had avoided death, the trials that had been averted, the illnesses that had been driven away from them, at the

Lord's command. Yes, his care over them was beyond belief – it was clear he was beside himself in his devotion to them. His concern lest a rock should trip them[15], or a doubt should plague their minds! Sometimes it made good sense – shutting those lions' mouths for Daniel; they got that. But other times they simply must put it down to his obsession over them, his blind admiration that meant he could not see them as they really were. How the Lord's love was consistent and unchanging, through all the eras of time. Any harm that came their way he had permitted, and they were told it was for a greater good. Of course, some of the believers had died horrific deaths, but they were now dwelling with the Father and even used by him, consulted by him with regards to what was going on. Was that correct? For it was how it seemed to him. Intercessors in heaven, mediating as they had on earth. The Lord never needed input – how could he? – for he knows everything, but it is his choice to involve his people. What a profound mystery! Yes, this was his guess – that they had first-hand experience that he valued – they were even more useful to him than they were when they trod this dusty old earth, though it wouldn't make sense to those living here right now. Their perception was very limited, but as long as they kept their eyes fixed on Jesus, they would be all right.

Ah, well, this wasn't a bad abode, he thought to himself, flexing and stretching his wings and surveying the assembled group as they slept, before looking down at his charge again. It wasn't a patch on heaven, but as far as human accommodation went it was pretty impressive – more so, of course, because the Lord's presence was felt here in great measure. This home was used in service to him, which was what made it significant and placed it on heaven's map. It was a congregating spot for all of Jerusalem's angels, and they enjoyed the high ceilings, that meant they didn't have to duck their heads and watch their wings as they moved through the space. There was enough room for everyone, human and angelic beings alike.

'Praise to Jesus! Our Lord is awesome!'

'Hallelujah!'

Angelic worship had started up in the far corner, for it was hard to contain their gratitude towards him for long. Sometimes you cannot wait. The heavenly hosts had had the fortune of being around him since the creation of time. Oh, the celebration they had when he

---

[15] Psalm 91:11-12

created the world! How they sang, how they danced into the newly made night.[16] Even the stars proclaimed his glory, and they had not stopped – they could not stop. The hosts loved to hear him call out these stars in sequence every night – if they were near, they would hear him name them in order and would want to linger, just to absorb his voice. His creativity never stopped, new stars were always being formed by him, and they hovered to witness what he would call the young ones, just bursting into flame. The Lord could navigate his way through this vast universe without thinking – as angels, he would instruct them where to go, and sometimes it was hard to keep up. But how he loved those he'd made in his image even more – nothing could compare. He had been devoted to them ever since, laboured over their lives, wept over those that rejected him.

He had placed his heavenly concern for them in their angelic hearts too, so that they shed his tears. But oh – the joy when one discovered him for the first time! The utterances they breathed, the exquisite singing that went on for days![17] When humans grasped their sin, together with his overcoming love, when they invited him to come in and dine with them – that made it all worthwhile. As heavenly servants of the Most High, it was their life's purpose – what they were made for, and it brought them such joy. How they would love to read his salvation plans for each one![18] But they must steadfastly serve him, and know that, with their faithfulness and the prayers of the saints, the Lord would be merciful, for they were his plans, not theirs, and his love for them was more than they could comprehend.

There had been far more celebrations since Jesus' death and resurrection – oh, the multitudes that had come to faith in Jerusalem alone! Three thousand on the day of Pentecost, then many more soon after Cephas and John were arrested: estimates at that time were of 5,000 believers of the Way, even aside from the women and children. Not one of them had been missed. The joy on the Father's face, and for each one in turn! If they were in his presence they had to look away, such was the brightness that shone from him, and the sense of intrusion they felt. It was a deeply personal moment, one he had

---

[16] Job 38:4-7

[17] Luke 15:10 (NIV) "In the same way, I tell you, there is rejoicing in the presence of the angels of God over one sinner who repents."

[18] A thought that is inspired by the reference 1 Peter 1:12, "Even angels long to look into these things."

planned for each since before the beginning of time – some said that he designed their moment of salvation at the very time he conceived the idea of them – that the two went hand in hand, and he could not speak them into being, declaring their existence and his love over them, without planning their salvation, too. Of course, many of them missed their initial, intended moment – they were robbed of it, deprived, by believing the whispers of the evil one, but the Lord did not give up, and would try alternative means, speaking his love into them until they finally understood. It was better than watching the most beautiful sunrise he would paint into being, seeing the progression of their understanding, the small frail bodies brought to life, the hearts beating, then the lungs working, until the day they could hear him speak his love and at last accept and respond. Oh, he kept coming back to this! It was his favourite miracle of them all, by far. Every other miracle was to prompt them into believing – the ultimate aim in everything.

How many more days would go on like this until Jesus returned? He looked on a snoring believer and smiled to himself. What eras would pass between now and then – or could it happen tomorrow? How would life on this old earth change? But the human condition didn't seem to alter, whatever they were living through – they were still fallen, in great need of a saviour.

Daylight was starting to seep through the slats in the shutters and some of the believers were stirring now; one or two turned in their sleep, another threw his arm above his head and yawned. The human servants would be up shortly, and so it was time to listen into their plans, see where the angelic help might be needed. Oh, the joy in serving him! A team of them had Cephas covered, but he wasn't the only challenging one, and there was much to do. They would wait on the Lord, for sometimes the needs of the believers were not obvious to them. But with his help they would always be at the destination before they were needed. Never a dull day was had in following him.

Chapter Three
James

'James, will you please settle next to me and get some sleep. What good will it do, you pacing like this?' She patted the empty mattress she'd unrolled hours ago, that remained untouched by him.[19] 'It's getting light.'

'I'm praying for him, Zoe. I can't settle and sleep won't come if I try.'

'Well, it's almost too late now anyway – the day's all but begun.'

'The Lord has heard me.'

'Cephas is probably dead by now,' she said, her eyelids closing again, 'and your fretting won't make a bit of difference.'

'I'm not fretting – I'm praying, like I said. Let's not argue.'

'You need to get over your sense of guilt. I see it in you all the time. Jesus has forgiven you – you need to forgive yourself.'

He lay down next to her and listened to her breathing deepen and slow while he continued in his thoughts. But Cephas! The mighty leader no longer at the forefront of the church, but with the Lord himself. How the believers would be grieving... he wanted to be with them. Again, he was feeling a prompting in his spirit – that the Lord might be challenging him to take on more responsibility. More of an upfront role. The disciples had advised him to get some distance from the action and so he couldn't be sure of what was going on. As Jesus' half-brother, it was felt he was even more at risk than many of the disciples – especially the quiet ones. The resemblance between himself and his older brother was strong, and that provoked people. He stroked his stiff, greying beard – even *with* his obvious aging, it was clear they were brothers. They said that now he had Jesus' self-assurance, now he was right with him and claiming the authority of heaven, the resemblance was even stronger. This was the thing – he didn't need protecting. People still didn't quite understand the extent of his commitment. The yearning he had in his heart to serve. They

---

[19] It is highly likely that James had a wife – in 1 Cor 9 v 5 we read, 'Don't we have the right to take a believing wife along with us, as do the other apostles and the Lord's brothers and Cephas.'

were all in danger; now he felt what his brother had lived with for so long... How he hated himself for rejecting Jesus' message before – Zoe did have a way of seeing into him, knowing exactly what he was thinking. That they called Jesus mad[20] – it was often hard to get beyond that thought. They'd tried to humiliate him, but they'd only humiliated themselves. Oh, the fellowship they could have had, the joy they could have shared! As boys they were brilliant friends, but something took hold in him. He knew it as jealousy now. Looking back, what had he got? Regrets. Yet his determination to tell of Jesus' resurrection was stronger than many who'd pleased him from the start. He was like Paul in this respect – much to be forgiven, yet very passionate because of it. The Lord was calling him into leadership, and with Cephas gone he'd be needed all the more.

It was twelve years since the resurrection, and how that changed *everything*. It was awesome that Jesus bothered with the family then – he had no reason to, and he didn't appear to anyone else who'd been against him.[21] But he cared enough – always had. That was the thing. It was embarrassing – more than that – shameful, that the disciple John had been told by Jesus to look after their mother when he was dying.[22] Could he not have trusted them – were they that bad? But they were. Imagine using your remaining energy to make provision like that – and why? Because your earthly brothers are so shameful! Perhaps he knew that John would talk to her about himself with the right understanding of who he was, the purpose in what he had done. The brothers? Well, they were just angry, confused. Felt that Jesus had let their mother down in continuing with his claims, in not being able to let the thing go and walk away. In practical terms, John was there with her in Jerusalem while they were all back in Galilee, but it was more than that. Of course it was. He wasn't just providing for her in the short term, but in the long term, too.

It was a few weeks after the resurrection that Jesus had appeared to James. He'd heard so much by then – the disciples were back and sharing their stories. Everyone who'd had any faith in Jesus that he knew of was claiming to have seen him; they said he'd appeared to five hundred at once, and the stories grew bigger, wilder, and just wouldn't go away. He felt sure it was all true by then, but what could

---

[20] Mark 3: 21, 31-35.
[21] The resurrected Jesus appears to James: 1 Corinthians 15:7.
[22] John 19: 26-7.

he do? He'd missed his opportunity, made his decision while Jesus was among them. But then it happened – oh, it happened! Jesus appeared to *him*. Just strolled in like he'd never been rejected. Like their boyhood friendship was still intact, and he was as devoted as Cephas and John. It was as if he knew. And he certainly did – James had learned that since – other believers had spoken of the Lord's intuitive understanding to him. Some folk worry they haven't expressed things to Jesus, but he knows every half-formed, groping thought. Those that have led a life rejecting him, saying the most awful things about him, even dying in a moment of pain or disaster, or without the mental capacity to say sorry to him, to articulate in prayer that actually they now believe it all to be true – it was not too late for them, or thousands like them to come. He felt sure of that now. The heart and will can communicate with Jesus even when the mind cannot, whether because of pain, self-doubt or whatever obstacle. But how he wished he'd been like Cephas throughout. It had taken years for the believers to recognize the strength of his commitment, the true depth and reality of his faith. And now, here he was, away from the action, where things were really happening. He wondered if Cephas knew, or had given the believers any indication that he should be in leadership before he died.

***

'Shalom! Shalom! Open up, brother. I have news for you!'

'Does he want the whole street to hear?'

'Don't worry, Zoe. I'll see to it,' he replied, leaping from his mattress while she sat up on the floor and rubbed her eyes. He was out in the yard and unhooking the gate that everyone encouraged him to secure well, though these measures were pointless – if he were to be arrested it would take more than that to keep trouble out.

An out-of-breath lad stepped inside and struggled to get his words out. 'Cephas is safe – he's alive!' He leant forwards on his knees to breathe for a moment. 'We've seen him! He came to the gathering and asked us to tell you.'[23]

'Where is he now? Is he not still with you?'

---

[23] Acts 12:17

'Fled to safety.' The boy sniffed hard and wiped his sleeve across his face. 'They're saying there's plenty more trouble to come, that this is just the start of things. Jerusalem doesn't feel safe anymore!'

'It never did, lad.' James landed a heavy hand on his shoulder. 'You're not old enough to remember all that's gone on here. I'm coming back with you – you've got nothing to fear.'

'I wish Cephas had stayed. Imma says he has more sense. I wonder where he's gone now?' The lad clearly felt the weight of this – it was unusual to see a sense of burden in one so young.

'Take courage. Worse things have happened,' said James, placing his other hand on his back to steer him into the house. 'The point is this: The Lord has rescued Cephas! The Lord is on our side, lad. We can face *anything* with him.'

Zoe was in the courtyard now and looked out of the gate before securing it well with rope. 'We're okay,' James told her. 'Cephas is free – did you hear?'

'I don't understand how?'

'It was an angel,' the lad told them, and they took him inside and sat him down so that he could tell them everything, though in reality he knew little more.

'There's an atmosphere out there,' the boy said. 'It's frightening this morning. There are soldiers out searching and I had to hide from one on my way here. I thought he was following me. They're scared for their lives. Herod will kill them, they say. They think he really means it. It's not good,' he said, trying to mimic James' restraint. No doubt he would brag this story to his friends later, but for now he was feeling it intently and meant every word.

'You need to eat something – join us,' Zoe told him. 'You've woken us up – we haven't eaten yet ourselves. We have some dates here,' she said, getting to her feet and lifting a covering from a small pottery container on the side. 'I'll make some bread cakes in a mom-'

'Don't you see? You're in *danger* here.' His eyes were wild now, almost raging. With this passion he had the makings of a good preacher. 'I was probably followed,' he went on. 'And those soldiers are angry – if they can't find Cephas, they're bound to find some other believers to interrogate. Don't light a fire in the courtyard. Don't make any noise. Just be quiet and wait.' He was tearful now and he blinked hard, no doubt hoping that they wouldn't notice.

'Well, you're staying with us,' said James, shuffling across to sit opposite him so he could give the lad eye-contact. 'And I think we have something to celebrate. God is with us, lad. We mustn't fear like the rest of the world. He's set us free from all that. And if troubles come? It is an opportunity to show faith. To demonstrate joy. He wants us to endure through trials. To know peace. But never to fear. Do you understand?[24]'

'I think so.'

'If we're living in fear, how are we different? What freedom is ours? My brother didn't die for us to be tentative believers, dipping a toe into an ocean of boldness. We pray, we have courage, and we move on. The Lord *will* return. I believe his coming is near, lad. Look to him.'

He nodded, his hands clasped tightly, the most serious expression written into his young face, his brow wrinkled and his eyes still watering with tears which didn't quite tip over the brink.

'I'm not lecturing you! I say this not to burden you but to take the heavy load from your back. Have you ever heard Cephas tell his story about how he stepped out of the boat?'

He nodded intently again.

'You tell me what he learnt.'

'That you fix your eyes on Jesus. Not on the waves all around you. That when you are looking straight at him, you can go forwards, no matter how perilous it looks to everyone else.'

'Good. Go on.'

'If you look down, or look away, then you begin to sink.'

'That's right. Keep looking to Jesus. "Trust in the LORD with all your heart and lean not on your own understanding". It's from Proverbs. It's the only way for a fearful heart. Some of us have to work at it harder than others.'

'You of all people are not fearful, James,' Zoe told him, handing him a dish before sitting down again next to him. James wasn't interested in food, however, and placed it on the floor in front of him.

'I've had to train myself. Still do. I used to carry more than a burden of worry. I worried for him when we were growing up. My brothers liked to mock him – though I joined in, I was scared for him, too. I could see where it was all leading. I've never been good at speaking out. I feel things keenly though. When I do speak out,

---

[24] See James chapter 1 for my inspiration for our protagonist's outlook.

there's a whole lot of thinking behind my words. They may say I'm bold, but then I never was good with words. If I need to get something out, impress something on people, I really mean it. And I've learnt the hard way. Believe me, I have.'

The lad hummed impatiently and began worrying a small flap of skin beside a fingernail. 'So are we going back this morning? I'm meant to be at the house, serving.'

'Everyone cares for your welfare. You know that, don't you? We wouldn't risk your life, put you in the way of danger unnecessarily.'

'I do think the soldiers will still be out. Perhaps we should wait here for a little while.'

'Fair enough.'

The lad looked relieved and dropped his hunched shoulders.

'It's good to see you have *some* sense,' said Zoe.

'Here, have one of these,' said James at last, handing the lad a small barley cake. Made yesterday but still fresh.'

'I'm not hungry really,' said the lad, folding his arms across his stomach as he sat squatting on the floor.

'These are excellent,' said James. 'Quite sweet, with figs and honey.' He put the cake in the shallow dish again and went over to the window. He wanted to look out from the roof really but realized that posed something of a risk. Of course he wouldn't see anything from here.

'Try it,' said Zoe to the boy with a kind smile. 'You're not putting us to any trouble. I don't want to light the fire to cook, like you said – it draws attention to the fact we're home.'

'Thanks, but no.'

'You still troubled?' said James, squeezing in next to him, though there was no need to.

'Maybe. A bit.'

'Go on. We've got plenty of time.'

'Well, it's this. I do think the Lord could make things easier for us. I mean, if he really cares – as we know he does –' he interjected quickly, 'then why does he let bad things happen? Why does he allow the persecution? Do you know what happened to the other James?'

'Of course we do. They say that Herod had Cephas arrested because it pleased the people so much, having James killed like that.'[25]

---

[25] Acts 12:1-3.

'And at Passover. First Jesus, now this. Did Herod want to mark the date or something?' He pulled at the loose flap of skin again and looked at it closely.

'It's the Paschal Pardon, to release a prisoner at this time.'

'Exactly,' said the lad, getting heated once more. 'He's meant to show mercy now, not ramp up the persecution. It's outrageous!'

'Quieten down,' said Zoe. 'I thought we're meant to be lying low.'

'But anyway. If God is completely good, why does he allow bad things to come our way? What's all that really about? I want to trust him, but I need to know that I can. I mean, he helped Cephas but not James. Why was that? And how do I know if he'll favour me or not?'

'You're no less favoured by God if you don't live out long years on earth.' James got to his feet now and began to pace around the room as he spoke. 'We die, we're with him. Simple as that. Our next experience will be to find ourselves his loving presence.'

'A bit more of that loving presence now would be good,' said the lad, realizing that he could say anything to these believers and they wouldn't be fazed. 'I mean, if the next life will be overwhelmingly great, can't God spread that out a bit – you know, make things a bit better now?'

James laughed at that but stopped when Zoe shot him a look.

'The Lord doesn't love James less than Cephas. Cephas has a whole lot of demanding service ahead of him, while James is enjoying glory. And if we don't allow God to be God, who is he?' James stood still for a moment to deliver his next thought, looking at the lad as he did so. 'Isaiah says, 'Does the clay dispute with the one who shapes it, saying, "Stop, you're doing it wrong!" Does the pot exclaim, "How clumsy can you be?"'[26] He wouldn't be God if we could outthink him, understand everything he does. As if *he* needs *us* to direct him! Not everything is going to make sense in this life, but we do know this: he *is* good. His love is seen in its completeness in Jesus. He loves each of us so much that he died on the cross for us – and he'd have done it for us if there was no one else to die for. He'd have done it just for you.'

The lad was looking tearful again now and he swallowed hard.

'There's a battle going on,' continued James, walking again. 'There always was. Jesus has won the ultimate victory, and at any

---

[26] Isaiah 45: 9

moment he could step in and say "Enough!" But while he doesn't, remember this: he planned each of us, and that included when we would be born and live and die. He thinks we're up to the task, or he wouldn't have given it to us. Understand that.' James turned on the spot and looked in his direction, just to be sure he had understood.

The lad nodded earnestly.

'I wish I'd listened to Jesus when he was alive,' James went on. He sat down next to him to explain the rest of his thinking to him. Now it was his turn not to let the tears show. 'I do know this: he said we would have troubles. That he would give us the words we'll need, even though we'd be hated,[27] and those opponents may not listen. We should be about pleasing him, not the world. He also said to take one day at a time,[28] and that's very sound advice. If we listen to our fears, or to the fears of others, we will be heavy-burdened. He doesn't want that for us! It's not his best plan for the believer. Oh, he has so much more.'

'That's terrible but awesome all at once. I know that he's big enough to help me.'

'You can rely on him for that.' James took his cake now and broke it in half, though he appeared not to want to eat it. 'He'll give you exactly what you need, when you need it. And if the end comes, we have nothing to fear. Jesus said that he'll return when things get really bad. "So when all these things begin to happen, stand and look up, for your salvation is near!"[29] It's such a privilege to belong to him. We can take what comes, in his strength. Learn your Scriptures too, lad. It will help you. Start with this one: "For since the world began, no ear has heard and no eye has seen a God like you, who works for those who wait for him!"[30]

'He is awesome, it's true. I'll learn that one.'

'That's good lad. Keep your eyes on the Lord. Always take your thoughts and fears back to Jesus. It's the only way.'

'I will. I'm going to be different, because I do believe in him. I'll ask him to help me be bold.'

'You know something?,' said James, eating at last, 'I'm going to be bolder too. I know the Lord wants me to be leading his church

---

[27] Luke chapter 21
[28] Matt 6: 34
[29] Luke 21: 28.
[30] Isaiah 64:4.

more. Cephas is rarely around, and I think we need some permanent leadership. I want to stay here, though I know it has its risks. I feel closer to my brother living in the city, and I can serve him here. Will you help me?' he finished, brushing the crumbs from his hands. 'We can learn boldness together.'

'Of course I will,' he replied.

***

Note to the reader:
John chapter seven, verse five shows us categorically that James didn't believe in his brother while he was with them. We know from Acts 1:14 that all Jesus' brothers came to faith after the resurrection, and would probably have been with the believers at Pentecost, as we see them in the Upper Room. James seems to be a key figure in the family, and it was crucial to Jesus that he knew that he was forgiven; he needed this understanding to have had the boldness to take on leadership in the early church. (See Galatians. 1:19, Acts 15 v13 and 21v18.)

James is certainly recognized as a believer in non-Christian sources and was living a radically different life after the resurrection.[31] He was known as James the Just and 'camel knees' because of the time he spent in prayer.[32] Many commentators also

---

[31] Josephus wrote, *"But this younger Ananus, who, as we told you already, took the high priesthood, was a bold man in his temper, and very insolent...He assembled the Sanhedrin of judges and brought before them the brother of Jesus the so-called Christ, whose name was James, and some others. When he had formed an accusation against them as breakers of the law, he delivered them over to be stoned."* Antiquities of the Jews 20.200.

[32] Eusebius writes the following in his work entitled *Church History* (c. 325):
"But Hegesippus, who lived immediately after the apostles, gives the most accurate account in the fifth book of his Memoirs. He writes as follows:
[James] alone was permitted to enter into the holy place; for he wore not woolen but linen garments. And he was in the habit of entering alone into the temple, and was frequently found upon his knees begging forgiveness for the people, so that his knees became hard like those of a camel, in consequence of his constantly bending them in his worship of God, and asking forgiveness for the people."

believe that it was Jesus' half-brother James who wrote the book of that name.

You will have noticed a line in this story in which I include that contemporary Christian thought that Jesus would have died for each of us alone. 'While there is no Bible verse for this sentiment exactly, the parables of the lost sheep and the lost coin (Luke 15) explain the Lord's rejoicing over the one who turns to him. The message of the Bible is that each person is profoundly valuable to him. James is trying to explain his faith in simple terms to someone who is very young.

Chapter Four
Jerusalem Revisited[33]
Galatians 1:13 – 2:10

'You need to understand how I'm seen in Jerusalem, Titus.[34] I'm still the enemy as far as many of the believers are concerned. Don't you see?' He stopped walking then to look at him hard, and rubbed a hand vigorously over his already balding head. Titus shrugged his shoulders and began walking again, feeling sure the believers would welcome this man, who'd led him to believe in Jesus, more readily than they welcomed himself. Barnabas made another of his encouraging comments, but Titus was beginning to feel a little anxious about meeting this first community of The Way. 'Most of them were too afraid to see me after I'd found the Lord,' Paul went on, striking the ground with a stick as he walked. 'I saw Cephas and James and that was it. As it was, it took me three years from my Damascus Road experience until I actually turned up there – I'd much to work through.' He said nothing for a long moment. 'I'm probably the most hated man in the city, even still.'

'It will help that you're bringing financial aid,'[35] said Titus.

'Of course it will,' said Barnabas, practically springing in the air with each step, his way of lingering as no one could match his usual long strides. Had he any idea how long this walk was going to be? 'Everyone trusts you now,' he went on. 'Your reputation goes before you. And they'll just be so relieved to have some resources again.'

Paul barely seemed to notice their reassuring words, his eyes squinting at the distant horizon and his thoughts on all that had gone before, as if they weren't with him at all. They still had the entire

---

[33] This story is set seventeen years after Paul's conversion. See Bible verses for this in context. My notes at the end of the story also give details of the timings of the Jerusalem events in Acts.

[34] In Galatians 2:1-10 we read of how Titus went along with Paul and Barnabas to Jerusalem. I agree with Tom Wright that this reference connects with the story in Acts 11. It is the most obvious explanation. See *Paul, A Biography*, P.95.

[35] Acts 11:30.

journey ahead of them, and Titus studied the marble pavement under his feet, wondering how long it would be before he saw it again. Or if, indeed, he ever would. He glanced back at the colonnade – they'd still see it for miles, he felt sure.

'I only stuck around for fifteen days last time,' Paul went on, 'and that was many years ago. Everywhere I went people were trying to kill me – Damascus, *and* Jerusalem, and believe me, it took a while before I had the courage to go there. That was partly why I waited so long. It was the Greek-speaking Jews who were after my skin there, but it made no difference. I had to get away – I wasn't welcome, I wasn't trusted. I wonder if that has changed?'

'It probably didn't help that you'd killed so many of the believers – or tried to anyway.' said Barnabas, with his usual carefree approach. Well, that didn't go down well! A bit of a risk, joking like that but sometimes Barnabas couldn't stop himself it seemed. Titus did wonder about the friendship between the pair – their opposing characters on the whole made them a good team, but just occasionally it made for tension, and this was one such moment. Paul shot him one of his angry looks, the sort he must have worn when he was dealing with members of The Way, when he was on the other side.

'I wonder how bad the famine is?' said Titus, trying to move the conversation on.

'Bad enough for the Lord to have prompted us through Agabus,' said Paul. 'It hasn't helped matters that the believers sold everything they had in the early days of their passion, keen to show their commitment to the Lord and to each other. It would have been better if they'd held onto some land, a few more buildings, that kind of thing. Still, the family of God extends beyond Jerusalem, as we're about to show them.'

'It's easy to get disheartened,' said Barnabas. 'But I'm sure the Lord will use this situation to draw many more to himself. He always works like this – never an opportunity lost. We look at circumstances and are prone to despair, but the Lord…'

'Perhaps the end times are upon us,' said Paul. 'Jesus spoke of 'famines and earthquakes' coming before his return. He *will* be coming back. I want to do all that I can to hasten it, if that were possible.'

'No one doubts your drive,' Titus told him. 'It's as if you would hasten his coming single-handedly sometimes.'

'Well, I have much making up to do. If I can build his church as much as I destroyed it, I'll begin to feel remotely pleased with myself. And I've never been one to sit idle.'

They laughed at the thought and Paul allowed the corner of his mouth to twitch into an almost half-smile. 'There is talk of corn having been sought from Egypt; pomegranates, figs, fruit that keeps, from Cyprus, which sounds odd – I think everywhere that's heard of the famine is stockpiling, in case it spreads to them too. I'm worried our people will have been sidelined. Let's hope our money will be good enough and the believers are not exploited when they go to purchase.'

'The *Christians*,' said Titus. 'I wonder if they're calling Jesus' followers that in Jerusalem yet too!'[36]

They laughed.

'Actually, I quite like the term,' said Barnabas. 'To have something of our Lord's name about us is a privilege. I rather hope it catches on.'

'Anyway, I'll make sure they are provided for. If they recognize me, I don't think they'll quibble. My past assertiveness does have its uses.'

'It's hard to work earnestly for the Lord when your stomach feels like an empty pit and clamours for your attention,' said Titus. He was already starting to feel hungry himself but felt he must keep quiet and wait until they had walked for at least a couple more hours. He knew that their provisions may have to last them for much of the journey – they had no idea quite how far the famine had spread, though everything looked green as far as the eye could see. 'A dearth of food has to be the hardest thing. I think I might rather a beating than ongoing hunger. At least a beating is over quickly.'

'Titus, you haven't lived,' said Paul. 'We're going to need to bring you up to speed with the persecution that's happened in Jerusalem,' he continued. 'I know I'm partly to blame, but the place feels more like a battleground for the Lord. It's where it all culminated for Jesus, after all.'

'Anyway, has it not occurred to you that the Lord might be using this?' said Barnabas, suddenly serious for once. 'He's making people

---

[36] In Acts 11:26 we read 'It was at Antioch that the believers were first called Christians.' It's thought this was a term of insult at first. The word Christian in the original Greek is '*christianos*', meaning "little Christ".

aware of their mortality. Their hunger is showing them a deeper gnawing inside, it's setting off a craving. Many of them don't know what it's for yet, but they will. Oh, believe me, they will.'

'I hope you're right,' said Paul. 'The Lord can use all things for good. I'm always telling people about this. We know that God causes everything to work together for the good of those who love him and are called according to his purpose.[37] Believers need to hear this,' he continued, his words still punctuated with the regular and purposeful tap of his stick. 'Why do we always feel entitled to perfect circumstances in this life? Jesus never promised them – he said we'd have trouble, but that he'd be with us. That's the main thing. If *he* is with us, we can face anything.'

'So Titus,' said Barnabas. 'Have you understood this visit could be somewhat challenging for you?'

Well, the prospect of hunger was the biggest challenge for him, though he dare not say it. 'I know that I'm young, and young in the faith too,' he said. 'And being a Gentile might be something of a challenge of course. I haven't thought much about it – it hasn't been an issue before now,' he said.

'It's true, your very presence will be a challenge,' said Paul. 'I was thinking you perhaps sounded anxious when we set out.' So he *was* listening earlier. 'As if mine isn't enough of one. But it makes sense to deal with several issues at once – it's not a quick journey, and I have plenty of other places I want to get to.'

'You'll be fine, Titus. It'll be fine,' said Barnabas, placing a reassuring hand on his arm as they walked.

'Now I am getting worried.'

'You don't need to be,' he replied. 'Yes, you'll be a challenge. But it's *you*, Titus. How can they not love you?'

***

The build-up did cause Titus to worry, but the believers were welcoming, and he was humbled by the meal that was prepared in their honour on the day they arrived. Could they really spare their provisions in this way? He noticed how hungrily Cephas ate as he sat at his table with them. And here was another thing – he had

---

[37] Romans 8:28. I think the knowledge that Paul expounds in his letters would have been present in his thoughts before he had written it down.

anticipated trouble on that level; that's what Paul and Barnabas had prepared him for as they'd walked. But he sat at *the same table* with them. 'The Lord has spoken to me about acceptance,' Cephas told him now. 'Praise his name! I feel the Jerusalem church is ready to catch up with you all from Antioch,' he said. 'For the Lord gave me a vision a few years back, when I was staying in Joppa. I saw a large sheet let down, filled with creatures, both clean and unclean. Reptiles even. "Get up," the Lord told me. "Kill and eat them." So my thought of what was clean and unclean was challenged. What I'd do to eat a feast like that now!' There was an uneasy silence for just a moment. 'For though I have no taste for pig... Well, the next thing I knew there were men waiting at my gate, and the Lord told me to go with them. They took me to Cornelius, a Roman officer. The Lord wanted me to go into his house – a *Gentile* house.'

Titus felt uncomfortable at this point and hoped his disapproval didn't show – they *should* be accepted, seen as equals! It was the way Cephas said the word; as if there was something inherently dirty about it. There was nothing magnanimous about this action of his, associating with a Gentile, going into his house. Why did they even need the Lord's prompting in this area – shouldn't it be obvious? Cephas continued – 'Yes, the Lord wanted me there. For he was speaking to Cornelius, but he was also speaking to *me*.' He stopped talking to look at them and they all heard coughing and a scuffling of feet out in the courtyard, but he was too caught up in his delivery to give it a second thought, though Titus wondered what it signified. 'Faith came to the man's house, Cephas went on. 'There were baptisms that day – I baptized them! They had received the Holy Spirit, and I can see that you have too, Titus.'

'I'm glad you can see it.'

'Indeed, I can.'

Titus looked at his bowl of food, and for once he had lost his appetite. He would finish eating in a while, when his emotions had stopped churning inside him.

'I can't promise the believers here will be quite as forward-thinking as me,' Cephas went on. 'For when I returned to Jerusalem I was in trouble. Word had already reached the believers here, and I had some explaining to do.' He took a deep breath and puffed out his big chest, pausing to look at them all, as if enjoying his storytelling and wanting to see its effect on their faces. 'There was criticism of *me*, their leader. "You entered the home of Gentiles and even ate with them!"[38] they said, accusation in their voices. They came round when I explained the vision, the prompting from the Lord, the salvation that came. They praised God with me! For they accepted that the Lord has chosen to give eternal life to you Gentile people too, should you reach out to him.'

Titus smiled at him and waited for Paul or Barnabas to speak on his behalf, for it was clear to him that no matter how they were accepted outwardly, they were still seen as second-rate citizens. He knew in his innermost being that this was not how the Lord saw him. How many other believers felt this way, because of their class or gender or race? Yet it was not the fault of the Lord, but the believers' own limited perceptions. He had never thought they were particularly radical in Antioch, but now he could see that they were.

The latch rattled and they all turned to see the door open and a group of four men burst inside. A servant who had come with James ran over and shrugged his shoulders in an apology at his leaders, for there was no way he could have prevented this happening. 'Brothers,' said Cephas, stumbling to his feet. 'What do you think you are doing? For this meeting is private!'

'That's what we're worried about,' said a stout, hairy man in a brown tunic. He took a wide stance and held his arms defensively in the air, as if expecting a fight. His voice was deep but he seemed to be making it especially commanding for the purpose of rebuking his leaders. 'Conducting important church business behind closed doors! We know what's going on. It's the talk of our community.'

'Were you spying on us?'[39] asked Paul, now also on his feet. James, who had remained in the background until now, looked startled and was clearly deep in thought. He joined Cephas, standing behind him and rubbing his beard as he worked out his own response. He was the brother of Jesus and it was interesting to see him under pressure like this. His thoughts were clear and his comments uncompromising, if the last hour had been anything to go by. But now he said nothing. Titus remained seated and soon dropped his head as the conversation went on around him. He knew it was a bad idea to

---

[38] Acts 11:1 -3.
[39] Galatians 2:4. John Stott on this verse: "This may mean either that they had no business to be in the church fellowship at all, or that they had gate-crashed the private conference with the apostles". *Reading Galatians with John Stott: 9 Weeks for Individuals or Groups* by John Stott. P.33. (IVP Connect (25 July 2017))

have come – why did he allow himself to get talked into it? The smell of the stew hung in the air like a taunt to these local believers, and he didn't want to see them take in just how much food had been placed in front of each of them.

'Paul, we've come to accept you, appreciate you even, over the years. But *this*! Bringing a Greek with you and sitting him down at a Jewish table! You need to remember the rules, the boundaries.'

Perhaps the extra value they now placed on all their resources wasn't helping.

Astonishingly, Paul said nothing. Instead he sat down, as if unfazed by what was happening. Titus saw him between his own flickering eyelids – the Holy Spirit was upon him, reassuring him of God's own acceptance of him. This behaviour wasn't what he knew of Paul – perhaps he simply understood his opinion would trump theirs, or was it to reassure the object of their rage? James joined him, as if following his lead. Titus dared to glance up now and watched Cephas as he closed his eyes for a moment and took a deep breath, probably saying a silent prayer. 'We're not doing anything wrong,' he said at last, turning to each of the men in turn, who were now spaced evenly around the room, looking down at the seated group from all four walls. 'But I think you are. Barging in here with your accusations! What conduct is this?'

'If we hadn't then we'd have no proof,' said another believer, a tall man with a scar that was evident, just visible beneath his long beard. 'We've seen you all eating together. This isn't done, Cephas. You should know that. It's inappropriate to say the least.'

'It's not the first time you've complained of the company I've kept.' A vein was twitching in Cephas's temple, suggesting he was more hassled than he appeared. He pulled back his shoulders and composed himself, pausing before he spoke. 'You must remember my time with Cornelius and his household. This is nothing new. You accepted it then – or I thought you did.'

'This is different,' said the first man.

'How?'

'That was unavoidable. It's how you're mixing things up. They can repent – even approach God now. But we are separate communities...' said the tall man.

Finally, the oldest member of the deputation spoke, and with no reservation. 'I hate to say it, but Paul, you bring trouble with you! Why can't you leave us to it?' He shook with anger as he spoke, no doubt remembering the persecution they'd suffered at his hands many years earlier.

'You wouldn't be saying that if you knew how they've just resourced our church,' said James. 'Come on, lighten up fellows. This is too much.'

'Are you circumcised?' said the first man directly to Titus.

That was going too far, Titus felt. 'Well, no,' he replied. 'It hadn't been seen as a problem.'

'Then you're not saved,' said the old man again. 'How can you be? It's a half-hearted effort. You're not a proselyte at all. You're an imposter and you're diluting our faith. What would Moses say?' Getting no rise from him he turned to his leader. 'Cephas, you'll be letting slaves sit at our table next.'

James glanced at the attendant who seemed especially loyal to him, as if to show his own acceptance, but he was now looking at the floor.

'Jesus came to complete what went before,' said the tall man, nodding in agreement. 'He never meant to replace it – start a new religion. This is all very dangerous.'

'I can't help thinking you're forcing things to a head,' said Cephas. 'We're trying to keep up with what the Lord wants – understand it. We wouldn't have even been addressing this tonight, for to my mind it is a secondary matter. But know this: we are not about regulations. The old has passed, we often say; the new has come. Jesus has radically changed *everything*.'

'But this is pollution! We don't throw out everything that our God has taught us over the years. We are meant to be a holy people – set apart. Our God does not like compromise. This young man wants to become one of us – well, we can accept that. But he must show his commitment to the one true God by being circumcised. How else will we know that he is serious?'

'*He* does have a name!' said Barnabas.

'Well, we don't know it,' came a muttered reply.

'Meet Titus,' said Paul. 'Your brother in Christ!'

Well, that was bold.

'He is like a son to me,' he continued. 'A son in the Lord. Rarely will you find such faith and devotion,' he said.

'And quite frankly, this is ridiculous,' Barnabas went on. 'How would the Lord Jesus feel about this?'

'That again?' said the oldest among them.

'I'm starting to doubt the genuineness of faith in many of you,' said James.

'Circumcised he will not be,' said Paul. 'The Holy Spirit is in this man – I witness it daily and you would do well to follow his godly lifestyle. In Christ, there is no longer Jew or Gentile, slave or free, male or female.[40] I know this to be true in my spirit and we cannot quench *his* work. The compromise would be to allow you all to have your way. This is God's church – not yours. Not mine.'

'Paul is right,' said Cephas. 'But I can see how the Antioch believers are further on in this discussion than we. Further on than many of you are ready for. Paul and Barnabas, I believe that God has given you special responsibility for the Gentiles, while we here in Jerusalem are to reach the Jews. While I'm unhappy with the conduct of these brothers here, we cannot force the pace. Is that understood?'

The Jerusalem brothers hummed and muttered their consent and even looked slightly smug, folding their arms over their chests and giving the Antioch crowd a knowing nod, as if they had won. Were they really that obtuse?

James nodded at the servant who opened the door for them and the four filed out. Cephas put a finger to his lips so that no one said a word until they were out of earshot. 'You can't trust them to be gone,' he whispered after a minute. 'I suspect they were listening in for a while before they burst in too,' he said, sitting down with them at last. 'We have a problem on our hands.'

They sat in silence now, Titus staring at his bowl of now-cold stew and feeling even less inclined to eat, but Cephas picked up his and continued to eat ravenously. The guests followed, knowing that no small amount of sacrifice was involved in the meal that had been set before them.

'I fear it will be many years before they have truly grasped equality in Christ,' said Paul finally, wiping his bowl clean for a second time with a piece of bread. Titus looked across at James and Cephas who were saying nothing.

'Don't you think, brothers?' said Barnabas.

'You have to understand where they are coming from,' said Cephas, looking replete at last. 'They feel any big changes should be

---

[40] See Paul's words in Galatians 3:28. No doubt his thoughts came out in his speech as well as in his writings.

prompted by the Jerusalem church too. For it was established here, and they feel they must guard it loyally.'

'I understand that, but it is a misplaced loyalty, as mine once was,' said Paul.

'Go on,' said Cephas.

'They seem to want all believers to become Jews.' Paul got to his feet now and started walking around the room, as if the movement aided his explanation. 'Then they're allowed to be a unique kind of Jew, a Jew with a Jesus layer on top. It's all wrong,' he said, moving his arms around as he spoke. 'We're not an exclusive club – we were never meant to be. You know, this may rumble on for years. I don't see it going away any time soon. But I never was out for popularity!'[41]

'They fear any old rabble,' said Cephas. 'They think the Gentiles won't understand how things are done. They think their leaders have got it wrong. That we haven't thought this through. They struggle to grasp his love is for everyone. It reminds me of a story Jesus used to tell, of two brothers. One is outraged that his father will welcome home his wayward brother when he has tried to obey the rules all along, and isn't praised for it. He's so angry that …'

'But that suggests we Jews are more worthy – less in need of a saviour,' said Paul, interrupting. 'Jesus couldn't have been using that as a metaphor for Jews and Gentiles. We're all sinners, each as needy as the next man. We'd do well to remember this.'

'I question whether they are believers at all,' said Barnabas, stretching his feet out on the floor. 'Could they be outsiders who have made it their business to stir? Who are looking for a bit of excitement? We must remain men of integrity, and always seek the Lord's will, no matter how unpopular that may make us.'

'But I feel it's important that you stay here with us for a while,' said Cephas. 'Our unity speaks volumes, for any believer of any age here remembers the animosity there was once between us. Many a night we spent praying for you, at the peak of your persecution.' Paul looked away – could this strong man's eyes be watering? 'Besides, you've had a long journey,' he continued. 'They must see that we are united.' He got up now to walk over to Paul and extend the hand of friendship. 'If you can, stay and oversee the distribution of your gift – that will go a long way in softening their hearts.'

'I'd be pleased to,' said Paul, taking Cephas' outstretched hand.

[41] See Acts chapter 15.

'If only people could grasp how generous and how great our God is!' said Barnabas. 'We attach all sorts of strings and conditions to his salvation. How dare we? What purpose is there in setting out requirements that exclude some, or in ranking believers in importance?'

'It is human nature,' said James. 'But what my brother accomplished on the cross was complete. We must seek him more on this, ensure we have a right understanding. He is the leader of our church, after all. It is not us. The day we think it our church is the day we're not fit to lead it.'

This comment caused them all to stop talking for a moment. Those seated around the table looked into the flame coming from the lamp that had been placed at its centre. It was growing dark outside, and their shadows flickered on the wall.

'While it's good to join together like this, it would try our patience to stay too long in Jerusalem and work with you here,' said Paul, sitting down in the group again. 'Our calling is to the Gentiles, while you are doing a good job here with the Jewish believers. We should always run with the work God has most equipped us for, where we see the most fruit, feel the most compelling tug in our spirits. I feel Jerusalem is old ground for me too. I need new challenges, new territories.'

'I'm happier here, anyway,' said James.

'The believers will always accept you here,' said Barnabas. 'You're Jesus' half-brother – they want that. They like it.'

'We've witnessed how the Lord has raised you into leadership here,' said Cephas. 'I feel you are right for the Jerusalem church. I may well be travelling myself in years to come. Expect the Lord to confirm this to you, but be ready.'[42]

'Do you have any men who could bridge the gap between the two groups, James? Someone of a calm temperament, a peacemaker? Young preferably, not set in their ways at any rate.'

---

[42] FF. Bruce writes of the transition of leadership in the Jerusalem church, as led by apostles then elders. 'The two stages overlap: the elders appear (Acts 11:30) before the apostles leave the scene. The transition between the two stages is provided by the record of the Apostolic Council, where the responsibility for deliberation and decision is shared "by the apostles and the elders" (Acts 15:6, 22.f.) In the church of the apostles Peter is the dominating figure; in the church ruled by elders, James.' *The Church of Jerusalem in the Acts of the Apostles*, John Rylands University Library of Manchester (1 Dec. 1985) P.642

'There's my cousin, John Mark,' said Barnabas. 'It will be good to see him again. My aunt's the most hospitable woman you could wish to meet. We gather at her house, so you'll meet them tomorrow.'

'He's a sound lad and feeling the frustration of life here,' said Cephas, with a certain warmth in his voice. He sat down too, apparently more at ease now that a plan was coming together. 'I hadn't thought of him.'[43]

'It's been years since I've seen him,' said Barnabas. 'No doubt he's quite the young man now. I know something of him, for he writes to me. He's gifted in administration. A modest, reserved type. His mother wants him to record some of the goings on here, the establishment of the church since Pentecost.'

'Barnabas, you think the best of everyone. And he's your cousin? I need a better recommendation than that!' said Paul.

'His faith is mature for his years,' Cephas told them. 'His mother told me about his writing, and I plan to tell him more of my times with Jesus. For I'd like him to make a record of everything. What he has at the moment is an unfinished story. But it is all in his head. I must see to it that he records everything properly before I am very old.'

'We're all part of an unfinished story,' said James. 'It's an unfinished story until he returns. We will pass the torch on to the next generation, and they the next, until *he* declares the work is done.'

'But some years are especially important,' answered Cephas. 'I want a record of my time with Jesus, no matter how that shames me. It is only *he* that needs to be seen in a good light, after all.'

'So, John Mark, then. We could try him out,' Paul replied. 'If you can spare him, that is, Cephas. We may even take him on a journey with us, if he grasps the Gentile mission.'

'See if you like him first – it would be wise,' said Cephas.

'Yes, but I've no time to dither. My feet are itching now, telling me it's time to move on. It feels as if we've already accomplished what we set out to do here. I think we'll return to Antioch first, but I don't intend to stay there long. The Spirit is making me restless. I know he has more for me – for us,' he said, looking to Barnabas, who was clearly tired and opened his eyes wide at this eager declaration of intention, and after such a long day.'I will seek him on this; on

---

[43] It's thought that Peter was related to Mark too – see p.172 of Tom Wright's *Paul: A Biography.*

what he wants from me. Many of you are called to belong in a place, to dwell there with integrity. But I've always been restless, and I know the Lord can use that. It's down to each of us to ask him where he can best use us. I just know the rules and hair-splitting of Jerusalem are not for me. Besides, I'm too well known here. But they don't *really* know me, and that's the problem, as I see it. I need new faces, new challenges almost daily. Am I alone in that?'

The others made the appropriate noises, not out of any lack of commitment to the Lord, but they had had a challenging day. Titus had wondered if Paul ever slowed down... but having journeyed with him and been in his presence continually for days and nights now, he could see that the man was just made differently. He supposed his own lack of energy, of rigour, didn't in itself make him any inferior, but the zeal of this man, the passion, could not be matched. It was an honour that Paul had seen something in him – had decided that he was worth taking under his wing and training. He could not yet see the Lord's purposes for his own life, but just following Paul along was an education in itself, and it was fascinating. Barnabas was always reassuring and kind, and when Paul spoke sharply or lacked understanding in the human frailty of the rest of them, this friend was always good to have around. And Cephas and James? They too had had a long day and he couldn't blame them for their lack of empathy on the Gentile issue. They certainly had their hands full with some of those unruly believers, if you could even call them that. What a day indeed. Titus was the first to admit that his own character contained many flaws, so he would try to be patient with them. They were all a work in progress, after all.

Note to the reader: Tom Wright places the Great Famine in AD46[44], while it is widely held that Cephas' escape from prison was around AD42. Luke writes 'About that time' (Acts 12:1), which together, I think, give me license to place Paul's arrival after the prison escape (Acts 12:1-18). I don't claim to have the answers and simply hope to promote your own research!

What does the early Jerusalem church speak to us about in our own circumstances? For me, the strongest themes to emerge from this study were issues of equality – what does true unity look like? – and freedom from fear.

---

[44] Paul, A Biography – p.94.

MACEDONIA
Acts 16:6 - 40

HEAR ME WHEN I CALL
From Philippi – A Desperate Prayer

God of the universe…
God who made the stars –
if you're there?
I believe that you are, but other than these signs in the sky and in
each leaf and bud, I've little to go on, no one to guide me.
If you are there, would you send someone?
The slave girl has been calling out her unwelcome thoughts and
predictions; today she saw me and had a go.
She says that I will die alone,
with no business,
and nobody to love.
That no one will ever want to live with me.
That my servants are only with me because they have to be.
I'm troubled and I so want all this to be untrue. Everyone thinks me
competent and strong; they have no idea what goes on inside of me.
Will you help me? Oh, hear me when I call, as the poet says. Hear
me when I call.

Chapter One
Troas

'What's the matter?', 'Go where, Paul?', 'It's the dead of night.' The voices merged in shared confusion as the group came round and tried to take in what they'd just heard. 'Sooth, that's my arm you're treading on!'

'Sorry, Luke, is that you? It is dark in here.'

'It's me, brother.' He yawned, more to make a point than anything, and sat up in the darkness.

'So then, listen, all of you – we're going to Macedonia,' said Paul. The shutters were now pulled back and he was up and rolling his mat in readiness of a quick departure. 'I believe dawn won't be long – it's not so dark now, you'll find.'

'We *are* a bit tired,' said Timothy, ever the tactful one.

'What? Now? Can't it wait, Paul?' said Silvanus.

'Not really.'

'I know you're a man of action, but can't we finish sleeping the night away first?'

Luke was surprised by Silvanus's boldness, still feeling he was getting to know the group, but his directness was welcome; it seemed he spoke for all of them, and Paul needed grounding with practical advice.

'And why the change of heart, Paul?' asked Timothy. 'You said…'

'I saw a man in the night – just now in fact. Standing over *there*,' he replied, pointing to the corner of the room. 'He was from Macedonia and –'

'You had a dream,' Silvanus told him.

'No not a dream – I was awake. I'd been praying. I know it wasn't a dream. I haven't been asleep yet.'

'You can see all sorts in the shadows. Especially with your eyesight,' said Silvanus with a challenging smirk.

'God communicates through dreams anyway,' said Timothy, intent and serious, apparently missing Silvanus's attempt to make light of the situation. He was working through the credibility of

Paul's encounter aloud. 'Either way, it was, perhaps, the Lord convincing you of something. What di-'

'It couldn't be a man from Macedonia!' said Silvanus. 'It had to be an angel – he's not still here. A man would have walked out the door, and why would he be in this house? It makes no sense otherwise.'

'Don't be so literal,' said Timothy, in the way you could only speak to a brother. Luke got that he was rarely outspoken; ever cautious, he had to be sure this direction was coming from God himself or he wouldn't want to be a part of it.

'So what did he say?' asked Silvanus.

'"Come over to Macedonia and help us!"'

'I'm sure he didn't mean right now – he must've known we should be asleep,' said Luke, emboldened by the others' attempts to instruct him. Telling others what to do was his job, and he'd deliberately tried to hold back in this situation, but now he couldn't help himself. 'I understand – you have found your purpose again; I think your exhaustion was as much from disillusionment when I found you yesterday. But just slow down.'

'A complete pagan land. Not a believer amongst them,' said Timothy.

'All the more reason to go there. Besides *we'll* be there, that's four believers, and there'll soon be more. That's the point...' replied Paul.

He was making an assumption here, but no one challenged him. Luke felt an energy in his spirit now, despite the early hour – he hadn't experienced this since the day he came to faith in the Lord Jesus. At last the others seemed to be catching onto Paul's vision, too. 'God doesn't call you anywhere unless he has a job for you to do,' said Silvanus. 'Something exciting is afoot, I'm convinced of it. All this dallying, and at last, finally, we know what the Lord wants next.'

'Afoot for sure,' said Luke, laughing. He watched as Paul sat down and rubbed his feet absentmindedly. 'They've been giving you bother – I was watching you hobble about through the evening. You need a doctor! Someone watching over you at all times. Your feet are cankered, Paul, and you have no physical reserves.' He was at least listening – it was that doctor's authority and Luke still couldn't get used to it, even after all these years. 'In truth,' he went on, 'there's no flesh on you at all. You are allowed to rest sometimes,' he said. 'I'm convinced sleep is good for you. And go easy on yourself once in a while. It's important. Just remember that, Paul.'

'A doctor travelling with us? It's not a bad plan,'[45] said Silvanus. 'It could save us a lot of bother, all the injuries we've sustained on our travels.'

'You'd be very welcome to join us,' said Paul. 'In fact, I assumed you would. And not just because of your medical skill. You seem like a godly man, and you know this region better than we do. You could be invaluable to us, if you wouldn't mind, that is.'

'I prescribe a little more sleep, for now, fellows,' he replied, and went over to close the shutters, his decision made. 'A burnt-out servant is no good to anyone. Just as a house is damaged by fire, so is a body by an owner that knows not how to rest.'

***

The ease with which they found a merchant ship making its way to Neapolis was startling. There was space for just four more passengers, and they would be leaving that morning. There was no time to question Paul's vision any further, and they paid for the voyage and listened to the shipmaster as he explained the passage. They would lay anchor at Samothrace, a mountainous and volcanic island known for its religious practices. The others could see this had set Paul's mind whirring. When the man had left them, Paul said he would like to stop there and educate the people, but that the original purpose was pressing, explaining again his encounter with the Macedonian.

The journey proved smooth and uneventful, the crew commenting on how they'd never had the crossing so good. Before nightfall they

---

[45] 'So we decided to leave for Macedonia at once,' we read in Acts 16:10. This had been a 3rd person account until now, with the word 'they' being used in a more detached way. Now the writer of the text (Luke) includes himself in the narrative. We don't know any more about this and commentaries speculate, but that Luke was a doctor is a given, and this would have of course been a help to Paul in his travels. I imagine Luke was keen to be involved where God was at work dynamically and may have even suggested that he accompany the group. Luke doesn't draw attention to himself in the text, and though he remained in Philippi when the group went on, this was probably with the intention of leading this new believing community. Paul later describes him as 'Luke, the beloved physician' (Col. 4:14).

were in sight of Samothrace, and Paul seemed absorbed by the significance of the place. Daylight faded on their approach, assuring them that it was the right time to stop and pressing on would be foolhardy. Lights twinkled from the windowsills of people's houses, like a warm welcome, though that was deceptive, they all knew. As the boat slowed and the ship finally moored on the northern side, so as to shelter from the wind, Paul asked a crew member if they were allowed to disembark.

'That won't be happening,' he replied. 'We'll be off at first light, we don't want to have to round up any passengers or crew.'

Turning from him, 'I will come back here,' Paul told the others, sitting down in the middle of them. Luke saw the sailor smirk and raise an eyebrow at him, though Paul was oblivious. 'There's a cult that operate from here,' he went on, as if they didn't know, 'and their practices are distasteful. *The cult of the great gods* – we're not even meant to pronounce its name. What have we to fear?' he finished.

'Don't jinx us,' said a voice from over his shoulder. Paul looked ready to launch into an explanation of the gospel, but the sailor had wandered off before he had gathered what he needed to say. It was unlike Paul to miss an opportunity, but it had been a long day and they had covered many miles.

'We might be able to see some of their carry on from the ship,' said Luke. 'They operate in the dark. I've been here before at this time of night, though it was a long time ago.'

'Why would we want to?' said Timothy. 'That they celebrate in darkness tells us enough.' Just then cries and screams were heard coming over the trees. 'Sacrifice,' he said, startled. 'They are not human cries.'

'It's eerie,' said Luke, pushing his heavy flop of hair from his eyes, as if wanting to see into those woods and beyond. 'Clearly they are suffering. It's inhumane.'

'How long did this journey take before, Luke?' asked Paul, shuffling onto his haunches, for the base of the boat wasn't comfortable and rope was getting under their feet.

'Like I said, it was years ago, but I don't remember it being this quick. It was a rough crossing too – I know I didn't eat for the entire journey and got off the boat feeling very weak.'

'Should've known better,' said a voice. Luke wasn't sure who'd uttered it but, to be fair, it was true.

'God is with us,' said Timothy. 'Talking of food, would you pass my bag over, Luke. It's behind you. I have a glut of dates and figs to go round, and more than enough bread. I'd packed plenty before you rushed us out of the house, Paul. I thought Philippi was days away.'

'When you're doing what God wants, living at the centre of his will, then sometimes his endorsement is seen, experienced even. I think this is one such case,' said Luke. He handed Timothy the bag and was impressed by the weight of it. Here was someone who knew how to prepare well – no doubt he was trustworthy all round.

'The contrast between this and our directionless wandering couldn't be more clear,' said Paul. 'I'm very excited for what is to come.'

'Aren't we all?' said Timothy, passing the bag of food back to Luke.[46]

'Silvanus, I think there's something left for you,' said Luke with a touch of irony, taking a flatbread himself and a couple of plump dates.

Luke saw him wince at his comment and he wondered if he had taken a dislike to him. He got up and took a step backwards to hold onto the side of the boat, looking out towards the darkened horizon, where just a seam of light glimmered. It was always a difficult balance, being approachable, and yet others knowing you were a doctor, expecting you to think yourself better than them; not that you did. He knew he was fortunate, to have had his education; that the Lord had blessed him. But it had always meant he could feel an outsider and people thought him stand-offish, when he was only trying to find a way in.

'He prefers to be called Silas,' Timothy told him, picking up on Luke's sense of rebuff. He had come over to explain, and the two of them sat down with the group again.

'Sorry – I know I sound like an old man sometimes,' said Luke. 'My father was very elderly when I was growing up. I hate my formality sometimes and I can only apologize.'

---

[46] The journey Paul and his companions undertook would have been daunting, and probably more so than anything else he had attempted at this point. They were crossing continents by sailing the Agean sea, from Asia all the way to Europe. Hughes says: "That they 'sailed straight for Samothrace' is quite revealing, because this is a nautical expression that means the wind was at their backs. So perfect were the winds that they sailed 156 miles in just two days, whereas returning the other way at a later time (Acts 20:6) it took five days.".

'Don't worry,' said Silas. 'I had you down as a learned type from the start, and the old father explains a lot.'

'It's hard when you're educated, isn't it?' said Paul with a smile. 'The assumptions people make, and the assumptions we make about people making assumptions.' There was laughter, and Luke felt reminded that he *was* in good company. Why did he ever doubt it?

'I have to say, I'm always happy when I have the opportunity to write. I was an unusual child, having parchment readily available and being encouraged to use it.' The others looked genuinely interested, having shuffled closer to listen, and so he continued. 'My father made it from reeds, – he was always experimenting with recipes – he made ink from gallnuts and berries too, and fashioned quills from the reeds and feathers. His products were always rustic, and he wouldn't sell them, though they worked well enough for me. But I would write on leaves and stones too – anything I could find. I had to ask for the parchment, you see.'

'Perhaps you'll be able to record our travels,' said Paul. 'Write an account of how the Lord is using us.' Paul brushed crumbs of bread from his lap and settled in amongst the ropes, as if getting ready for the night.

'I'm surprised you don't have anyone else already doing that,' he replied.

'Well, we did have. We do. I mean, well –'

'What he's trying to say is that there had been a bit of a falling out,' said Silas. 'Barnabas left him over it, and that's why I'm here. Paul needed a stand in, and since then, well, the team has grown to this.'

'It's not something I'm proud of,' said Paul. 'Who knows what the believers made of it in Antioch? New believers too. I'll do my best to make things up to them in the future, when I can. It happened a while ago – I really should visit, but we're miles away now.'

'Don't be hard on yourself,' said Luke. 'We can waste too much energy on old regrets.'

Paul nodded, though his furrowed brow told another story. 'And who knows,' he said, 'John Mark may well have written up what the Lord had been doing with us. He's not a bad man – far from it. It's just that – he wasn't really ready for the work. So then, we took him on, on the recommendation of Barnabas and Cephas. But they're related to him, which, in hindsight, is never a good idea.'[47]

There was a contemplative silence as the waves slapped against the side of the boat... 'I should probably write more myself,' said Paul. 'I think I will, though I'll need a scribe.'[48] He blinked and rubbed his eyes, the constant frustration of them not lost on his friends. 'But I would rather write letters of encouragement than records of what's going on. And it does seem a bit self-important, which is not something I like. I'm more of a do-er than a reflector.'

'I'll happily help in that area too,' said Luke. 'As much as I can. As I said, I do like to write myself. It's not self-important though – in truth, it can be an act of devotion, when it's done right, with good motives. We're all gifted differently.'

'Go on,' said Paul.

'You're the first to admit that this is the Lord's work, not ours. You just happen to be very well used by him. It's your duty to keep a record of what's going on. These are significant days and believers may well be looking back on them for inspiration for a very long time,' he finished.

'I don't want it to be about me, though,' said Paul. 'That's the danger. People always like adventure and drama in a story – they always have; I suspect they always will. By all means make notes on what happens, but let any narrative be about him, not me.'

'You'll have to be in it, though, Paul. It's unavoidable. In truth, people will want to know about your exploits too – they can learn from them.'

'So don't paint me in a particularly good light – let them know something of how gracious our Lord has been, taking me on, allowing me to serve him. Ultimately, my presence must be in the background, and that starts here.'

---

[47] It's thought the visit to Philippi happened around AD55-6.

[48] It is known that Paul had others write for him – for example, Tertius wrote Romans on his behalf. In Galatians 6:11 Paul writes, 'Notice what large letters I use as I write these closing words in my own handwriting.' See Ellicott's Commentary for English Readers: 'The latter part of the Greek phrase means "in" or "with" letters--*i.e.,* characters of hand-writing--and not "a letter," "an epistle," as it is taken in the Authorised version; (2) The former half of the phrase means "how large," strictly in respect of size.'

I think Paul's 'thorn in the flesh' could well have been poor eyesight, and this is the idea I run with.

There was laughter among the men – 'You can never be in the background, Paul.' 'Just how is that going to work?' 'How much detail do they want? How much of the bad?'

But Paul was serious: 'The attention has been on me too long; I don't like it. Let people read of the lives the Lord touches through our adventures. If you can keep the focus on the Lord and these other ones, you are welcome to it, Luke. I have enough to be contending with, leading as I do. And I fear my eyesight is getting far, far worse.' That issue really seemed to get him down. You wouldn't expect such a strong leader to have low moments, but he did. 'So I'll leave it with you from here,' he finished.

It felt a God-given task to Luke and he knew these were the days the Lord had been preparing him for. He would record the lives of others, then, and show how salvation came to them, for he felt sure that was what lay ahead. He would write of Paul, but only where it was necessary. He would remain anonymous in it himself, for he was inconsequential, and no one would want to know of him.

Chapter Two
Philippi

It was a hot Sabbath day and Lydia and a group of women had congregated on the riverbank to pray, as they usually did. The river was slow-flowing at this point, and provided the perfect setting for their meetings. The sound of the flowing water filled their gaps and silences, and the tall reeds swayed rhythmically in the light breeze. Swallows would even congregate in these reeds at times, after skimming low over the river, and water lilies were just visible in the shallows, landing pads for bugs and even the occasional small bird. Today the visiting insects were a welcome sight, aiding thought, though presenting a distraction for some. Yet there was another reason why Lydia preferred to meet here – the prayer house was appreciated in the cooler months, but everyone was always so much more relaxed outside, and women they knew were tempted to come along and sit on the edges of the group, just within earshot. There was something about stepping inside a building that made people feel uneasy, but outside was everyone's territory, and never threatening.[49]

Today some newcomers were walking towards them but, strange to say, this was a group of men. The leader was a confident fellow with long strides, despite his stature, and he strode up to them and asked if they may join them. 'My name's Paul,' he said, 'and these are my friends,' and he introduced them. He asked their names and Lydia told hers readily, but she could already see some of her group were looking uneasy. This Paul and his friends sat down with them on the grassy bank, and he began to explain their reason for being there. That they were believers in Jesus – God's son, he said, who had lived among their people, died for the sins of all and had risen again.

---

[49] There is some debate about whether there was a physical building there, but the following resource is useful on the subject: LYDIA AND THE 'PLACE OF PRAYER' AT PHILIPPI BY MARG MOWCZKO, https://margmowczko.com/lydia-and-the-place-of-prayer-at-philippi/
Mowczko explains that the word *proseuchē* is used for a building where Jewish believers met.

'Where was he now then?' she asked, and they said he was in heaven, but he surely was alive. Lydia felt something taking place on the inside of her – it was hard to define really, but it was, she supposed, an inner conviction. It was as if her heart was being opened up and restored. Losing her husband a few years prior had made her keep a tight grip on her emotions, for waver slightly and her lip would tremble and the tears would tumble. She had learned that it was best to show no emotion at all, but here, today, something was changing in her, and she really didn't mind. But it was when Paul told of a man who had appeared to him and instructed them to go from Troas to Macedonia that she felt really touched. She asked when it was, and it was only three days ago… that was the same night she had called out to God in prayer to reveal himself. Their voyage had been uncommonly fast – to start with, just a day across the sea from Troas to Samothrace. They bedded down for the night, dropping anchor, and on the following day sailed onto Neapolis. As these are safer waters, they sailed through the night, the crew being more confident. From there, they had walked to Philippi without stopping. It felt as if they had done it just for her. But more than that – that God had sent them, that he was reaching out and revealing something of how much he loved her. She really couldn't argue with that. Please could they tell her how to follow, what to do? She was sure this was what she wanted; she'd never felt more certain about anything.

Lydia had been so caught up in what they had to tell her that she had barely noticed her female companions, but now she realized that they were all edging closer to her and trying to catch her eye. They didn't look happy – in fact, they were most unsettled and their eyes were imploring her, though she didn't know why. She then heard them mutter to themselves things about her. 'She never did do anything by halves,' said Demi. Oh, she'd heard them, but she pretended not to notice. If it wasn't for her generosity, she doubted they'd be her friends at all, for there was always an underlying jealousy that she tried hard to ignore, though she felt it keenly enough. She'd wondered at times if they were really seeking God like she was, or if they were simply seeking patronage. Their voices grew louder and bolder now: 'Lydia, we have to get on home,' said one. To what? she thought. What could be more important than this? Her disappointment in them must have shown in her face, for they felt the need to explain. 'I need to check in on my uncle – he is ill you know'; 'I should be with my family – time is getting on and it *is* the Sabbath

– my husband expects it of me' – but he wasn't Jewish –; and 'I need to visit my mother now, it really won't wait'.

Lydia straightened her back and gave them each in turn a long look, but it did no good. At least, not for now. Perhaps they'd listen one day, but it wasn't going to be this one. The years of trying to stand shoulder to shoulder with the men in the guild gave her a degree of confidence and an air of authority, but she felt she needed more than that to get through to these women.

A small red damselfly hovered over the water in front of them and gave Lydia and the menfolk something to look at while the other women slipped quietly away. Soon Lydia was the only one left speaking to these men, but she didn't mind. Few people wandered out this far, and she'd felt an outsider in their community for a long time now – ever since she took on what other people called 'men's work', though out of necessity rather than anything else. She used to travel here with her husband for the novelty of it, never knowing she would need the training, that wasn't really that at all. It was the same for her back in Thyatira, enduring that feeling of not fitting in, but at least she had two homes to go between. When it got too much in one place, she would often go to the other, and she could easily justify it to each household by telling them of some work-related problem or issue. In fairness to herself, there always was a need that she could think of without too much effort.

'I worry about being the only believer here when you've gone,' she told them. 'The only follower of Jesus – how can I do that on my own?' She explained how she'd lost her husband, how she was running a business, but always longed for a better sense of community. It seemed wherever she was, whatever she was doing, that she sat just a little on the outside – that she never truly belonged.

'We won't leave you till we feel sure you are properly set up,' said the man who they called the doctor. 'In truth, we're glad to stop travelling. And I never was one for the sea!'

'This is a good spot for a congregation,' said the young, quiet one. 'Perfect for baptisms, with the river here, and shelter when you need it.'

'Though I like to think you'll outgrow this building,' said Paul. 'As a place of worship, it won't do for long.'

'But what is worship, if it isn't our very lives being lived out to bring him glory?' said the doctor.

'Yes, let it never be about the building,' said Silas, who was the striking, memorable one among them. He didn't need to say much – his passion said it all.

'The Jerusalem church has been scattered – I trust that those believers will be as close to the Lord as they ever were,' Paul told them. 'Worshipping together as a large community is good, but we have eternity for that. Now is the time for living our lives out faithfully, all the while remaining in close communion with him. Nothing brings him more glory. The important thing is that our own walk with him is alive – then no circumstances can stand in our way. We could be imprisoned and it wouldn't matter.'

'Let's hope not!' said Silas.

'Our home life can be worship too,' said Paul. 'As head of your household, you will lead and everyone else will follow. We have found such unity in our number – slave and master, old and young – the Lord brings fellowship where he chooses, and it does please him. Just wait and see what he can do.'

They made it sound so easy – so natural. Yet their enthusiasm was compelling, and Lydia sat quietly, averting her eyes to the river as she waited for them to fill the silence she'd left.

'My writing is worship,' said Luke. 'It's often how I express myself to God, and I ponder the deep things about him as I write. I hope salvation will come through what I write one day. Your work can be worship – if what you do and how you undertake it is done in reverence to God. It seems you are very self-sufficient in your life – this is good – a help, if you will. Our faith isn't dependent on who is or isn't around us. We can access our Lord immediately, without anyone else leading us.'

Lydia told them now about the loneliness that had followed her around. How she never fitted in with the trade guild, and hated the banquets, the come-ons. 'People always say I look miserable, like I'm still grieving and that I can stop now– I'm not – well, I've accepted my lot, anyway. And I know how to have fun, believe me. But I can't pretend to approve of their flirtation – I can't play their game at all. Why do men assume that women are incomplete without a husband? Or that they will automatically want *them*? I am an individual in my own right. I've made my own happiness – or, at least, made the best of a difficult lot.'

She noticed Luke raise a doubtful brow. 'Life was easier before I was widowed,' she told him. 'Yes, I'm comfortably off, but it was a fight at first. My husband hadn't shown me how to run the business, not really – he'd had no need to. I had to rise to it, for there were still bills to pay, and opinionated workmen who wanted to tell me their versions of how things should be done. There was a Haman or two amongst them, believe me.'

They talked long into the afternoon. She told them about her home, wondering how to invite them over and whether they might stay with her there. They offered to come back and help explain the gospel, but she said it was something she had to do on her own. Her household needed to hear her own conviction, not that of a group of strangers. They agreed that tomorrow they would come, but that Lydia must address them on her own first.

And so, after spending much of the day in engaged instruction and debate, Lydia knew she had to return. The task ahead had begun to distract her until she could put it off no longer. Would they see a difference in her before she even spoke? Would she be glowing with this new life, this joy? She really hoped she could be coherent in her explanations, for it was weighing very heavily on her now. Best get it over with, she had decided.

***

'Mistress, let me wash your feet,' said Maia on her arrival, as Lydia removed her shawl and wiped her now-damp hair away from her face. 'You've been gone ages in the heat of the day.'

'Thank you, Maia.' Lydia stepped out of her sandals and allowed the girl to perform her duty, though her thoughts were elsewhere.

'You must take a rest,' said Yolanda, coming through to welcome her home. 'Supper is being prepared and you'll find the house is in good order.'

Lydia's attention seemed to be held instead by a mosaic of Dionysos riding a panther that was built into the floor. She never did like it – all his wine, debauchery and merriment. What sort of god was that? Its only merit was that she could stand on it, place it under her feet. 'I want that mosaic gone,' she said.

'But it's beautiful,' said the first servant.

'You are tired and the day is a hot one,' said the second.

'Do you want it incorporated somewhere else in the house, or outside?' continued the first. 'We will find a craftsman who can take it apart piece by piece and mark out a map so it can be recreated elsewhere, just –'

'No, thank you, Maia,' she replied. 'You don't understand. Something has happened today, and I want you all to be aware, for it affects everyone. I am calling the household to a meeting after we've eaten. I want everyone present, and no excuses. Until then, please let me pass?

'I will be in my room – in fact, you'll find me in my pattern room should you need me, though I would prefer to be left alone.'

Lydia made her way upstairs to her special chamber where she rarely went. The day was most significant – should she dress accordingly? Wear the little-worn necklace that her husband once gave her, to signify by her dress that this was a momentous moment? But why, when the change that had happened was on the inside? She used her brass mirror to check on her reflection – she looked exactly the same, her face as mournful as ever, but she knew she *wasn't* the same, as for once she felt light and joyful. She changed her tunic and tied a neat belt, all the while rehearsing what she was going to say… But no, they wouldn't understand it like that. Though wasn't it a simple message? How exactly to convey it? What had Paul said to her? If only she could remember his exact words.

There was a tension in the air as Lydia ate her supper, seated on her own as usual. How she longed for someone to truly share these times with – someone who was accepted as on her level. She could hear whispers and hushed voices, nervous coughs, the shuffling of feet that stopped, then the feeling of someone's gaze on her from behind. She found it hard to eat, though she knew they had gone to great trouble to prepare this, and so she chewed and chewed her juicy, flaking fish into a ball, finding it was now impossible to swallow, like tough old goat meat from the most aged creature. She asked for more wine to wash it down, which in turn made her feel, at least, a little more relaxed.

At last she was finished, and she beckoned for her bowl to be removed, got to her feet, and asked that the household be gathered in the entrance hall. They assembled in no time and she stood on the third step of the main staircase, so that she could be seen and heard clearly by everyone.

'Today I had, what was, the most significant encounter of my life,' she started, with the opening line that she had finally settled on and rehearsed beyond measure.

'She's getting married again,' said one slave under their breath to another, as he leant against the carved limestone pillar.

'No, this is not mere human attachment,' she said, giving the young lad a glare, for her hearing always was sharp. She felt it stemmed from her own days in slavery, for her first place of service wasn't as happy as this one.[50] 'Today I heard about the Lord Jesus Christ, how he lived here on earth and died for each one of us. He was the Jews' promised Messiah, and he's made it possible for us all to know and encounter the living God. I was told about him by a group of men who had travelled across from Troas – in fact, they had travelled much farther than that. He was resurrected from the dead you know –'

It wasn't easy, conveying articulately what she knew to be true, this conviction in her spirit, this certainty that they must now live for Jesus and incorporate him into their lives, as he had each of them. That he had given up heaven on their behalf! Paul told her he had given up his 'divine privileges' to die 'a criminal's death on a cross'. It was astonishing, and she knew with utmost certainty that this was true. But just look at them! They were going to take more convincing than this, though of course they would do as they were told. It was not for them to question their mistress, but she still wanted them on side; to genuinely share her conviction, and not simply be commanded to comply, in the traditional way.

The old white cat seemed to be the only one who warmed to Lydia's message, rubbing against her legs and purring to himself. She picked him up and stroked him on the head before landing him firmly on the floor.

'How can you trust these men, these *strangers*,' said an old slave named Cletus, who always looked out for Lydia's best interests and who proudly bore each callus and wrinkle that had come about through his dedicated, hard service. He looked vulnerable, the way he stared at her square on and leant onto his stick with both hands, peering up at her from under his thick white eyebrows.

'He's right,' said his younger brother, whom Lydia had bought from Thyatira and had brought over so the two of them could be

---

[50] This is speculation on my part and that of many commentators. The suggestion is that her name, Lydia, that of a place, was given to her because of her servitude. Slaves were, at times, named after their place of origin. Of course we don't know if this was Lydia's situation, but she is certainly a free woman by the time we meet her in Acts 16.

reunited. He had learned quickly to imitate his brother's boldness. Why should she tolerate their doubts though? There was no need, and they should trust her judgement. She was not a conventional mistress, and she knew that. Perhaps they took advantage of it, but she could not – *would not* dictate without trying to engage their will first.

'You know that I cannot tolerate liars,' she told him, taking the opportunity to remind them all as she cast her gaze around the room. 'Dishonesty is my greatest hate, but they have no reason to lie. What's in it for them? They have travelled miles to bring us this news and I truly believe it's no accident that they are here. I intend to be baptized as soon as it can be arranged, and I really–' Lydia was distracted by a hushed conversation – she heard it all but chose to ignore it –

'Why's everything so urgent with her?'

'What if I don't want to be baptized,' came the reply. 'That's where this is heading.'

'We have no choice; of course we don't. She'll only make out that we do.'

'Everyone, I will want you to listen to these men,' she went on, with even greater force now. She blinked hard and straightened her back, making herself feel taller as she looked across the assembled group. 'I have found faith in the Lord Jesus Christ, and as my household I need you to listen yourselves and believe. Tomorrow they will meet you all. After Paul has spoken, I'm going to be baptized in our river, beside the house of prayer. I would like it if you would do the same. A household cannot have two masters, and so we all need to understand what's said here and take this step of faith. It's not possible for you to serve me and follow a different god.'

She could see from the blank expressions, the defensive postures with arms folded over chests and backs half-turned, that many remained none too impressed. The day was still warm, but that was not the only reason for their gleaming brows and the wetness of their hair, she knew. Of course, it was a stressful prospect, and it felt as if they had to change their religion without warning. Oh, what should she say?

'He is the living God – the one who can truly help us, who loves us beyond compare. Please listen to our guests tomorrow.'

***

Chapter Three

Everything *seemed* to be going to plan... at least, it had to start with, and here lay the confusion. Things *were* going to plan until today. Luke's days of being the local doctor were on pause at last, and the adventure was just what he had needed. Lydia had done a good job of convincing her household, and they seemed persuaded even before Paul had stood up to address them. She appeared surprised by it when they spoke the next morning, telling him they were a wilful lot, and were only paying her lip-service. But as a doctor he knew a night to sleep on things often brought great clarity, and they had at least had this. Perhaps it had been the Spirit working on them, but soon this one native believer had genuine support and fellowship within her own household. Thus it had all begun.

Luke was happy to record as much, but from here things had got complicated. Wasn't the idea to befriend people and demonstrate God's goodness? Had they not talked about respecting the local people and taking things at a steady pace, observing the infrastructure, learning the 'lay of the land' before doing anything too bold or dramatic, showing respect before causing a stir? In all fairness to Paul, this they had tried to do. They had been very tolerant of the girl who'd followed them around, interrupting to such an extent that she was a spectacle, and no one could really concentrate on what Paul was saying. What would Lydia think of them now? In truth, that was the least of their worries. Here he was, supposedly picking up the pieces and not knowing where to start. Indeed, it had all gone badly wrong, very badly indeed.

As a doctor, the situation had been fascinating to watch. The power of Jesus' name was visibly demonstrated, bringing the girl freedom in a way medicine never could have. But he felt uneasy – most uneasy, if you will. Her so-called owners had dragged Paul and Silas away to who knew where, the crowd siding with them and manhandling them, and now few people remained, except Timothy and the girl, of course. What would happen to these brothers? Had it occurred to Paul to even consider where this might lead? It could be a very short mission if this angry crowd had their way. No, this really wasn't part of the plan. Luke would step back here and quietly observe – reserve judgement as best he could; after all, Paul was right. Any narrative must be about the people the Lord reaches, not themselves, and here they were, getting in the way of that. He would watch from a safe distance and hope that he wouldn't be arrested. But what foolishness! He couldn't leave her – besides the knowledge that he should be imitating Jesus, he was a *doctor* and had a job to do. No, he couldn't leave a patient like that. Professional distance now, a healthy detachment so that no one could accuse him. Did the locals even know he belonged to Paul's group? A large part of him hoped that they did not. For now, the crowd was starting to gather again – smaller than before, but quite a presence nonetheless: a group who wanted to gawp, having lost interest in what was happening to Paul and Silas – perhaps that was a good sign – had the action died down? The two of them might return soon, and it was indeed his duty to take care of the girl. For them to see him ignoring her like this really wouldn't do.

***

The ground felt cold beneath the girl's hands and as she shifted her weight and raised her head from the floor her cheek felt sore. She touched it with tentative fingers and, finding blood on them, she tried to sit up. There was a crowd of people around her; looking about her she felt dizzy, disorientated. Why were they looking at her in this way? What had she done now? She couldn't see either of her masters, only lots of unfamiliar faces with smiles and laughter directed at her – but not in a good way. It wasn't worth the effort and she slumped back down, all her concentration going into trying to work out where she was and what had happened.

'What's your name?' said a commanding voice in an accent she couldn't place.

She didn't know – she'd never really had one.

The voice came again: 'I say, what's your name?' A young man was squatting beside her and had lifted her hand. He didn't seem in any hurry to go, and she felt he was protecting her from this crowd that was pressing around her, somehow emboldened by the fact she was awake and feeling vulnerable – did it show? It must, or why would they behave like this?

The man spoke softly now and a little nervously, but she wasn't listening, for she was caught up in that first question of his. Her name? She couldn't remember anyone ever taking the trouble to *name* her. She could see the city was in chaos, and from what she was gathering from the voices around her, it was her fault somehow. Everything was her fault. It always had been.

'I don't know,' she found herself saying. 'I don't know who I am anymore. I don't know that I ever did.'

'You must have a name,' he said. 'Everyone is given a name. It will come back to you – just try to relax now.'

There was jeering from behind her which she did her best to ignore.

The man took her other hand and helped her to sit up. Now he had placed a hand on her back and knelt in front of her, stretching his arms wide to give her a circle of space as all the people pressed in. He was tall and thin, like his parents had kept him in a small, cramped box and he'd kept growing up towards the light.

'Step away everyone, I'm a doctor,' said another voice. A stern glance was given to all around from beneath a heavy flop of hair, in a tone that suggested he was used to telling people what to do. His eyes were dark and penetrating, if a little severe, and to her astonishment the people around them did begin to back off. Then he crouched beside this other man and looked at her with that serious way of his. This felt uncomfortable and went on longer than she liked, before at last he began to speak. 'You've had a terrible shock,' he said, 'but you're over the worst, and you'll be glad once you've understood everything that's happened.'

The man smelt like he'd been running for his life and was catching his breath, as if he'd been caught up in this problem too. 'Thanks for watching her. There's no sign of them,' he said to the first man, and then to her, 'I'm Luke and this is Timothy. What's your name?'

'I don't know. I don't think I have one,' she said again. 'I'm... not... my own. I'm not...Where are my masters? I should be with them.'

'You don't have a master anymore – you're free!' said the first man, with the joy and the simplicity of a small child.

'Free?' Her voice croaked like it had been overused, though she had no recollection of how exactly. She remembered these men that she worked for. She remembered how she would draw a crowd, a bit like the one peering at her now over the shoulders of these new men.

'They say they don't want you, now you can't earn them any money,' said the young man, like it was really a good thing. His Adam's apple moved up and down as he spoke. She started to cry at this – it made no sense. And where would she live? What would she do?'

'You can come with us,' said the doctor man, perhaps sensing her anxiety.

She rubbed her eyes so she could get a better look at him. 'Are you my new master? Are you... do you?' she said, her confusion hard to articulate. 'What do you want me to do for you?'

'We don't want to own you – or use you. We want to help you!'

She couldn't quite believe it. That didn't happen. People always wanted something from you. They would hurt you in some way, put you in a dark corner, make you do despicable things so that you might be fed. This much she knew, didn't she? Or was her mind making it up in her attempt to understand?

Somehow this doctor did seem to understand her fears, for he gave her space and spoke very slowly and gently. 'It's going to be okay,' he said, taking time over each word as if he were rolling it around in his mouth like a stone. 'Your life gets better from here. You have been set free, not only from the demons that held you, but from your slavery. We're Christians and you've been set free in Jesus' name. I know the Christians here will look after you. They may give you some work, but not until you are feeling physically strong and mentally well-recovered. They will provide you with somewhere to live. A life of purpose and hope – that's what the believers stand for.'

Well, it was nice of him to speak kindly to her. He probably *was* a good man, and he meant well, but he couldn't possibly mean all that he was saying. And he couldn't speak for other people either. She must have shown the doubt in her face somehow, for... but what was he saying now? They were forming a plan, debating what to do with her. She must concentrate –

'We need to talk to Lydia,' said the doctor man to Timothy. 'I think she'll be at work. Are you up to a walk?' he asked, turning to her. 'You're looking winded. Here –' he said, extending an arm to her and helping her to her feet, taking each of her hands in his.

Yes, he certainly seemed kind. Of course, all this could change at any moment. She felt sure that it would.

'We need to get away from here. It's too chaotic, and people are still staring.' He sounded flustered, like her problem was becoming his own. 'Besides,' he went on, 'the others will know where to find us if we head back to Lydia's place. And the servants will know where she is if she's not home. Let's try her shop first. I'm surprised she didn't hear all the commotion and come and see what was going on,' said the doctor.

'Perhaps she had a fair idea. She's lost her reputation as it is,' said Timothy. 'Associate with us strongly enough and she might lose her business entirely.'

Who were these strange people and what problems were they causing? Was she really any safer, any better off? Now she needed to start life all over again. And no one was trustworthy – not in her experience.

'She's wonderful – you'll love her,' said the doctor to her, again sensing her unease. 'Calmness and stability – it's just what you need. Her house is full of it. And there's so much space. She has the most beautiful courtyard, and her hospitality – well, it's God-given, if you will. It really is God-given. Second to none, I'd say.'

'You won't be any trouble there,' said Timothy. Why did everyone always equate her with trouble? It was like it was a part of her, followed her around. 'And I'm sure, once you're better, she'll be able to find some work for you to do.'

It was interesting, listening into their conversation as they walked. Who were Paul and Silas? They sounded like they were too bold for around here, too outspoken, and they'd got into some real trouble. She did recognize the names, though. There was so much that was locked in her thoughts, that she couldn't quite access. The doctor was saying he needed to get to the two of them, to tend to them too, from what he'd gathered from the crowd. Timothy told him they wouldn't let him, that he wouldn't be able to. 'Besides, we need to get you sorted first,' he said, turning to her.

This part of town was unfamiliar to her, but she felt safer with these men than she had in a long time, she knew that much. There were shops all along this road selling cloth and ready-made garments that they hung from hooks outside. There were shades that she'd only ever seen on flowers or in her imagination. The customers looked well-dressed too – now a woman had stopped in front of them to adjust her sandal and she smelt of the sweetest fruit that she'd only seen others eat, dripping juice down their chins as they did so.

'It's just around the next corner,' Timothy told her.

'You wait here, both of you,' said the doctor man to them both when Lydia's premises came into view. And so they waited, just outside the gate, and both silently took in the scale of the place, that suggested Lydia was running quite some significant business. What surprised them was that they could hear the conversation between the two, for Lydia must have been found in her courtyard just the other side of the wall, though of course she couldn't see them.

'We have someone we need you to take in,' said the doctor.

'Oh? Go on.' But might she guess they were waiting here like this? It was unlikely, and at least they would hear her honest answer. It would be quite telling.

'It's a young girl. You probably know her – she was a problem about the place, you know, the possessed one who kept interrupting when Paul was preaching.'

'What, that crazy, frightful being? I doubt she's a girl at all. I don't think she's human.'

If she had the energy she'd run away, but she had no energy whatsoever. She wasn't used to this, and she dug her nails into her palms to slow her breathing, in a way that was familiar to her from days before.

'I think you'll find she is,' said the man speaking on her behalf. Well, it was nice that he believed in her – he was a doctor too, of course. Surely a better judge of what's in a person than most people, for they were men of insight, she knew that. But what use was he as friend – what use were either of those men? They were trying to find her somewhere to go now, for *they* couldn't look after her. What was that he was saying? She was what? 'She's been set free, released. You must have heard the commotion it's caused.'

'That would be like her. The Python Girl – that's how they speak of her. She causes chaos all about, like a snake that comes out of nowhere.'

'Only now she has *nowhere* to go,' the doctor continued, ignoring her last comments. 'Her owners don't want her. We've no one else to take her to.'

'I have no need for any more staff. I don't know what I'd do with her.'

'She's not up to *work* yet. Maybe in time, but my medical opinion is that she needs rest and much care. What was removed from her was so evil that there's not much of her left. She's a frail little thing – it's hard to imagine her causing so much trouble.'

'I'll think on it.'

'It's what we followers of Jesus *do* Lydia, – look out for one another. Care for the lost.'

'The last time I saw her, she pronounced doom over me. It's what made me pray to God that he might intervene in my life and reveal himself to me. I think it's why you all came here, ultimately. It was an answered prayer.' She paused and it felt like a very long wait, wondering what exactly she'd say next. 'What's she like now? Is she shouting vile things, swinging her head around uncontrollably, jerking her arms and legs so you don't know which way to walk around her?'

That wasn't right, surely? She must be talking about someone else.

'You wouldn't recognize her – that's the thing – she's so changed. She's subdued, almost lifeless. There's no aggression in her spirit now. And of herself, she's not articulate at all. She really needs someone to take her in and well – you *are* the main convert here, you're the right gender to mentor her, and yours *is*, in actual fact, the only believing household. Consider it your calling.' He coughed in a way that suggested he had embarrassed himself. 'This is beautiful cloth, by the way. I know how to make some dyes myself – on a quieter day I will show you.'

There was another awkward silence for a moment before she spoke again. Had the doctor slipped her some money? For 'Of course,' she said. 'Will you take me to see her? We'll take it from there. And what time will you all be home tonight? I need to pass on instructions for the meal.'

'It's just Timothy, the girl and me. Have you not heard? How can you not know?'

'Know what?'

'Paul and Silas have been arrested. I fear our stay here may be a long one.'

The conversation ended, the gate swung and the doctor reappeared. 'It's all sorted,' he said, 'I told you there was nothing to worry about.'

'We know, we heard,' said Timothy, placing a reassuring hand on her shoulder. She looked up at him and realized just how tall he was – as tall as the tree he was standing beside.

'You're looking pale and quite lethargic,' said the doctor. 'I'm concerned about you doing any more walking now – you need to rest.

149

Perhaps I can take you back inside and you can lie down until Lydia is ready to return home.'

'Please don't do that! I'll stay with you until later. Please,' she said, searching for all the words she could to vocalize her fear.

'You should be safely out of sight of the crowd, anyway,' Timothy told her. 'It's the best option.'

'Take me to the house now then,' she replied.

'It's quite a walk and you could do with a rest. That's doctor's orders.'

And so they arranged for her to stay with Lydia who would take her home when she was ready. The workers stared when Lydia asked them to make a bed for her on the workshop roof. The glances and raised eyebrows said 'and why can't she do that for herself,' but this was nothing compared to the reception she received from Lydia's staff when they finally made it to her home. They must have recognized the girl, even though Lydia had already given her a clean tunic and disposed of her ragged one. She stood behind Lydia and watched while the servant washed her feet, dreading the moment that was coming, hoping to sidestep it, but she instructed that her feet be washed too.

'It's alright, I can do it myself,' she remonstrated, which only confirmed to the staff that she was one of *them*. She could sense their attitude without even looking at them. In the hours that followed that day, she noticed something: if she stayed close to Lydia's side, they were at least pretending to be respectful. But the moment Lydia walked into another room she could feel their glares, and would look up to see them staring from her head to her feet and back. 'What makes her so special?' and 'We've served her for years – we don't expect to be elevated, so why's this one any different?' It's the company she's now keepin',' said the old man named Cletus of his mistress, in a voice that was too loud for the room. He was a self-important one, and she could already see how he performed for Lydia, then showed a different side to the rest of the household.

'You know who it really *is*, don't you?' said Lydia's chief maid, whose name hadn't yet been spoken. 'See, I heard what happened in town this afternoon. Surprising it hasn't reached the rest of you.' This was more than she could cope with, and she ran to Lydia's side and begged that she let her go to bed. 'I'm very tired,' she said. 'The day, it has been difficult. Difficult, though wonderful,' and the mistress smiled kindly at her before removing her snake bracelet and discarding it like a used kitchen utensil, to be cleaned and put away. 'I would ask someone to show you to your room, but I would like to do it myself.'

The next morning, she woke with a disorientated feeling before remembering where she was. The room was beautiful – spacious with a high ceiling, and light was flooding in through the slats in the shutters. She looked at the oil lamp that was placed by Lydia beside her bed – 'hers' she had told her – never before had she had anything to call her own, and she'd stared into the flame until she slept, not wanting to blow it out. It was a small brass lamp with a lid that slid over the bowl, but its value was not in how small, how exquisite, how perfect it looked.

Someone rattled the gate outside and called out to the young gatekeeper. 'Come quickly, come! Let us in!'

Must the day begin already? When would Lydia require her to be downstairs? If she could just enjoy this solitude for a bit longer. Soon enough the household would be sizing her up again, questioning Lydia's decision to take her in.

But whoever was at the gate had caused quite a commotion, and now doors were slamming, footsteps were heard rushing up and down the stairs, shouts were heard: 'They're back! Would you believe it? They're back!'

There was nothing else for it but to get up then – at least the focus wouldn't be on her, for this was surely Paul and Silas, the men she'd heard all about. Timothy and the doctor would be up, and they would look out for her. But would Paul and Silas be as kind? She'd heard they'd been arrested because of her. Granted, they were out now for some reason, but whatever they had suffered was all because of her.

She dug her nails into her palms, stood up and straightened her tunic before making her way down the stairs. She could smell fresh bread – no doubt some of the staff had been up preparing that before it was light – but the smell turned her stomach and she pushed her muscles so that it gurgled, for the thought of eating anything now was just too much. The household had already assembled – she could see this from her view over the high bannister – and Lydia was there with the two men, busy making them feel welcome as was her way. 'Why are you out so soon?' she asked them. 'I mean, we are delighted, but –' and before they'd had time to answer she was onto her next concern – 'You must be starving! Breakfast is ready and cook will make you something more – there's –'

'We've eaten – rather well, actually,' said Silas. 'We're not used to eating a meal of honour in the early hours.' He smiled a wry smile, clearly knowing something that they didn't and apparently enjoying the moment.

Lydia looked confused and everyone was silent as they waited for an explanation.

Two more steps, and so far no one had noticed her – not even Lydia, who had been so attentive to her needs the previous day. Timothy was at the bottom of the staircase and extended an arm for her, guiding her to sit in a space beside him, but she wanted to turn and run back upstairs. For Paul and Silas had been badly beaten[51] – Paul could only open one eye and his whole face was bruised and swollen; so much so that from the whispers around her she knew that he was barely recognizable. 'Is it really you?' the doctor had said, examining Paul up close before stepping back and leaning against a pillar, ready for this explanation that had to be good, going by the strange look on his face – a mixture of repulsion with satisfaction somehow, and a smile that spoke not of relish at his misfortune but of astonishment. Silas was cradling his arm as if it were sore, and their arms, faces and legs were all covered in gashes. Timothy was holding onto her arm now and had nodded his reassurance at her as he held her gaze and smiled; there was nothing to do but stay and listen with the rest of them, and she *was* rather curious.

As Paul walked into the centre of the room it was clear that he was limping, too. 'We're not meant to be here,' he told them. 'We've been asked to leave the city, but I'm not used to being told what to do.' There was laughter here, and a look of 'don't we just know it' on the faces of his friends. 'Besides, we needed to make sure this young girl was being taken care of,' he went on, gesturing towards *her*, 'and of course catch up with our team and the rest of you.'

She had shrunk towards the wall then at being referred to by him – were they really that concerned about what had happened to her? It was telling that they seemed interested in all Lydia's household, too. Timothy placed a hand on her back and, as she turned, she could see

---

[51] Acts 16:22-24 tells us something of how severe Paul and Silas's punishment had been: 'A mob quickly formed against Paul and Silas, and the city officials ordered them stripped and beaten with wooden rods. [23] They were severely beaten, and then they were thrown into prison. The jailer was ordered to make sure they didn't escape. [24] So the jailer put them into the inner dungeon and clamped their feet in the stocks.' (NLT)

Lydia sending her a kindly glance from where she stood beside Silas, just to the left of Paul. So they all settled in and listened to him tell the story of their imprisonment, with Silas interjecting here and there. Luke, she noticed, was writing down words and phrases, as if wanting to record this event for the benefit of others at some later point. Paul told of how they'd been placed in an inner dungeon, as though they were dangerous men who had committed a terrible crime. Their clothes had been removed and they had been beaten. Strangely their attire looked freshly laundered and the audience's sense of puzzlement must have been picked up on, for 'These belong to the jailer,' Silas said, which caused even more confusion. 'His best attire, but then he couldn't do enough for us.'

'So, he came to faith, see,' Paul explained, as if now everything would make perfect sense.

'Don't forget the earthquake,' Silas told him with laughter in his voice. He clutched his rib and winced before cradling his left arm again. He was a handsome man, despite the bruises, and the girl felt herself blush as she found her gaze turn to admiration. He had such an easy way about him, like he had not a care in the world, yet he had lived through the most dramatic thing. That was what made him attractive, she decided.

'Oh yes, the earthquake!' said Paul. 'Did you feel it here?'

Some of the household nodded, though the girl had been fast asleep – she wasn't used to sleeping like that. 'But that didn't happen of its own accord,' Paul went on. 'We were singing praises to God, as one does in these challenging situations' – the company looked confused, but he hadn't noticed – 'and praying out loud. This alone was of much interest to the other prisoners in there with us. *Then* the earthquake happened. It wasn't your ordinary earthquake; the chains fell from all of us as if they'd been made of shrivelled grass. The doors swung open. This woke the jailer, unsurprisingly, and on seeing what had happened he took the sword from his belt as if to kill himself. He was bewildered and called for a light – though looking back it was very bright in there, strangely. "Stop! Don't kill yourself! We are all here!"' I told him. At this he brought us out into the courtyard and beneath the stars asked us, "Sirs, what must I do to be saved?"'

Paul was visibly choked by this remembrance, so Silas went on: 'Of course it's so simple and he was saved already really, for his heart now belonged to God. "Believe in the Lord Jesus and you will be saved, along with everyone in your household," we told him, and then continued the strangest of nights, as he gathered his entire household and asked us to explain to them what we had said to him. This man had sunk to his knees, pleaded with us, his prisoners, and finally he washed our wounds, and with the same water we baptized each one of them.'[52]

At this, Silas was now weeping and Paul continued. 'He took us into his home and had a meal set before us – choice dates, fine wine, soft bread and cheese – and then we all praised God, singing the saviour's name, and praying together. We had no inclination to sleep after that, and news travelled fast, for before we'd even left the house this morning officers came to tell the jailer to let us go. "The city officials have said you and Silas are free to leave. Go in peace," the jailer said. But I told him, "They have publicly beaten us without a trial and put us in prison—and we are Roman citizens." – Did Lydia sigh at this point? The doctor certainly rolled his eyes as Paul went on – "So now they want us to leave secretly? Certainly not! Let them come themselves to release us!" I said. When they learned that we are Roman citizens the magistrates did come and find us at the jailer's house and apologized. They were rather squeamish and keen to rectify the situation. I told them the thing to do then, to set things right in our minds, was to talk to the jailer about how he had come to faith, and how they must too, for we know it is good to start sharing your faith from the moment of salvation. Instead, they implored us to leave the city, as if we are some kind of threat to the peace!'

'The reality is they want us gone,' said Silas. 'Much as we would like to stay here, we feel our work is done. And going by some of the sentiment we've experienced in this town, it wouldn't take much for trouble to be stirred again.'

'Not all officials are as kind as those,' said Lydia. 'Believe me.'

'Be encouraged,' said Paul. 'The Lord is here with you. He released us from that prison cell, and he will remain here when we have gone.'

Then the household gathered around them, with Timothy and Luke joining them in the centre of the room. Luke stretched out a

---

[52] Luke suggests the baptisms happened 'immediately' after the jailer had washed their wounds. I am making an assumption here, but I think the events were placed side by side deliberately. There is the thought that there would have been a pool within the confines of the jail (Ellicott and Gill's commentaries on Acts 16:33, available online.)

hand to place on Paul's back, but then withdrew it, remembering his wounds, though perhaps it was more than that. Then, 'I'm not sure I'm going,' he said, from beneath his heavy fringe. 'I feel a connection here, and the church is yet young. Would you mind if I remain and continue the work you have begun?'

'However the Spirit leads you,' said Paul.

'Conversion is just the beginning, we've discovered,' said Silas. 'Discipleship is what you and Lydia can provide the church.'

'You can oversee the complete recovery of this one,' Paul told him, gesturing towards the girl where she sat on the bottom step to observe all that was going on. 'Girl, come here,' he said.

There was nothing else for it, and she went to join them. Expecting a quiet rebuke in her ear now she was close by she looked down at her feet and began counting backwards. And yet he placed a hand on her head and said a blessing over her. She felt a soft arm across her shoulders and looked up to see Lydia smiling at her. 'It is good to see that you have bonded,' he said to them. 'I think our work here is done.'

***

Their work here was done. It was good to see that they had bonded – well of course he would think that. Wasn't it neat, convenient for them? Yet they had to go, and she couldn't have expected any more than that – it was unfair of her, and at least Luke had stayed behind.

She rolled over on her mat and realized that it was still dark. Another broken night, then, and another moment for taking stock before the busyness of another day. Lydia felt she had truly earned the title of parent in these few short weeks that'd passed since that momentous day and night. The journey had been nothing like she'd expected. She could not forget the instance she first saw the girl, after the deliverance – it was as Luke had said – she bore such little resemblance to the demon-possessed-girl-about-town. She looked so small and, well, helpless. There was an innocence about her and a vulnerability that really didn't go with what she knew of her. She seemed much younger too – a genuine child, which she had been, of course, all along. Luke had carried her in there in his arms, for it seemed like she might faint. Perhaps that was, in part, down to the fear in her. Once they'd met, she had assumed that fear would go, for there was nothing frightening in her own character – most people found her easy to overlook and she'd had to work at asserting herself, but most things now intimidated this girl, and as Lydia lay in the quiet she realized why she'd come round, for noises were escaping from the end of the corridor. She got up from her bed on the floor and opened the door – how could she not have realized? For she sounded like the Python Girl again, calling out, thrashing around in her room. What had fallen on the floor now? Was there anything in there left to break?

There was nothing else for it.

'Calm down,' Lydia told her, entering her room and pulling back a shutter to let in the light of the moon. 'You're having a nightmare. You're alright – you're here with us now. You belong to Jesus – remember?'

She looked bemused as she came round from her dream, her eyes relaying her confusion as she looked about her and tried to place where she was. Lydia pushed the girl's hair from her face – her skin felt cold and clammy. She wondered how long she'd been like this.

Sitting down next to her on her mattress on the floor, she put an arm around her – 'oh, it's wet,' she said after settling in a comfortable position, her knees up in front of her. In a moment she was on her feet. 'I think you've had an accident. We'll have all these things washed in the morning,' she said, pushing away with her foot the cloak that had fallen off her in the night. 'We'll scrub the matting then and dry it in the sun. There's a clean tunic here, you should get changed.'

But the girl was crying now and demonstrated no readiness to sort herself out.

'It was just a dream,' Lydia told her, wondering when the girl was going to show signs of normality. No one had told her just how much work would be involved, taking her in. She could, of course, leave all this to a servant, but that wasn't her way – it never had been. Grantedly, she felt she should be spending more time with her each day, but she was still trying to run her business, and she did what she could to prove to her she cared. 'We'll get you through this phase,' she said, but still there was no response. She crouched on the floor next to her, where it was dry. 'It will be okay, it will be okay,' she said to her, but the girl didn't lift her head.

'If... I... can...,' she faltered, 'just spend... a few weeks with you, I... can be gone.' She ended with a long sniff, then rubbed her eyes with the back of her hand.

'We don't want you gone,' said Lydia, still watching the girl intently and waiting for her to look up. 'This is your home now.'

'It's not really,' she mumbled into her arm onto which she rested her already sleepy head – she seemed to have come down from the fright very quickly. 'What do you... get out of it?'

'*You.*'

'But you don't really want me,' she said, looking up at Lydia now.

'What makes you think that?'

'Oh, I know these things.'

Lydia shifted in her crouching position and put a knee on the floor. Was the girl still psychic? Did she need further deliverance? Of course it was hard looking after her at times, and she had to admit to herself that more than once she'd regretted her decision...She hated being confronted with the reality that what the girl had uttered might be true. But she *did* want her. She was tired, it was the dead of night, and clearly the Lord had placed her in her care. It had been easy, being responsible only for herself, but it *was* lonely.

'They say Jesus told a parable once,' Lydia told her. 'They call it "the prodigal son".'

'I know it.'

'Oh?'

'I heard Timothy explain it last night, to a boy... who was spying from the gate. He went outside and sat next to the lad...passed him a hunk of bread that he'd been picking at himself.' She paused, not used to stringing so many words together in a row and for them to make sense. That normally only happened in the girl's head, from what she'd told Lydia. It was strange, knowing someone so well again, understanding their ways, the odd little pauses and stops. The curious thing was there was undeniably a similarity there. She knew her own thoughts had a habit of racing on and sometimes she would keep people waiting for an answer, as their quizzical expressions told her. 'The boy looked hungry,' the girl said. 'I watched them from the courtyard...heard every word.'

'I think the father in that story is a picture of God the Father. This is important, you know. It's how he welcomes each one of us. None of us are worthy, you see. He drapes a cloak of forgiveness over each one of us – his best cloak, the one that has cost him dearly. He places the best ring on our finger, and he welcomes us home.'

'That's beautiful,' said the girl, and she paused. 'But I don't see... how that changes anything... for me now.'

'You're worthy. God sees you as worthy and so do we.'

The girl was silent, and Lydia wondered what she needed to say to get through to her. She looked at the little pile of clothes she'd given her, all made for her and placed on the shelf beside the door. There too sat the pot of hair pins and the carved comb that she'd presented her with – what did she really need? Why wasn't it working? Her efforts continued to snatch and tangle in the same way the ivory comb caught in her hair. The girl would at least let her try to tame it, but to try to rein her in in any way seemed pointless.

Lydia straightened her back and regained her poise, as she often did when she was about to say something that promised to be important. 'I want to give you a name, to show you that you belong. Will you let me?'

'I had hoped my name would come back to me. It's lost. I don't think it ever will.'

'How about Abigail? It means father's joy.'

'But I don't have a father.'

'You have the Lord. He adopts all of us, if we let him. It's a very freeing thing, you know.'

The girl was silent again – she clearly hadn't warmed to the name.

'Netanya, then. That's the other name I like for you. It means "gift of God". That is who you are.'

Another long pause, before she said, 'I like it, but it's not really true.'

'Perhaps you'll grow to understand it, but it's true to me.' She wondered how much to share with the girl; being honest with her, being vulnerable with her herself seemed like the only way. 'I have never had a child of my own – I've never been able to bless anyone with a name before. I'm surrounded by people, but, like you told me once, they are only here because they have to be.'

The girl looked confused, and Lydia didn't know how to begin to explain. She wasn't used to opening up to anyone – in fact, she preferred not to. That had always been her way, but increasingly more so, since everything that had happened to her.

'When my husband died, that was it,' she said. 'I was alone in the world. I would like it if you felt you belonged to me – not out of any sense of duty or obligation, but because you are loved. Will you think on it, Neti?' Had she used the name on her without permission? But she had been toying with these names for so long in her mind that it just, sort of, well, came out. And she hadn't expected to confide in her so fully. Her inner world always had her several steps on from what was happening in reality. Didn't the scriptures say that 'God places the lonely in families; he sets the prisoners free and gives them joy'[53]? They could be their own little family, of sorts. And they'd both been prisoners in their own way, too. Perhaps the Lord was solving it all at once – though she could just say no, find this all too much. This child might not want to belong with anyone – she was too bruised, too hurt. Yes, she'd gone through too much and no one could blame her for wanting to protect herself. Lydia had played that game with her own emotions for long enough, before she finally recognised her loneliness and told the Lord about it. Oh, why did she always get so carried away in her thoughts?

But it seemed the girl had accepted her name and more besides, for she had taken hold of Lydia's arm and was sobbing. Lydia put her other arm around her and allowed her to lean on her for the first time. Years of pain and rejection jolted through her as she cried, the hurt that no one possibly thought she could have felt, admitted and released as she took on the idea that she could, just possibly, be loved.

***

It was the start of a happier era for Neti – she felt almost secure now, though occasionally doubtful thoughts crept in and she wondered how it would all end. She hadn't completely shaken off the first words Lydia had said about her: 'that crazy, frightful being' – that's what she had been to her. Worthy of nothing, except perhaps keeping your distance from. 'I doubt she's a girl at all,' she had said. 'I don't think she's human.' So why this kindness now? She said it was 'because of Jesus – he was worthy of everything, but that didn't mean deprivation, but joy.' That he had 'changed her heart' and she knew 'his plans were the most fulfilling.' Neti sincerely hoped it was true. She would never tell Lydia what she had overheard her say – let her life speak the truth of it. It was better that way.

Neti could hear the household was up and about and she would find Lydia now – avoiding the servants if she could. She could hear them, sweeping outside, banging the dust from the carpets, laughing from the kitchen, but Lydia had so many that they were impossible to avoid completely. One or two of them still made her feel uneasy: kind

---

[53] Psalm 68:6.

of strange... unworthy; that was it. She knew it was all because of Lydia's mercy that she was here, but she was constantly reminded of it by their hard-working efforts, especially when she entered a room, as if to make a point. They would scrub harder and sigh, wipe the often-imaginary sweat from their brows. More than once she'd caught them stop and glare at her when they'd thought she'd left the room. She would glance over her shoulder just to make sure that what they thought of her was true.

Lydia was descending the stairs when Neti left her chamber and that made her feel relieved. She waited for her to catch up, mid-stair. 'What are you going to do today, Neti? You may come with me if you like, just for a little while.' Hearing her new name made her smile; it always did. It had been a few weeks now, but it always did something in her. 'I've a new dispatchment of cloth arriving from Thyatira,' Lydia went on, 'and you could help me sort through the colours. It's the older madder root that makes the most intense dye, but some people like the more subtle shade. The variety is quite incredible.'

'I was thinking of exploring today,' she replied. 'I remember this place in part, but it's not real to me. It's like a weird dream. I need to see if places are where I think they are.' She wanted to go back to the agora in the hope it would help her remember any of her former self. She didn't want to, and yet she did – it was a strange fascination, but if she could remember it might help her to move on. There were memories when she first came around after her deliverance, but they soon went. She just couldn't understand that 'wild' version of herself that people spoke of, and she needed to. Besides, who didn't like a good market, with stalls to dodge between and under – she might even be able to find somewhere new to hide, should things ever get too much, and she need a bolt-hole.

'Why don't you play with the jailer's children?' Lydia said. 'I know they'd be glad to see you, Neti. You could ask them to show you around. Children always like that. And besides, I'm keen for you to have some friends of your own age.'

'I could do, I suppose.'

'They are the only other believing family that I know of around here. I've been shunned by so many people since finding the Lord that I feel the need more than ever to cleave to our own. If it wasn't for people wanting my business, I'd be accepted by even less. There is a certain snobbery that means some people do still *want* to associate with me, for they want to be of my class. But it's not genuine.'

It was hard to go against Lydia's wishes – she was doing so much for Neti that she had to oblige where she could, though in all honesty she would rather be alone. And so, when Lydia had left and the servants were making her feel uncomfortable again, Neti made her way out of the house, looking left and right out of a triangular shaped chink in the gate before venturing out. At least the house was situated at a quiet spot, and Neti looked out across the plain, watching birds following an invisible line in formation, swooping and diving as if at play. Neti did know the way to the jailer's house, as she could see it from here at the top of the hill – Lydia had pointed it out to her often enough. You could make out the path of the river too in the opposite direction, meandering its way out of the town. That was where she preferred to wander but that was for later – she would reward herself with a walk that way after she had done this for Lydia. She liked to walk to the small prayer house where nobody else seemed to go much during the week. It was her own special spot, and she would gaze into the river and imagine the big baptism when the whole household went down into the water there. She would think about when she might be able to do it herself; the thing was, she didn't want many people watching, for she felt a spectacle even without that invited attention. Could she be baptized with just Lydia there and Luke, the kind doctor? He was the last of those men to stick around, and Lydia said he was trying to help strengthen the new church. Neti wondered if he had a particular interest in Lydia too, though she wouldn't say it. Still, she liked his quiet way, and from what she could see, he took a special interest in everyone.

Baptism then, she thought, swishing the long grasses beside the path as she made her way along the track– wasn't the point of it that you were making a public statement? There was little purpose in her doing it at this stage, she felt, if she wasn't prepared for anyone to watch. She'd heard it said that you could give a short message too – she didn't know what she'd say or how she'd say it. What message did she have for anyone?

The jailer's house was getting closer – it looked very small and cramped compared to where she was living, but she knew she'd fallen on her feet there. The jailer and his wife seemed to have many children and she could hear them laughing and shrieking already –

she was surprised they put up with the noise in the courtyard and didn't send them out to play.

Neti began to count in her head backwards. She didn't know why she did that, but she associated it with her past, with getting through something. It did seem to calm her down, though she found she always dug her nails into her palms at the same time. Nineteen, eighteen, seventeen – she knocked gently on the courtyard gate, and was about to turn and walk away quickly when it opened and a girl of about her age opened it wide for the others to see, as if she was there to be gawped at. That was how it felt. The girl held a rope as if ready to skip, but this made Neti wince for some reason and push on her stomach muscles. Sixteen, fifteen, fourt-

'It's the girl from Lydia's,' shouted the smallest of the boys. 'What've you got in your bag?' Neti touched the small fabric bag that hung from her neck, that Lydia had once put over her head, feeling its reassurance, all the while looking at this child of the jailer's, whom Lydia was so desperate for her to get along with.

'Nothing,' she said. He was holding a sling shot which made her feel decidedly nervous. But more to the point, didn't they know she had a name? She'd heard Lydia tell their mother – they *must* know!

'I've come to visit, if that's okay.'

'Why?' said the oldest boy who must have been at least as tall as Timothy. He was older than her and his voice was already breaking. This made him even more intimidating, and she watched his Adam's apple move up and down as he talked – 'What makes you think we'd want you with us? You forget who you were. Who you *are*.' He was nothing like the quietly spoken, respectful Timothy, despite the physical resemblance – he couldn't be more different. This lad thought himself grown up, behaving like this, trying to impress his little siblings. How ridiculous!

'We're going out to play,' the girl who'd opened the gate called out, and they all followed her through, leaving Neti bewildered – presumably she was meant to go with them... Or should she just go home? That was enough rudeness to be going on with and she didn't know if she could cope with much more.

Neti turned to go, not even bothering to look at them, when a young voice piped up, 'No, wait a minute.' The girl was not much bigger than a toddler, but she had the confidence of all the others – perhaps you would if your father was the jailer and could take any problem in hand. 'We can have some fun,' she said. They whispered amongst themselves for a moment or two and sniggered.

'Can you tell me what I ate for breakfast,' said this little girl. Her broad grin and matching plaits made her somehow endearing, forgivable perhaps? Was she to know any better? Neti, having given her the benefit of the doubt, sighed and turned to leave again, but then the smallest boy was in front of her, running circles around her. She ignored the question and hoped they'd move on from it, but they only thought of more ways to interrogate her.

'Tell me how old I am,' he now said, stopping dead in his tracks and staring up at her, as if she was a statue he was trying to provoke in a game, not a real person. He put a stone in his slingshot and pulled it back, aiming at her with great concentration.

'No, that's lame, Theo. Tell me how powerful I'll be!' said the oldest boy.

Surely he was old enough to know better? And she wasn't even sure how many of them there were – they moved so fast and even when they paused, they couldn't stand still. It was as if this was a practiced art, this teasing banter. She suspected they weren't all the jailer's children either, which was even more worrying. She felt a target already and didn't want to become so for all the local children.

'Tell me what I'll be known for in this life,' joined Theo now, getting the hang of this. 'Tell me all about my future and make it good!' His stone fell to the floor and he stamped his foot, more concerned about having to reload his sling than whether Neti might answer him or not.

'This is ridiculous!' she said to him. 'I've been set free from all of that. You're meant to belong to a believing family. I don't see much evidence of it – your parents would be appalled if they could hear you. Is that why we've left your courtyard?'

'They've put *me* in charge today,' said the big brother whom they all looked up to. He should really be a young man, but clearly he had a long way to go. 'I *am* the parent while they're out of town,' he told her.

'What makes you think they'd believe *you* over *us*?' the oldest girl added. 'We could say you were casting spells over us. Nobody trusts you. *Everyone* thinks you're strange.'

'Yes, you're not going to find a good reputation *that* quickly,' came another voice from behind her.

'You're meant to be like Jesus,' she replied.

They all laughed at her, but for a brief moment they didn't know what to say.

'There's plenty of time for all that,' said the oldest lad. 'When it looks likely we'll die we can reach out for him.'

'What makes you so sure you'll have the opportunity?'

'What makes you so sure we won't?' said the girl who could look at her at eye-level. She held Neti's gaze with such antagonism that she had to look away. Did her fear of them show? 'Anyway, we've been baptized,' the girl continued, '*you* haven't. Our names are logged: Antonia is mine, you'll find.'

'I don't think they'll let her be,' said the big brother again. 'I mean, you're not a true believer. We've heard what Lydia's servants say about you.'

'A true believer!' They had Neti's full attention now, and she wasn't scared of any of them. Something of the old Neti was rising in her – the Neti well-practiced at self-defence, and not afraid to speak out. Her outrage at the injustice made her want to spit at them, only now she was beyond all that.

They were looking at her and laughing again, doubled up with mirth. 'It's the same girl – like she always was!' said the girl of her age. 'It's the way she shakes her head and looks like she's going to explode. And that hair! She can never be tamed.'

Neti began counting in her head again – it wouldn't do to give in to the provocation. She had to remember Jesus and how people tried to get a reaction out of him. At home they'd talked about how the same children he'd grown up with would have been in the crowd who tried to do away with him, and on his home patch. They no doubt explored the local hills and caves together when small, went up to the steep banks and cliff tops that their parents would have warned them about. A familiar dangerous edge they later tried to throw him from.[54]… 'Would you mind relaying to me the conversation we've just had?' she said, getting them back to the line of conversation. She would remember Jesus now – he would help her.

'Nobody wants you around,' the lad replied. 'You should think about where you are going to go, what you are going to do. There's no future for you here.'

'Yes, there is. Lydia is training me in the business.' Lydia hadn't really said that, but how else was she meant to respond? Why would

---

[54] Luke 4:28-30.

she want to show her the new materials if she hadn't a plan to let her work with her? Navigating this 'doing right' all the time was proving hard.

'You'll be bad for her reputation!' he said. 'Just think on it... everyone knows what you were, who you *are*,' said the vindictive boy again. 'It's like I've already said. It would be very selfish of you to stick around – think about it.'

'You are all missing out,' she told them. 'You're the ones who should be pitied. *You* just think – you could have all the excitement of a believing life, have *the God of heaven* on your side. Aren't you even a little bit impressed by the miracles, by the wonders? How could life get more exciting than following the believer's path?'

Again, they were silent for a moment until '*Neti*,' said the older one and the little group all laughed. 'Neti. What sort of name is that?'

'You can be our servant if you like,' said young Theo.

'Servant?' said Neti.

'Well, slave if you prefer. That's what you are really isn't it, though somehow you got away.'

'She could be our *prisoner* – let's play that game!' the younger one said to his big brother. 'Abba has left some of his spare things in the house – I know where he keeps the ropes and chains.'

'I've got this skipping rope, *der*,' said the older girl to him.

'No thanks,' replied Neti. 'I'm going home.'

'Home?'

'You don't have a home!' shouted one from behind her again.

Neti was off up the hill, walking at a brisk pace – she wouldn't give them the satisfaction of thinking they'd actually intimidated her. 'If you want to fit in, you need to submit to us. Let's face it, that's what you're destined for. Submission!' Their voices were getting louder the further away she got. 'You always were!'

'Python girl,' they shouted, in one last ditch attempt to get at her. It seemed desperate, but that was a name she particularly hated. She'd heard Lydia use it on that first day – *She causes chaos all about, like a snake that comes out of nowhere*. Why could she remember that but not what she wanted to?

Neti started to run now but still she could hear their taunts just as clearly, their shouts keeping up with her. She knew they had a point – it was a shame they weren't really following Jesus, but perhaps their words had an honesty to them that she needed to hear.

She looked back to see the oldest one was following her – she had to get away; running straight back up the hill was not a good idea, and he was gaining on her as it was. *It will be okay, it will be okay* she said to herself. Without any time to think, she took a path that led behind a shop selling wineskins and water bags, knocking one to the floor as she went. There was no time to stop and pick it up, and they'd only think she was stealing. She grazed her arm pushing past a date palm so as not to collide with a couple of men coming towards her who were engrossed in discussion. Another narrow alley to the left now and Neti took it, holding herself as flat against the wall as she could, all the while looking through the gap to see if she'd managed to lose the boy. She was behind some small, obscure temple and could smell something burning – a sacrifice perhaps? The smell made her want to cough, which was made all the more difficult because by now she was out of breath.

The minutes passed and she felt almost safe again, her breathing slowing at last. Nobody seemed to come up this path – it was a dead end, and she sat on her haunches to think. Why hadn't Lydia taken her in as a servant instead? Who were they trying to fool, that they could be a ready-made family, that she could become something of a daughter to her? What did they have in common, after all? Perhaps she'd got that wrong, anyway. She could never be a daughter to her. Her most endearing childhood years had passed, and now, here she was, no longer a child really, but with all the problems and hang-ups of someone not ready to be of use. She would be a burden and Lydia had only taken her in out of pity. In fact, it sounded like out of a sense of obligation at first – she remembered that bit too. She really wasn't that willing… had to be persuaded. Still, girls not much older than her married, didn't they? But who would want her?

She shut her eyes for a moment, took in a deep breath and sighed. 'Well look, if it isn't our little prophet of doom!' came a voice.

Neti opened her eyes to see a face that was all-too familiar, staring at her. He took her chin between his finger and thumb and drew her face close to his – his eyes were bulgy and his breath stank of rotten fish. 'Well, well. We were glad to see the back of you, but now you look like a proper little madam! Look at your shining face and neat little outfit – scarlet edging, eh, and matching bag? And there's not a bruise on you! Seems I could use you for different purposes now.'

He grabbed her arm at the elbow now and Neti let out a little scream. Then his face was over her mouth, up close: 'Don't even think about it,' he said, clamping a hand across it.

She struggled and tried to trip him at the ankle with her foot. This at least meant he let go of her mouth. 'I can give you something valuable, if you –'

'That you can,' he said with a long, leering look, and he moved his hands to her waist and upwards.

Neti started to run now, though she wasn't quite sure where to go – in fact, she didn't really know her way around at all, because she preferred to stay back at the house, out of the way. If she'd known how much trouble this outing was to bring her, she'd have stayed at home today, for certain. She headed for the noise and bustle, thinking she would be able to immerse herself in the crowd very soon. One advantage of her skinny limbs meant she could run fast, and squeeze between some rather narrow gaps. Here was another market with plenty of people loitering, like they had nothing better to do. The building housing it all looked pretty formal, but she had no choice, so in she ran. Old men were sitting on the marble floor and playing a board game that was etched into the floor – she tried not to knock over their pawns as she made her way past. They were smoking something that made her feel like choking. So many awful smells around here! She could lose him in here for sure... But this could lead to another dead end... Neti looked about her and discovered the man had yet to make it into the building, but he *had* seen her, for their eyes met. She shouldn't have looked back. There was an open gateway ahead and some steps leading down, so Neti took it, not knowing where it would lead. She really had no idea where she was either – which part of town – but she would sort that out later.

On she ran, past merchants selling their wares from trays on the ground or from bags slung across their shoulders, between women gossiping or deep in innocent conversation – she could not tell which. There was the smell of faeces in the air and lots of young men milling around. The building in front of her had a huge entrance – should she go inside? She decided not to chance it and to keep going, hoping no one had seen her – following the walls around Neti dashed past the public latrines – the building seemed to go on forever, but the man wasn't following her, from what she could see. Soon enough she had reached the north side, and the building opened up onto a busy street, with more people selling their wares. A large portico led back into the building, and men were gathering there and limbering up, ready for some sporting competition inside. Still she felt conspicuous, but she was out of breath again and needed to rest.

'And here you are,' came a voice from behind, savouring each word. Or perhaps it was just that *he* was out of breath, but he seemed to be enjoying himself. 'You never did know your way around very well. It was worth keeping you medicated, or we had no peace. If it wasn't for that crazy mane of yours, I wouldn't have recognized you.'

He had grabbed her wrist and shoved a knee into her back to make her walk. Neti could vaguely remember a bitter-tasting herbal drink that they would give her at regular intervals. She never knew what was in it and didn't have the energy to argue. It was strange that she could be so wild and outspoken then, and yet at other times subdued. At least things were starting to come back to her.

The man was now panting from the chase, somehow more out of breath than when he'd found her…That brought back some horrid memory too. Oh, he was vile, and she had to get away! If she could just find her way to the riverbank, her safe place. She knew that area intimately and could probably shake him off on the way, if she could just get close. She'd promised herself she'd go there today anyway, though not like this.

She would trip him up in a moment – catch him unawares.

In no time her opportunity came, for two old men were having an argument on the street and a small crowd had started to gather around them. Neti stuck out a foot behind her and hooked it behind his leg, pushing him into the crowd as she went. The man grabbed her wrist tighter. 'It's no use trying to get away! I'm bringing you back until we can decide what to do with you. Though I think I know where to start.'

He leered at her again and Neti's thoughts jolted onto a new tack. 'I can give you something you can sell and make money from,' she said.

'That used to be you,' he said with a laugh that seemed to come from deep inside him. Seeing she was unamused, he replied, 'It would have to be good.'

'I mean an object or two,' Neti said, trying not to let the panic show in her voice that had a habit of squeaking when she was under pressure. 'Something gold – something valuable, like I said earlier. If you'll just let me go! I have a life now. I'm wanted – properly wanted.'

'I doubt that.'

'You let me go. You said I was worthless to you, that's what I'm told. Now please.'

'So, what exactly can you bring me? As I said, it will have to be good.'

'Jewellery, probably.'

'Probably?'

'Definitely. I'll bring you something gold, with rubies in it. I know just the thing. Then you'll leave me alone?' That snake bracelet haunted her, and she knew Lydia didn't like it anyway. Perhaps she wouldn't notice it had gone – she certainly wouldn't put out a search for it.

'We will,' he replied. 'I can't trust you to come back though. I'll be waiting outside at an arranged time. And if you don't emerge, I will cause such an outcry that you'll regret the day your mother ever brought you into this world.' He paused. 'As she probably did,' he said, and laughed through his rotten teeth. 'Always a burden. People always wondering what to do with you... Don't get too comfortable with her, you know. It won't last – it can't.'

Neti ignored the last comments, for the prospect of needing to deliver the item into his hands, unseen, was bothering her more. 'But I might not be able to bring it straight away!' she said. 'There are servants, many of them.'

'Oh really? Then perhaps I deserve more. I always knew she was rich, but t-'

'Well, not lots of them, but a few.'

'I'll decide when you bring it to me. And if that's not enough, I can always send you back for more... and more,' he said.

'I'm not even sure of the way back from here,' said Neti, the pitfalls of the situation now overwhelming her.

'Oh, I know where you live. I've known for ages – you're with the Christians, aren't you? And that woman who sells purple cloth. It was only going to be a matter of time before we came for you. Unfinished business is never good – it hangs over one, don't you find?'

Neti said nothing.

'Now walk to the end of this road, turn at the leather worker's shop on the corner. I'll be just a few steps behind and will tell you where to go.'

Could he be trusted? Would he really direct her to home, or was something more sinister going on?

The walk couldn't pass quickly enough for Neti. He got closer behind her, so close that she could smell that breath again, and he could tell her things she most certainly didn't want to hear. There was no way she could escape him now – that just wasn't an option. Had she really walked this far when she came to find the jailer's children this morning? Was he simply trying to confuse her, or taking a longer route because he was enjoying his power over her yet again? It must look odd, her dressed in her neat outfit with her scarlet bag slung around her neck, him looking like an impoverished down-and-out, which he was. Had she been his only source of income? As they approached the house the situation didn't go unnoticed, for neighbours who had grown used to Neti as part of Lydia's household thought it strange and did stop and stare. 'We thought you were as good as dead,' he told her. 'I didn't expect you to recover; *I* wasn't going to be the one clearing your corpse from the street. Besides, we had to deal with that man who had the *nerve* to release you – what made him think he had the right to meddle and destroy our business?'

Again, Neti said nothing – what was there to say? It was best he didn't hear that Paul and Silas had been released from prison, but perhaps he already knew.

'Cat got your tongue?' He laughed to himself at the expression and Neti hated to be reminded of his self-congratulation. He loved to gratify his own desires, to please himself only, and Neti hated to think on where his perverse thoughts took him. Now the memories were flooding back it was very hard to stop them. He always did silence her, when she had every right to object. 'Do you know the origin of that?'

'No.' Neti thought of the old white cat that roamed through Lydia's rooms. It seemed to have a mistrust of her – perhaps rightly so.

'No, but then you don't know much! They say it came from Egypt. That years ago, those who lied or swore had their tongues removed and fed to the cats. Now that's a worthy punishment! Egypt has some pretty grand cats. Personally, I'd have sold you to the mines if I'd known,' he went on. 'Or someone dealing in prostitutes. It was never really my way – I'd have had to invest in the right clothes for you, tidy up your hair, which still needs doing. *The famous python girl! Tame her if you can!* Do you remember that chant?' He smiled to himself again and Neti looked away. 'It really did draw the crowds. Not that you needed any help. I'm astonished you look as you do now, to be honest. If Juro hears I've gone all soft on you and allowed you to return, I'll be in big trouble. So, like I say, you'd better make this worth my while.'

Neti concentrated on the feel of sand between her toes as she walked, glancing down to see if her sandals could scoop up the dirt as she walked. She didn't want to look at him again if she could help it. Dust seemed to be hanging in the air today, blown in from across the sea from what people were saying, as if some countries were more dusty than their own.

'You should be glad I'm not a Roman,' he went on. 'We could have had you crucified, or branded if we were feeling kind. They could learn a lot from us Greeks, wouldn't you say?'

At last, the house was before them and Neti couldn't wait to run through the gate to the courtyard and secure it. If only a gate was all that was needed to keep him out!

'You will find me waiting outside at sundown,' he said. 'Meet me underneath this huge plane tree. Do *not* let me down. Try anything on and it will be much worse for you – understand?'

***

The house was its usual calm, cool self – it was as if nothing changed inside this building and that was good. Neti untied the knots on her sandals and stepped out of them, enjoyed the feeling of the cold marble beneath her hot, swollen feet. Believers said the sense of the Lord's presence here was tangible and Neti knew it herself, but she couldn't think about that now, for it would interfere with the task. Nobody stopped to greet or even stare at her on this occasion, for they were completely absorbed in preparing the supper and polishing the floors in the rooms beyond. Neti walked through the entrance hall and up Lydia's own staircase, hoping that no one glanced at her once she had passed. At the top landing she paused to look down from the gallery, but all was well.

Neti put her hand inside the red cloth bag that she wore around her neck – it was empty, but just what she needed now to conceal the item she'd planned to take. Lydia had pressed it on her once as a sign of her acceptance, and she had protested, though now, quite unexpectedly, she found it was just the thing, for if anyone caught her in here they wouldn't suspect. She couldn't shake the memory of how Lydia put the bag over her head, insistent that she must have it. Lydia had told her it was to demonstrate how valued she was, and how she wanted to share her home with her... Neti felt heat flood her cheeks now and she pushed down on her stomach muscles, as if to expel the shame. It was just a one off. Lydia wouldn't notice if an item of jewellery went missing – she owned so much, after all. Even this bag she'd given her showed her outlandish wealth – 'it's just made of a scrap,' she told her, but Neti had never dreamt of owning a stitch in this colour, let alone an item to wear. Yes, if she could just get today over with, they'd be left alone to get on with life. Neti would be out of her hair one day, but not like this, with *him*. She had to do all that she could to lose him, and this, it seemed, was the only way.

Neti listened at the door first, her ear up close, then pushed it very gently with the hand that was resting on it. She peered through before stepping boldly inside. No one was around, and the sooner this was done, the sooner she could get life back to normal.

Oh, but this was such a beautiful room... it was what girls dreamt of, and though she'd been living under this roof for several weeks, she had never been inside Lydia's personal chamber. This was a special room, and it seemed even Lydia didn't use it all the time. She had taken to sleeping in a room close to her own since her arrival. She'd said she wanted to be near to her. There was a drape on the wall made up of cloth patches that suggested a sunset – it incorporated the range of her madder shades, from the palest almond blossom through to deep garnet. On the opposite wall an array of shawls on a taut string billowed in the breeze from the open lattice. This window overhung the house and contained its own little seat from which to survey the valley below.

Neti fastened the door with a plank, then looked all around her to take in the grandeur more fully. Lydia clearly came in this room, for there was evidence of her creativity everywhere, though she had never seen her make her way up the stairs. A low table with sketched out designs sat in the middle of the room, and fraying snippings of cloth were found here and there on the floor. It was as if no one was ever allowed in here to tidy up, but the room was no less beautiful because of it. Beneath Lydia's shawl collection there was a wooden box that sat on a low stool and Neti went over to examine it. Its lid was inlaid with a darker wood, and from its centre shone a flat, smooth piece of iridescent shell. Could this be mother-of-pearl? She lifted the lid with both hands, and all Lydia's trinkets and jewels shone from inside. There, gleaming from underneath a string of coins, was the snake bangle, coiled and ready to fit around a small lady's wrist. It was wriggly at one end, as if real – she stepped back from it and pushed with her stomach muscles... It will be okay, it will be okay, she said to herself... Neti took some deep breaths and tried to calm down. She hadn't seen Lydia wear it since the day she allowed her to live here. And she herself didn't like anything to do with snakes; not after what she'd been called. That was still the only name she could remember anyone using for her. Did she really have a life before she was owned? Perhaps she was one of the many abandoned babies – one mouth too many for a family to feed. She knew she should be grateful that she hadn't been 'dispatched', but it didn't feel easy sometimes, this not being wanted. Unless you've felt it, you cannot really know.

She could give the bangle over as she said she would. Or run away with it! She picked it up again and felt its weight in the palm of her hand. And those were definitely large rubies for eyes. There were green stones too along its length, forming the suggestion of snake-like stripes. If she took this, it would provide enough for her to start over somewhere else. Lydia wouldn't mind – she was making life easier for her really. She was being considerate. That was the thing. Now, where could she sell it? She knew they made coins here in Philippi – did that make the gold less valuable, it being commonplace? No, this new plan was ludicrous. Of course, she should just hand it over, as arranged.

There was a noise from the other side of the door – the clearing of a throat, then a nonchalant whistle. Neti dropped the bangle and saw it roll to the other side of the room. She stood as still as the temple statue her masters had compared her to, in a moment of public flattery. She had as much heart too – what *was* she doing? She tried to control her breathing, but the person must have heard the clank as it landed on the floor. Neti now drew herself back against the wall so they would not see her feet under the door and began to count. *Nineteen, eighteen, seventeen...four, three*. Whoever it was seemed to have thought better than to enter Lydia's chamber, and light footsteps sounded, perhaps aided by a walking stick, away and down the stairs.

Neti had to get out as soon as they were at a safe distance. What if they thought they'd better come back to check? How quick could they be? No, there was a walking stick tapping down the length of the corridor, she felt sure of it. That was probably Cletus, Lydia's most long-serving slave, she now knew. At least he was as deaf as the old white cat that lounged around downstairs... Still, she couldn't chance it. Placing the bangle in the bag around her neck she counted down from one hundred and crept out of the room, watching from the gallery to ensure no one was passing underneath before making her way downstairs.

***

Cletus whistled to himself as he approached Lydia's workplace, today taking the most direct route through the street of potters, his stride purposeful and quick. This was a sure way to win more favour with the mistress – she hadn't noticed him for weeks, it seemed – not so much as a broad smile or one of her knowing nods; no more than two words had he exchanged with her in recent days. Sometimes he wondered if she'd even remember his name without prompting.

It was a long walk from the house on the hill down to the clothing quarter of town. Other members of the household grumbled that she should live where she worked, like most people did, but Cletus was glad of the fresh air, and liked the prestige it brought her, for some of it, surely, rubbed off on him. He usually preferred to find his way in via the bakers' street and take in the smells of the breads, cakes and pastries that were cooking. Today, however, he was in too much of a hurry – a pedlar selling strings of onions from around his neck was walking too slowly in front of him and he wanted to push him out of the way. In his hands he carried a basket, too carefully, for it couldn't contain anything of value. Cletus stomped behind him, brushing past so that the man appeared to lose his balance – he halted to glare at him, then bent down to gather up his bunches of herbs. There was no time to stop and help him. Admittedly, this wasn't Cletus's usual behaviour, but his mission was an important one and people just needed to get out of his way. Conversations were taking place in doorways, channelling more people through a narrow gap on the road, and no one seemed to be in a hurry. Except Cletus.

After a few more minutes brisk walk, Lydia's shop came into view... not a moment too soon! But inside the place was especially busy and Cletus knew he had to wait his turn. Surely they should have worked out their budget before coming? And how should Lydia know when her next new batch of cloth would arrive? Lydia dealt with them in her usual tactful way, and now at the desk stood a portly man who went on to explain the length of his most difficult of journeys, the meticulous standards of the customer that *he* was buying for, and his need to see Lydia's complete range of available cloth, including any winter weight fabric, for he wouldn't be back for quite some time – well, that was a relief at least. Cletus knew better than to whistle at instances such as this, but he caught Lydia's eye and she must have sensed his concern. 'Excuse me a moment,' she said, 'Is everything alright at home?'

'Yes, Mistress. Well, I think so. That's why I'm here.'

'I'll talk to you shortly, Cletus.' Then, turning back to her customer, 'Now, where were we? Winter weight cloth. Yes, I have a couple of good varieties if you can just hold on. I need to climb some steps out the back – Cletus, perhaps you could do that for me?'

Cletus made his way through, pulled out the steps, and was pleased to see that Lydia had followed him through. 'On the top shelf, Cletus. Underneath the new silks. Please be careful up there.'

'I've come to talk to you about that girl you've taken in,' he said, pausing with a hand on the ladder. 'Caught her up to somethin' I did. See, I thought you should know.'

'Just wait with that thought,' she said. 'Let's help our customer first please.'

Cletus obliged, astonished that Lydia could seem so unconcerned, so willing to wait it out. As soon as the man had gone Lydia joined him again in the back room, where he was tidying the stock and returning the unwanted items.

'Now, tell me again what it is that's bothering you.'

Cletus climbed down the steps so that he could look Lydia square in the face and convey the gravity of what he had to say.

'The girl you've taken in. I caught her – she can't be trusted you know.'

Lydia laughed out loud, throwing her head back so that her curls shimmered all the way down her back, in that beautiful way of hers. Then she looked at him, all serious like. 'I won't hear of it, Cletus. Trust, Cletus, trust. It's a very freeing thing.'

'But she was in your room, the special one that no one goes into.'

'What makes you feel so sure?'

'I watched her from under the door, Mistress. The cat had started to go upstairs, and I decided to follow. You know how rare it is for him to ever get up from his spot in the sun – his intuition has always been good, just like mine.' Cletus smiled his best smile so that his eyes would twinkle – that's what his mother used to say of his smile anyway. 'It looked like he didn't want to bother but felt he really should. I do think this is serious.'

'Well, what was she doing?'

'Looking through all your things. Poking around. I saw quite enough, but I'd recommend that you go up there later and make sure everything is where it should be.'

'And if it's not?'

'Well, it seems to me that she's freeloaded on your charity for long enough. I would perhaps consider allowing her to stay on as staff, or suggest she sling her hook.'

'Thank you, Cletus, but I'm sure that won't be necessary. If you see the girl, say nothing out of the ordinary to her. I need to work on this afternoon here and I do trust her. I will see you back at the house later.'

'It's an honour to be of service to you, as always. I do hears more than I let on. That reputation of being a deaf old fool serves me well – or serves you well, I should say, my mistress.'

'Be on your way then, Cletus. I appreciate you coming all this way, but I'm sure your fears about the girl are unfounded.'

'You promise me you'll follow up on this? With the greatest of respect, some of us feel you are love-blind towards her. Don't forget what she was. I'm not so sure such impurity can ever be washed out of a person.'

'Well *I* am, Cletus. I am. Now please be on your way.'

***

The light was fading now – there was a dirty haze forming over the town, as if it would soon be veiled from view. If only it would fall thickly and fast, concealing herself and what she was about to do, for it was very nearly time. Neti knew she couldn't be waiting outside too early, or the staff would suspect. But the house seemed quiet, and she would chance it now – slowly though, heading to her room if anybody spotted her. She wondered if old Cletus had been taking too much interest in her this afternoon as it was – 'Let me carry that for you, young Neti. You'll do yourself an injury and then the mistress won't be pleased.'

She would wait behind the wide trunk of the aged plane tree, as agreed, which would obscure her from sight of the house. She sat down and leant back against the trunk, placing her hands in the clusters of bark that had fallen to the floor. They looked like they could be pieced back together, if only she knew how. She picked up a fragment and traced its pattern with her finger, before tossing it away in a rush of fury with herself.

She couldn't sit still like this – it was impossible. She stood up and felt the hot summer breeze hit her face, shutting her eyes for moments at a time, as if to make the situation feel less real, but it only felt more so. She could smell the jasmine-like scent wafting from the courtyard, from the vine that clung to the walls and clambered towards Lydia's upper chamber. Lydia said it wasn't jasmine but Stephanotis, and that its name meant 'fit for a crown'. It suited her residence, and she herself was fit for a heavenly crown, that no doubt the Lord had ready for her arrival in his courts one day. Everything about Lydia was good and true, and here she was betraying her, who had been kinder to her than anyone else in the whole world. Oh, but Neti mustn't think like this – at least, not for now. It wasn't helping the situation. She felt conscious of how her back was turned from the house, and with her eyes still closed she made fists of her hands, but the scent still reached her. Yet this was about her survival, and she felt sure Lydia would understand… though perhaps she was too pure to? Had evil motives ever entered her mind? Was she capable of appreciating what it was like to be in her position, under this much pressure? It was circumstances that were making her do this, and there was no way around it.

Neti opened her eyes now and there he was, approaching the top of the hill with dust flying up and around him from the ground, as if he were emerging from the dirt, from the murk of this world. Oh, and she could smell him, too! She pushed on her stomach muscles and felt the palms of her hands grow sweaty. She tasted the spiced beans of supper in her mouth, acidic now, and wanted to retch. She must compose herself and get this over with. Then she could repent and move on.

The man was repulsive – everything about him, from the way he looked at her from sideways on, not releasing her gaze, his knowledge of her both too full and familiar, to his now-filthy clothing. Did he always look this bad? He looked impoverished, and for a brief moment she wondered again about his livelihood but stopped herself.

She would not have pity on this man – he didn't deserve it and never would. Neti handed him the bracelet at arm's length, but still his breath stank, and more besides. She knew it was hard to keep clean at this time of year, but really!

As he took it from her, she jumped back a couple of steps from him and observed him. He turned the bracelet in his hands and inspected it – the fool. When was the last time he held anything this prized, this valuable? But then, 'I need one more thing from you,' he said. 'You see, this isn't quite valuable enough. You must be able to see this won't feed me forever?' He twisted as he spoke, never quite able to stand still, as if evil thoughts were constantly jostling inside of him. Was he deformed? She didn't think so, but he never looked quite *right*. He needed deliverance himself, for sure.

'Well, that's hardly my responsibility,' Neti told him.

'Do you want me to go and find your mistress? I can demand more from her!'

'We had a deal!' Neti felt a piece of bark under her foot that had found its way into her sandal – she kicked it out, and he moved to one side, as if he thought she was going to kick him. Now that wasn't a bad idea! But he was out of the tree's concealing reach now, though she wasn't about to correct him – he would only wander further into view of the house.

'This wasn't what I was expecting,' he said in a cool and measured tone, with such ease, inspecting the perfect bracelet again. How could he object to such a beautiful item? He was just trying it on because he *could*. Because he could see where she lived and how well things had worked out for her. But her lack of response was rattling him – that was the thing about him – he could turn at any moment. He always was so unpredictable! For now he was looking angry again and Neti was worried that he was going to lose it. 'I can't just go in and find you another piece, just like that,' she explained. 'There are people around, the house is busy.'

From looking at him she could see this answer really wasn't going to be good enough. She pushed with her stomach muscles as she remembered the ultimatum he often gave her – 'You want me to give you food? Again? But I gave you some yesterday! Well then, you know what you have to do.'

'I can try,' she faltered, hating that she was giving way to his demands once more. 'I can't promise more than that. Wait *out of sight*, just behind this old plane tree.' The emphasis she placed on her words seemed lost on him. 'If I don't come back tonight it's because I can't.' Neti noticed that the light was fading and the sky was beginning to look like the wall-hanging in Lydia's special room. Sunsets would always remind her of that now. There was an amber light tonight, as the dust hung heavy in the air – it bizarrely spoke to her of hope, though her deed had been a betrayal. 'I will meet you the same time tomorrow, if I don't return,' she said. 'I promise you that I will. I'll be true to my word.'

The look he gave her was most unsettling… He narrowed his eyes into little slits, and veins bulged in his neck, like he was trying to contain his anger but was really struggling. He was sweating and she could see a small tremble in the arm that held the precious bangle – *Lydia's* bangle. Oh, what had she done? She couldn't be sure he would behave as she'd requested, but what choice was there?

Neti ran for the house, looking back over her shoulder to see that he was waiting where he stood as their conversation ended, not where she asked but in plain view. She would have to be quick – she'd make her way up the stairs deftly. She knew where to look now; it really wouldn't take so long. The chain of coins was most beautiful, though Lydia would be sure to notice that was gone. Perhaps anything she hadn't seen her wear – for she obviously didn't love what she didn't put on. She had to be business-like, matter of fact. One more hurdle and this whole episode would be behind her.

She was back at the door of Lydia's private chamber now, having taken two stairs at a time, though without making a sound. She stopped and looked all around her – over the gallery, along the corridor – but she was definitely on her own. She knelt on the marble floor to peep beneath the door: the room was empty, and she proceeded to enter.

She had forgotten just how enchanting this room was! She wouldn't come inside again for quite some time – it wouldn't do any harm to look around first, just for a short while. She needed to choose her item carefully, after all. Something that looked valuable, but that Lydia didn't like or wouldn't want – that was the objective.

In the fading light the room had a different sort of beauty. It made the place seem mysterious and other-worldly; almost temple like. The search would take time, for she had to lift each item as if it were a precious artefact, take in every detail to make sure no jewels had fallen out of their settings, that the metals really were silver and gold, and that any tarnish would rub off easily. Neti knelt on the floor among the snippings of purple and set to work unpacking the jewellery box that lay on the stool. It demanded deep concentration. And what was this... the box had a hidden floor! Something very valuable must lie beneath, and it was obvious Lydia wouldn't miss it – at least, not for a while. In the darkness of the box, the stones winked like the eyes of wild animals hiding in bushes at twilight, waiting to pounce on whoever disturbed them. This was a necklace that spoke power and pronounced its value. She held it in both hands and lifted it up and down – it certainly was heavy, and what's more, she'd never seen Lydia wear it.

Neti shut the compartment, closed the box and placed the necklace on its lid. She'd come back to that. But no – why not put it on? She would wear it while she continued the search, to *feel* if it was the right one. She thought that it was. Yes, it was important that she made sure she had found the right item to take to him, and to deprive her of her most significant piece did feel risky. Neti pulled the piece over her head in one motion – if it wasn't so solid it might have broken. It hung from a sturdy chain, and she found the weight of it reminded her of the much heavier chains that at times her owners had her wear. She tried to brush the thought aside by allowing her eyes to drink in the beauty of her surroundings.

Looking around the room she saw the shawls again in varying shades of purple. But of course! Why hadn't she thought of that? And yet he clearly knew Lydia's occupation. If he'd wanted purple cloth, surely he'd have asked. The thing was, there was so much of it here that Lydia would never know. But then getting it out of the house could prove difficult. And they did say that this wasn't the most expensive purple – *that* came from the murex shell, but Thyatira dealt with dye from the local madder root. He probably knew this. Lydia had garments in both, and Neti thought the madder cloth was actually more beautiful – it was the colour of autumn leaves on the local grape vines, not of the grapes themselves. It was far more sophisticated, but they said it was the effort, danger even, involved in the harvesting of the shells that made it more desirable and costly.

Neti had lost her sense of urgency now, so absorbed was she in her explorations. She lifted the scarves in her hands and felt the fineness of each... Oh, there at the back *was* one of the expensive kind. Neti pushed the others out of the way and untied this one with her clammy fingers, before wrapping it tightly around her neck, just so that she could feel the delicate fabric against her skin. The necklace swung from beneath the scarf and she touched it with her hand – it felt cold and refreshing and she kept hold of it while she ran her fingers through the scarves again. Perhaps she could find a tunic to go with it? Surely the beast would be happy with that?

There was a large woven box beside the door with a fabric lid and this was the obvious place to store items of clothing. Neti lifted the black embroidered lid with its bright flower patterns and found an array of tunics inside. Delving deep she found one that matched the scarf exactly. Without hesitation she put it over her head – it was way too long and draped along the floor behind her. It made her feel like royalty or an ancient Greek god... oh, how her thoughts were slipping –

'I knew I'd find you in here!'

Neti turned to look, knowing full well who it was, and pushed on her stomach muscles as if to expel the guilt. Of course it was Lydia, standing in the doorway with her disappointment evident in the monotone delivery of her words and her downcast gaze. She wasn't enjoying this moment and would rather not be here – Neti could see it, *feel* it.

Lydia didn't say anything for what felt like a very long time. Neti had really overstepped the mark this time and she would definitely want her gone. She was working out how to break it to her, obviously. That's what it was.

'I'm sorry,' Neti said. 'I was just... trying it on. The purple, I mean. The colour... it's so...enticing.' Hadn't her vocabulary grown since they'd been together? She was now quite articulate. And all for what? Yes, she would be gone before the evening got much darker. Perhaps she would have to go with the man... but no! She'd rather risk life on her own than go back to him. She could manage, in time. Oh, how much did Lydia know? Had she been seen by someone, informed? Old Cletus had been stalking her all day – it must have been him at the door the first time, and then he kept appearing, as if monitoring her behaviour. But then he was only doing his job – she was to blame for her own actions; she couldn't pin this on anyone else.

'I won't keep you,' Neti said. 'I know I shouldn't be in here. I've let you down, and more besides.' She tugged at the scarf but then gave up, so tightly was it wrapped around her neck. 'I'll go at first light, if you don't mind. It will be safer for me. You don't know who's around these parts. It's all a-'

'Will you just be quiet and listen to me? You're not to ever think about leaving. Do you understand that? I want you here with me. You don't seem to get it – how I love you, how God loves you. Start to believe it Neti. There really is no other way.'

Now she was crossing the room to talk to her up close, and Neti pulled even harder at the scarf – what had she been thinking? It was impossible to remove – oh. She managed to shirk off the cloak as she wriggled and looked around her, wondering where to put it.

Lydia picked up the cloak and draped it over her shoulders again. 'Here, we can tie it like this,' she said, and she took a rope-tie from the low table, doubled it and looped it around her skinny waist.

'I'm sorry, I won't do it ag-'

'Nonsense,' she said. 'I should have let you into this room before now. I will be training you up in here in years to come. This is my pattern room, where I spend time designing when I'm at home. It's where I store my treasures too, as no one is allowed to come up here.' She gave an embarrassed little cough. 'I have to approve a sample of what's been made in recent weeks here. The colour suits you.'

Neti laughed at this – nervously. Most people wouldn't ever be able to touch fabric as rich as this, let alone try it on, but for some reason Lydia really didn't seem bothered. Now she was adjusting the scarf, first releasing its hold on her, then draping it in the latest style Neti had seen Lydia herself wear, and some of the other more classy women about the town. It was a loose hood that she spread over her left shoulder, then allowed to fall over her front, displaying its delicate beauty. But she must know she'd been in her treasure box, found its compartment, seen everything that was of any value to her. The necklace – her fingers must have touched it as she arranged the scarf! Why hadn't she reacted? It didn't make sense, and when she knew – well. Best to get it over with... but Lydia spoke first –

'I met an acquaintance of yours outside – or should I say, former acquaintance,' she said.

'Oh?' Neti could feel the heat rise up the back of her neck and she lifted her mane of hair in one hand. 'Who?'

'The man who owned you – well, one of them. I think you know anyway. Let's just say, you won't be seeing him again.'

'You paid him?'

'Rather handsomely, you might say.'

What could she possibly tell her now? She glanced up, just for a moment – 'It's true,' Lydia told her. 'If you stand in the window bay and peer to the left you can just see in front of the house. He really has gone.'

Lydia gave her a gentle push in her back and Neti stepped over to the window as requested. The fragrance of the Stephanotis was wafting through and she shut her eyes and inhaled, rather than run the risk of seeing him yet again. He was probably still around out there. More to the point, would Lydia get angry now that her back was turned? Was this for dramatic effect, was it a cruel, controlling moment such as those regularly inflicted on her by the masters?

'I'm sorry – I'll work for you now,' said Neti turning, able to bear the suspense no longer. Better it was over with. 'I was fully expecting to from the start, anyway. I'm much healthier now. I'm so grateful for all you've –'

'That I will *not* allow,' said Lydia. 'Nothing has changed between us. I wanted the man gone, and to be sure he would never be bothering us again.' She patted the mat next to her for Neti to come and sit on, as if she wasn't angry at all. Neti sat down like this was the most natural thing in the world, all the while a ball of anxiety building in her stomach that she wanted to expel. Was that it then? She could say nothing, and it would all be over. But if she told, then there was much danger. Lydia would really know who she was, what she was like. Surely then, after confessing the rest, she would not keep her. The best thing had to be to say nothing. Yet she couldn't do it to her – the Lord Jesus, he was watching this moment and he deserved better. So did Lydia. Why did she try to fool herself that it was okay to sin, so long as she repented after?

'I gave him something of yours,' Neti said in a quiet, almost imperceptible voice.

'I know.'

'What do you mean, you *know*?'

'I know that you gave him my snake bracelet. I know also that he wanted more. That you'd come to my room to find a second item to pay him off with.'

'I'm so ashamed,' said Neti. She concentrated on the heavy weight on her chest that Lydia had obviously been overlooking until this point – she could still flare... owners usually did. They were used to playing games; of course they were. 'I'll be gone by the morning. I have more than outstayed my welcome. I have exploited your kindness and I will trouble your life no longer.'

She got up as if to leave, but Lydia put a hand on her arm and kept her sitting on the floor.

'That bracelet was very valuable,' said Neti. 'And it was *yours*.'

'I never liked it. It symbolised something evil... I always think of the creation story and the serpent in the garden. He was there to tempt, and you too were tempted by him.'

'To be rid of my past,' Neti replied. She picked up the smallest patch of purple fabric from the floor but let it drop – she wasn't entitled even to this now, and she knew it.

'You already were,' Lydia told her. 'You should have trusted me.'

'I know. I feel so guilt-ridden.'

'You don't need to. I'm going to let this go, and I'm only following the Lord's pattern. You see, this is what God does for each of us, time and time again. We ruin things, we let him down, and we think the only decent thing to do is to walk away, for he deserves better than us. But we are his choice, and in the same way, *you* are *mine*. And what's to say I'd have done anything different in your position?'

'I'll buy it back for you. I'll work hard, like I said. I'll do whatever you ask –'

'No, please don't. The point is, you are family to me, not some hired help. That's where things were always different. He has his python now – the one to make him money. The two of them belong together.'

'And there's *this*,' said Neti, holding up the pendant and swallowing hard. Here it would end then...

'I know, I've seen it,' said Lydia.

With fumbling fingers Neti unfastened the necklace this time – for the chain was tight when pulled over her head – and she placed it along Lydia's knees – 'Please will you put it on?' she said.

'No, it doesn't interest me like it does you. I'm just a custodian for it, really.'

'Please would you put it away then?'

'No. I want to tell you its story.'

Lydia played with the beads of coral in the pendant's setting as she began her tale. 'I haven't owned this necklace an especially long time. But it *is* special. It belonged to my husband's mother; she died when he was small, and it was all he had to remember her by. He said she wore it often, and when he held it, he felt transported back; the scroll work and the beads that swivelled were, of course, exactly the same, and he felt close to her, even though she had gone. He said he could remember the feel of it in his fingers when it was around her neck. He kept it hidden away from me when times were good.... there was no need then for him to have her at the forefront of his mind. He gave it to me when he knew he didn't have long to live. He said that threads of connection go on forever, and that love is stronger than death.' She paused and picked it up in both hands, feeling the weight of it as it hung from her fingers. 'And now, Neti, it is yours.'

'I could never own this.'

'Well, then keep it safe for me.'

Lydia took the necklace and placed it over Neti's head, lifting her mane of curls, then centring the pendant on her chest. 'You are family to me now, and this is its rightful place. It might be best if you unfasten it when you take it on and off though – your head is bigger than I thought.'

What could you say to this? And Neti thought she would *never* take it off. 'You are still young,' Neti replied after struggling to find the right words for some time. 'If you don't remarry, you could adopt a son. It could become his – his wife's. Think on that.'

'Neti, why would I want to do that when I have you to give it to?'

Lydia looked betrayed and her eyes really could spill their tears at any moment. Neti had to keep the conversation going. 'And that bracelet ... had you had it long? Where was it from?'

'It's just an object that my husband gave me. So is the necklace, really, at face value of course. Objects are often significant because of the people attached, with their beauty ascribed, though that snake bracelet never did charm me! Objects come and go... people do too sometimes, but I wish they wouldn't. I have known poverty in my life, before my husband fell in love with me. That was a miracle in itself, although sadly it didn't last. Objects cannot offer happiness really – I've been so lonely, living with all this wealth. I need people to love, and I need a purpose.'

'Your choice in me was a pretty poor one.'

'I want you with me,' she said again. 'I don't care what you were planning to do. Well, I do, but it doesn't change how I feel about you. I can see the man put you under immense pressure, and how desperate you were not to return to that life. What happened? Where did he find you?'

'I ran into him in town... I had to escape from the jailer's son, and in the process stumbled into him. He followed me, bribed me. He wanted to take me there and then and I knew he had the strength to overpower me. He looks like a weakling but he's not. He's not afraid to inflict pain, that's the thing. In fact, I think he enjoys it.'

Lydia's wide eyes were even wilder than usual, her gaze even more intense. For once her solemnity seemed appropriate, and that look she had that suggested she was about to cry. Neti thought in their early days together that she was about to cry at every turn, but soon learned this was just her way.

Lydia seemed to distract herself by seeing to Neti's new attire. 'Keep it clean,' she told her. 'I want you to have these garments, to keep them forever as a symbol of how loved and respected you are. Not just by me, but by the Lord Jesus. You'll grow into the tunic, but you can have the scarf to wear now.'

Neti didn't know how to respond to this, so she didn't. She wanted to cry, but she'd spoil the fabric, so she buried her face into Lydia's lap and allowed her to catch her tears. She really couldn't stop them, but again, Lydia didn't seem to mind.

They sat for a while in silence. Lydia had taken Neti's hand into her own and said nothing while she recovered. She seemed to know when it was the right moment to speak, and what banal thing she needed to hear, for 'Your nails are beginning to grow,' she said. 'Will you let me shape them?'

'Of course.'

'I have a pumice stone in my room along from yours. We'll find it later.'

'Thank you.'

At last the trivialities of life, as if everything else had been dealt with. 'Your hair was unhealthy to start with too,' she went on. 'All patchy and matted… I think you used to pull it out. You really were distressed. In the early days, I'd untangle it as you slept, and while I soothed you from your nightmares. It looks pretty much like mine now, wouldn't you say?'

Neti smiled broadly at her – she'd love to look like Lydia, but she could see that in some ways she already did.

'I'm starving,' said Lydia, pulling a bunch of grapes from her bag and offering one to Neti. 'You are putting on weight at last, I must say. To start with there was nothing to you – all sinews and knobbly elbows and knees. Completely undernourished, I'd say.'

'I think I look like a normal girl now – nobody would know my past by looking at me.'

'I want you to feel more than just normal. I want your life to feel exceptional. I'm going to teach you to read – give you every privilege that I've had.'

'I thought you started out poor?' said Neti, tucking into a handful of the large purple grapes.

'I did, though my family was very loving, and a clever but very elderly uncle took it upon himself to teach me to read and write. I lacked for nothing really.'

'You were fortunate. Even girls from the richest families don't have that.'

'And what are riches? As I've said, I think those are found in relationship, not possessions. I'm conscious that I haven't spent enough time with you, but I will. I want to.'

'You could hardly have been expected to look after me all the time. Lydia, why didn't you stay in Thyatira? What brought you here?'

'Philippi became more home to me after a while, though I'd spend time in both. Perhaps it's only recently that I've felt loyalty to here. But for a long time, I needed a fresh start. And Thyatira is too full of self-important people – military personnel, especially retired ones, and people who knew my husband and refused to do business with me once he had passed away.'

'That's terrible.'

'I did try my best. I even joined their trade guild... That was a bad idea.'

'What's a trade guild?'

'It's hard to be in business and not a part of one, especially in Thyatira. It's expected of us, and their influence is phenomenal. Yet they don't like Christians and gave me a particularly hard time when they heard I'd become one... I wasn't spending much time there as it was, by the time I had my riverbank conversion, for I hated much of what they are about, and I was already searching for God. [55] They hold these immoral feasts... I refused to go, yet they still treated me like I should be their property. You know that I've always dressed to

---

[55] See E. J. Banks' note on trade guilds in Thyatira in the International Standard Bible Encyclopedia Online: https://www.internationalstandardbible.com/T/thyatira.html See also the Free Online Bible Library: https://www.biblicaltraining.org/library/trade-guilds

please myself and not for anyone else – I appreciate beautiful fabric, so why shouldn't I wear it, and stylishly too?'

Neti nodded at her in full agreement. She admired the quirkiness of some of her outfits; this evening there was a slight ruffle on the top of her tunic that wasn't there this morning. No doubt she had sewn it herself. She had draped a layer of black beads over the top and stained her lips with something to match her belted madder tunic. Her straight back and ability to look anyone directly in the eye made her a challenge to some, and her quiet manner was taken for offishness or antagonism, when she was just taking everything in. Perhaps she was seen as a person to conquer.

'Yes, I dress for myself,' she went on, though Neti was of course on her side. 'Not trying to attract a man, though my attire is at least modest. You wouldn't think so though, going by some of the comments I had. What made matters worse, in Thyatira I had to live near them. My husband's family had been a part of them for generations, though he always left their social gatherings before things got going, shall we say.' Lydia looked away from Neti for a moment, seeming to want to conceal the emotion this memory had stirred.

'That's awful. No wonder you needed to get away,' said Neti, not entirely sure what she meant, but she had her suspicions.

Lydia spoke after a long pause, as if wondering whether to share the thought. 'You know, my husband is even buried in their communal grounds, such is the totality of life within the guilds.'

'That makes things hard.'

'It would have been a blessing if it were working well, but they were too controlling. They didn't just look after their own – it was more than that. But I've discovered I don't need them, though things can be hard when I return. I just try to accomplish my tasks quickly and get out of there.'

'I hate it when pompous or lecherous people run things and expect everyone to do things their way,' said Neti with a knowing look. 'It's often the wisest and most able people who are overlooked. Or perhaps misunderstood. Plenty of people shout loudly about themselves. It's one of the things I like about you. You just get on with it. I know you're valuable, but you don't seem to care who knows and who doesn't.'

'It's the Lord who gives us value, after all. That's very freeing. That, and the knowledge that this life isn't all about achievement.

We've got eternity ahead of us, which changes how we live life, how generous we can be with our time, our energy – our everything, really.'

'Having Paul to stay – that was dangerous, wasn't it?'

'I wasn't troubled. They had done so much for me that I wanted to help.'

'I suppose you *could* always go back to Thyatira if you felt persecuted, couldn't you? Just for a short time.'

'I don't think I'd want to. Not for long, anyway. We live what the Lord gives us, one day at a time, Neti. If we lived in fear of what people might say or do to us, we'd never do anything. There's no need for me to go back much, on a practical level. I still keep a house there, but I have employees running the business side of things. It feels like I have a new life here. Or it's beginning to,' she said, giving Neti a solemn nod.

Neti smiled at her. 'I won't be hard work from now on,' she said. 'I promise.'

'Well, I do understand. Neti, what do you see in your nightmares? Can you trust me enough to tell me?'

'It was him – he was the worst of my masters. It all came back to me in stages. I couldn't believe those experiences could be real, but when I saw *him* I knew that they were. I have felt safe here, more or less,' she said.

'More or less? I'd expect you to feel completely safe. What still troubles you – they'll never get to you again – you know that, don't you?'

'Of course.'

'Well, what then? I need to know Neti, or I can't help you.'

'I never really felt that you wanted me. I know that you *say* you do, but I did hear when you were first told about me. I heard what you said.'

'How? What did I say? Where were you? Oh, I wasn't thinking straight.'

'I was just around the corner, waiting with Timothy. No one expected you to say what you did. But I'm over it now.'

'Neither of us are who we were back then. Come on, let's go to my room now. I'm going to do your hair and nails – if you're not too tired that is.'

Lydia had swung open the door, and there, caught with an expression of surprise like a guilty child, stood the old slave, Cletus.

'Have you lost your way, Cletus? Can I help you?'

His skin turned the shade of a ripe berry as he looked beyond Lydia and into the chamber.

'I was just checking on your property, Madam,' he said to her. Then, having caught Neti's eye he spoke to her: 'What, you still here?'

'Everything's sorted, Cletus,' said Lydia, stepping out from the room and beckoning Neti out. 'I trust you will keep this matter to yourself,' Lydia told him.

'Sorry, Mistress. I didn't realize you were both in there when I came up to keep an eye on everything. But she – well, goodness, well…'

'As mistress of this house, that is my prerogative. A bit like the good Lord himself knowing, in his wisdom, who to allow into his heavenly courts. All of us are found wanting, Cletus. All of us. I think you'll find you're not perfect, if you look hard enough.'

'How does he know?' whispered Neti as he shuffled down the stairs.

'Not much gets past him,' she replied. 'And he's only trying to do his job. He did come to find me on more than one occasion recently. I'll allow you to work those out.'

Lydia and Neti descended the wide staircase together, their feet in step with each other, though Neti didn't know what to say for a while, as she felt sure that glances were being cast their way, as heads bobbed into view and out again from the ground floor.

Then 'Lydia?' said Neti in a hushed voice.

'Yes, Neti.'

'I want to get baptized.'

Lydia stopped walking and it took Neti a moment to realize, pausing herself a couple of stairs below. 'Not because of Cletus? You have nothing to prove. And he'll get used to everything.'

'Well, not really,' said Neti, looking up at her. 'I want to get baptized and at last I don't care who sees me.' She looked all about her, wondering if her testimony was to be heard already. She couldn't see anyone now, but she'd raise her voice anyway, just in case. 'In fact, the more who witness it the better. I will tell everyone how the Lord found me – how I know what *he* is like because of what you've done for me. I'll tell them what a sinner I am, though I think they have a fair idea.'

Lydia took a couple of steps to join her, then took Neti's hand in her own. 'Don't focus on your sin but on the Lord's greatness, his worthiness.' Her gaze was intense, her eyes bigger than usual and apparently on the brink of tears once again. 'Let what you say be that way around. And I worry you're doing this almost to clear your name. You don't need to do that.'

'I want to.'

'It won't make you any more forgiven – by the Lord or by me.' She sat down on the stair and patted it so that Neti joined her. 'I think it'll only cause you more problems if you go into detail about recent events too. Make your peace with the Lord – that's all I ask. Your salvation testimony is enough for everyone.'

Neti clung to the necklace and was silent for a moment, realizing its power in a new way. 'Lydia,' she said, hesitating for her thoughts to assess whether to say what was on her mind. 'Would you mind if I sold this to buy Cletus's freedom? It must be worth a bit.'

'Do you dislike him that much?' Lydia replied, laughing.

'No, not at all.'

'Or perhaps you think the necklace ugly? That's always the way with antiques – people love or hate them.'

'No, I love it, I really do,' said Neti, holding tightly onto the pendant again. 'I just feel for him.'

'He wouldn't want to go. I tried to release him before and he fell on his knees and wept, begged me to keep him.' Lydia's fingers played distractedly with a long curly tress, oblivious to her charms in her usual way.

'So why's he so keen to impress you?'

'Oh, he just wants to please – it's that simple. I want my household all to know that I don't need their gratitude. Let everything we do here point each other to the Lord Jesus. In the light of his perfection, we all have a very long way to go. Neti, I'm far more like you in my failings than you realize. I think we both want to be more like Jesus. Shall we help each other? Keep short accounts and be honest about the things that tempt and challenge us?'

'Of course,' said Neti. 'And now I know that nothing I do or say will shock you, or him. That unbinds me like nothing else. It makes me *want* to do the right thing too.' She straightened her back and gave Lydia a long, hard look in her face, hoping she'd see the resemblance. 'That's a very freeing thing,' she said, and smiled.

Note to the reader:
Read **Acts 16** for the biblical basis for this tale on Philippi. As with my previous stories, this is a blend of Biblical events and imaginary ones. While many of the characters are found in the Bible, we don't know that Lydia took the slave girl into her home, or what she was called. However, we do know that she was no longer profitable for her masters and had become a dead weight; I can only assume they would not have had much use for her. In the chaos that ensued, she may have been forgotten by them, or cast aside, for the focus was now on Paul and Silas. Either way, I very much doubt she stayed with them.

The church itself was young and presumably still very small. Lydia was hosting the missionary party and would be the natural person to approach for the slave girl's care. What we can be certain about is that the church was outward looking, taking care of social needs at every opportunity, from the young to the very old. They were concerned with a person's wholeness, and I imagine the slave girl had a way to go before she felt restored on every level. The early church would not have walked away from her, but would have done everything within their power to ensure she was taken care of, giving her all the attention she needed. I cannot imagine this any other way.

Interestingly, many commentaries believe the slave girl found salvation. It has been mentioned more than once that there is a cluster of three salvation stories found in the Philippi chapter: Lydia's, the slave girl's and the jailer's. While we read of Lydia and the jailer's household being baptized, we know there would have been many obstacles in life for the girl to overcome, but that God never gives up on the work he starts, and neither do his people, if they are really seeking after his heart.

Themes emerging from the Philippi location: Our responsibility for those who receive help from us as believers, affirmation, and living out the mercy we ourselves have been shown.

EPHESUS
Acts 19

Chapter One

'Get back, you don't want them to see us following!' As the smallest boy in the group, allowed only to tag along to make up numbers, Phelix certainly has the loudest voice.

'Why ever not? Abba says they're a complete nuisance –' this lad raises his voice – 'and should *go back to where they come from.* You must have heard him last night.' He throws his awkward adolescent arms around as he speaks in an attempt to mimic his father and the other boys laugh, knowing full well how opinionated the man is, though with the best of intentions. 'They think there's *power* in the number seven,' he says with a flourish. '*Desperate, that's what it is.*'

'Seven, Miles? There's seven of us!' says the youngest boy again, his lisp catching on the number. He's proud of his counting skills and looks at the others for encouragement.

'Dur! There needs to be if we're going to mimic them,' his big brother replies. He does get carried away when his friends are with him, but if Phelix is going to join them, he has to know his place.

'Look at them strutting,' adds Miles' best friend who always takes the lead from him and would be lost without him. 'All proud and purposeful. They're going through the old Wildman's gate, as if to make a point.'

The last in the line of seven men looks back at them and scowls. He couldn't deliver a wet fish in time for supper, let alone the wildest man on the planet. That is obvious. They cannot hold back the laughter now and double up with the hilarity of it, a new outburst coming whenever they pause to look up and catch one another's eye.

'Stop, look, it's old Wildman,' says Miles, always the ringleader of the group of boys. 'He's home! I'd like to see them 'deliver' him.'

They crowd round the open gate, left ready for a quick exit, they presume. 'I don't think they're that brave,' says Zeb, holding onto the latch. This lad always is one to stand back and comment.

'Shush, we're not gonna have long to wait, I don't think.'

The group of boys watch as the possessed man dances in front of them, even more provocatively than if he'd lived out their most outlandish fantasies. The oldest of the seven men doesn't hesitate but takes the opportunity to unleash his own perceived power: 'I

195

command you in the name of Jesus, whom Paul preaches, to come out!'

The small, leaping man pauses in his agitation to reply. They can see his anger rising. 'I know Jesus, and I know Paul,' he says, in a high-pitched voice that doesn't sound humanly possible, 'but who are you?' They couldn't have chosen better words for him – he's so predictable, in an exciting, dangerous kind of way. The lads laugh again, but the oldest boy puts out a restraining hand on his young brother. 'Wait. This is going to be good.' Their father is going to love this tale; he might even give them a reward if they could share it with sobriety when the believers gather later.

The old geezer starts spinning now, moving with more energy than one man can surely contain – perhaps what they say about him is true: that a whole regiment of evil spirits really lives in him. Now he's launching himself at them! Old Wildman, crazier than he ever was, lashing out with the strength of a thousand men! They're falling to the floor like skittles and he's kicking them, jumping on their backs, their heads…One man starts to wrestle with him, like they're at the palaestra, but he gives in quickly enough. Even together they're no match for his strength. But Phelix is going to have nightmares and Miles will get the blame. And so 'Get back, really get back now,' says the oldest boy to the youngest. At once there's a sound of running water and steam coming from the ground around their feet. 'Phelix, have you peed yourself?'

'No,' he replies. 'No I haven't. No I didn't. Shut up and watch.'

Yet for once there's no need to try to impress them – the older boys all scarper, leaving Phelix struggling to keep up, not knowing which direction to run in, for he won't stand alone. It's no good, though, they are too fast for him and inconsiderate. And so, resigning himself, he waits in the middle of the road, statue like, hoping the men won't see him. They don't. Young Phelix is, after all, the last thing on their minds and he watches as seven men flee the scene, their clothes torn and falling from them, blood dripping from open wounds…

***

'Where did you get to?' Phelix asks his older brother when he walks into his own courtyard a while later. But at least the lad has made it home safely – that's been on Miles' conscience, though what was he to have done? *Scarper, look after your own backs* – those always were the rules. They can't change now his little brother is tagging along.

'More to the point, what happened to you?' he replies. 'I thought you were with us. Imma and Abba will kill me if they find out! The whole thing with the Wildman is the talk of the town. I've heard people shouting when I've been on the roof. Have the men gone?'

'They have,' little Phelix says with a puffed out chest now and a commanding glint in his eye. 'I saw them go,' he lisps, somehow emphasizing what he's seen without trying. 'They couldn't get away fast enough! They were naked and bleeding. You should have seen them! Can you get me a drink?' he asks, heading for the open doorway.

'Proper butt naked? Hardly, Phelix. You can't expect me to believe that. He was crazy but he couldn't do that.'

'They'd all lost their cloaks and they were running around in short tunics like lunatics. They were torn right up to the butt –'[56]

'That'll do, young Phelix,' says a voice coming through the gate behind them. 'I could hear you half-way down the street. I've been racing to catch up with you.' The boys both turn to look, and confirm what the pits of their stomachs have already told them. But there seems to be some mirth in their father's voice, and he ushers them towards him, putting an arm around each of them so that his beard tickles their tender skin. 'Now I'd like to know what really happened. What's all this gossip that's doing the rounds? Where did you go? What did you see?' He looks happier than they've ever seen him. 'They say it's about those wretched seven sons of Sceva!'

'I saw it all, Abba! I can tell you everything, it's w-'

'Upstairs, lads. I need to sit down for this,' he says with a chuckle. 'Phelix, you're going to need to slow down a bit and take a deep breath.' Their father takes the outer staircase to the roof top and beckons them to come. Phelix brushes past him on the stairs, taking two steps at a time.

'I'm just getting a drink, Abba,' says the other son.

---

[56] '**Naked and wounded.** —The first word does not necessarily imply more than that the outer garment, or cloak, was torn off from them, and that they were left with nothing but the short tunic. (See Notes on Matthew 5:40; John 21:7.)' Ellicott's commentary.

'Bring the pitcher for him, Miles. Phelix, gather some cups – back down the stairs with you. Come on lads, I'm looking forward to this. Where's your mother?' he calls after them.

'Delivering another baby, somewhere near the temple I think. She left the house early, just after you.'

'Is that why you were able to run riot?' he replies, a resigned, rhetorical question that for once is accompanied with laughter. Miles is feeling relieved and soon they are all together, sitting on the rush matting on the rooftop under the goat-hair awning, the boys still half-wondering if they'll be told off for what they've done. For their father won't like it when he realises *exactly* what they've been up to, despite his present good humour. It's down to whether Phelix will land them in it. It's tempting to talk over him, but Miles has to let the lad say something and then he'll take over properly. Damage limitations.

But Phelix has launched into the whole tale already, and is relaying how all seven of the sons of Sceva had invited themselves into old Wildman's courtyard. He is very articulate for one so small, never striving to find the right words. It's frustrating. Their father looks like he's struggling to keep up, but at last he finds the lad pausing for a deep breath before his next long instalment. 'It does beg the question as to how you witnessed all this,' says their father. 'I can only presume you were following them?'

'Kind of,' says Miles.

'They were easy to spot,' adds Phelix, elongating his words.

'I think they enjoy having an audience,' says Miles. 'They're performers and they love a following.'

'And there's the thing. They are dangerous, boys,' says their father, his usual voice of caution now kicking in. 'As dangerous as Wildman with their incantations. They are not drawing on the Lord's strength – who knows what they've prayed to.'

'I don't think so. They're just after some glory, and a bit of money to go with it,' Miles tells him. 'The evil spirit in Wildman said he knew Jesus and Paul, but "who are you"? They're complete non-entities.'

'Trust the voice of experience,' says their father. He furrows his brow, forming deep horizontal wrinkles that make him look older than their grandfather. 'I mean what I say, and I feel this deeply. They're still dangerous. I still want you to keep away from them.'

'They won't be coming back Abba!' says Phelix in his excitable, high-pitched way, making their father smile again for just a moment.

'They couldn't get away fast enough – I saw everything!' At once the lad is on his feet and demonstrating by springing around the rooftop like his clothes are on fire, and now gesturing with persuasive orator's hands. 'Wildman beat them all up, single-handed,' he says, throwing punches in the air, 'it was like he was some superhero, and he was proper wild! There was foam spilling from his mouth and everything, and the men were bleeding and limping and na-'

'Stop getting carried away, lad. You're exaggerating. Of course he couldn't attack and injure all of them. One man against seven? How does that even work?'

Just then a voice from across the rooftops interrupts his flow: 'Bart, a word please! Would you mind popping over, so we can talk in private.' This is a neighbour who is leaning over his parapet, four houses along: Uri, the rude man who ignores them unless he has an errand for them to run. 'I have some questions to ask you,' he says, looking at the boys, as if what he has to say cannot be overheard by them. The man's voice quavers as he continues to speak, and his serious tone suggests this will not wait. *Always one for gossip, a man of no depth,* Abba usually says, but they all can see there's something more to this, and so their father is quick to his feet. 'Of course,' he replies, I'll be right over.'

The boys look at each other and hold a mutual stare while he makes his way downstairs, then break into laughter as soon as they see the gate swing behind him.

'Well, that could have been worse!' says Miles, watching his father walk the path to this neighbour's house. 'You didn't need to tell him everything – you should have let me take over.'

'He's fine with it. Besides,' lisps Phelix, 'I'm now the talk of the town!'

'The talk of the town?' Miles turns to face him and decides he is almost twice the lad's height. 'You? Why exactly?'

'I told old Yosef, and he must of told his wife, who's told everyone!' The lad struts around the roof with an imaginary following, his acting ability learned from admiring his brother and friends as they characterize the neighbourhood. Sometimes Miles would like to kick him! It is easy to forget to give him the grace he deserves, for his precocious statements colour your perception of him, despite the chubby infant cheeks and podgy limbs. Boys his age are always irritating, from what he can gather.

'I think lots of them saw it with their own eyes,' says Miles, stretching his legs out on the matting. 'And besides, they're not talking about you – you just happened to witness it.'

'Wit-ness?' he says, his head on one side. He stops to pick up a drying stem of flax and squishes a seed-head to remove its contents, before tossing the husks onto the street below.

'You *saw* it, you numskull. Here, put them in here,' he says to the lad, holding out a wooden bowl.

'Being a *witness* makes me pretty important, don't you think?'

'Well, I saw most of it,' says Miles. He gets to his feet and grabs a stem for himself to strip – there's always so much for their mother to do and they don't help nearly enough.

'You didn't see what I did, though!' The lad throws a fistful of empty seed heads at his brother, who in turn attempts to stuff some down the little lad's neck. It gets out of hand for a while, before Miles recovers himself, for what is he teaching him? 'The important thing is that we hear God in this,' he says. He stands taller and looks down on the lad, staring him straight in the eye.

'Hear *God*? You and the lads like the bad stuff. I've heard you talking. I know about your tokens that you keep…'

'I don't know what you're on about.' Miles crushes the seed-head he's holding in his fist this time and lets it fall to the floor. 'Just shut up or I'll tell that you've been bragging.'

'And I'll tell, too. You'll be in for it, I know it. You can't tell me what to do or I'll tell on you.'

Miles pauses before his reply. Imma has always said that part of growing up is not always trying to get the last word. *You can never really win an argument*, she tells them, always swiping away a curl that's fallen in her face as she cooks and corrects them. *Sharp comments always cause you to lose something with that person.* 'If you must know, yes, I have tokens, and I'm going to get rid of them.'

'Ha, I knew it,' says Phelix, dropping the stem he's holding and rushing to stand in front of Miles so that he can look up at him with his imploring eyes. 'Can you show me!' Would his grace always be lost on him? The effort it takes, and all for what?

'No, I can't. And I'm not getting rid of them because you know,' for here is the thing. 'I'm not frightened of you – or Abba – but I am frightened by what happened today. Of the Lord and his power. We know he's real now, Phelix, and he's not to be messed with. You're either in or you're out. Those men – they were just dabbling and it's dangerous... You've seen what God does through Paul – it's awesome, and it's because he completely belongs to the Lord. Dark powers are dangerous, out to trap you, but the Lord – he's –'

'Where did you get them, though? How did you pay for them?'

'Are you listening to me, Phelix? Why the fascination?'

'My friends have talked about them. If you own one, and manage to keep it secret – well, you're the top boy. There's big respect.'

Miles sits beneath the awning again and pats the mat for his brother to come and sit next to him. 'Phelix, I've learnt my lesson, and I know you don't look up to me, but you must hear me in this. I don't want tokens anymore because they're dark, *evil*. I want Jesus's power that won't set out to hurt me. Power I can trust.' For once Phelix is quiet and seems to be listening to him, though he's humming a tune to himself. 'Abba has seemed pretty extreme in his ideas sometimes, but I think it's just that he really knows the Lord, and understands it's a spiritual battle that's raging for all of us. Abba has learned stuff the hard way and doesn't want us to have to go down that route. He's overlooked and often misunderstood – I feel it too sometimes, that being underrated. He'll always be a bit opinionated, he'll never quite fit in, but today I'm seeing we're lucky he's been the one praying for us, bringing us up. And Imma of course.'

There's no time to discuss further, for the gate clicks and the boys both scramble to their feet to look over the side. 'Well, I never thought I'd see the day,' says Bart, entering the courtyard below, in a voice loud enough for anyone nearby to hear. The boys turn and watch as he ascends the stairs, wondering what could have happened next on this strangest of days.

Now he is with them, and the suspense is just too much, especially for one. 'What? What happened?' asks Phelix, jumping up and down on the spot in that annoying way of his.

'Don't wet yourself,' says Miles and his father scowls at him before continuing. 'He's come to faith. Old Uri has found the Lord! And all because the seven sons of Sceva have fled, frightened.' He's glowing with a holy joy and cannot contain his excitement. 'It's as you boys said. Uri has recognized the power of Jesus' name. I left him talking to his neighbour, the next roof along. Pretty soon the gospel will be gossiped right the way along our road. We need to pray for them, boys. These are exceptional times.' He is looking across the rooftops now to this man's house, as if looking will enable the new reality to sink in.

201

'So will Uri be coming to our meetings?' asks Miles, mimicking the man, his nose in the air, then catching Phelix's eye.

'He will – I've invited him along this evening,' says Bart, still staring in his neighbour's direction. 'He will walk with us.'

'Walk with *you*,' mutters Miles, quietly enough for their father not to overhear, though he must have guessed the lad has grumbled something. 'I won't have you making fun of him,' he says turning to face him. 'You hear me?'

'No, Abba,' the boys say in unison, after many years of practice.

'Of course not, we wouldn't *dream* of it, would we?' says Miles. Phelix is laughing.

'Miles, you're setting a bad example. *Again*. You really should know better, my son. Now, I have a job to do. Tell your mother when she's back that I might not quite be home in time for supper. I have business to attend to.'

'Business?' the boys both say at once. 'But she'll ask,' Miles adds, blocking the way down the stairs until his father has replied. 'Where will we say you have gone?'

'You must say nothing. She'll only worry.'

'That's no answer for Imma. She'll interrogate us so you *must* say.'

'Alright then, but only if she presses you. I'm off to see Wildman, to deliver him. The Spirit of the Lord is at work in our community and Jesus expects it of me.'

'Really, Abba?'

'Someone has to. It's no good if we're all frightened of him. What does that say of our gospel? Now, out of my way.'

'But Abba, he's attacked these men so they could barely make it out alive, all *seven* of them. Why do you think you'll be any safer?'

'Because I really am doing this in Jesus's name. I have his power and I'm not pretending.'

'Don't we know it,' says Miles under his breath.

'What was that?'

'We really know it, Abba. We're just worried for you. Won't you at least take someone with you?'

'You're staying here. I won't put you in any danger. You can be praying for me if you like.'

And that's that. He never would be guided, especially by Miles, who fears this won't end well. They watch from the roof as he heads off down the street. Do they follow – at a safe distance of course – or leave him to it? Perhaps they'll watch him go, see which route he's taking at least. Miles starts to pray – he prays far more than his father believes, but then he's not out to impress his father, is he? He never was. It would be nice, sometimes, if his father could see him for who he really is.

Chapter Two

'Boys? Are you home? Can you get the gate for me?'

There's no answer and Halle puts down her baskets of shopping and childbirth tools on the dusty path – the birthing bricks are heavy, and the bottles of oil and fragrant distractions don't help. She's weary but joyful – another child and mother safely delivered, with the Lord's help of course. She gathers her belongings, shuts the gate behind her and breathes out a deep grateful sigh as she looks around her. She doesn't really need to work; Bart brings enough home, and their living quarters are ample... embarrassingly so, she sometimes thinks, but the Lord has chosen to bless them, and they do their best to serve the believers here. But often there are not enough hours in the day. She's called to deliver babies – she knows that. Yet it's not the job of her boys to clean and tidy and prepare food, and besides, they should be studying. Could they be with their tutor now, or has he given them another day off to 'learn by observation and report back'? That's a worry sometimes... the boys should be learning with other believing children, of course, but how much of an education are they really getting? The gymnasium always was an unsavoury place, so she doesn't mind that the believers are doing things differently. And at least they are learning to read music from her.

Now, she needs to wash the tunic that's in her bag for soon the blood will stain, and she must finish the grain so that there's enough flour for the morning. Perhaps she could get ahead with the bread mix while she prepares supper. And the olives! She'd meant to buy more of those, too. The boys are always so hungry and grow so fast; she needs to let them have their fill, but keeping the house supplied is a challenge... She might go out again once she's done a few chores. She'd like to practice on her lute for a song is stirring in her heart; she's had some rhyming lines forming in her mind, but that's for another day. Now the goats are bleating and boisterous – has anyone fed them?

She takes a handful of grain from the tallest pot in the alcove and ponders her lot while she feeds them. Sometimes she thinks it indulgent, this musical whim of hers – perhaps a waste of time – but others tell her how her words are meaningful to them, so she keeps

205

going. It makes her smile when they sing her songs as a congregation, and it draws her closer to him to compose them. She knows it pleases the Lord, but so does running a good household, giving time to the boys, to her husband, and of course delivering all these babies. She's been told her small hands are designed especially for this and it makes her smile too, for if only they knew the trials of her small frame... that the birth of both her own babies brought her close to death, which in turn did bring her close to the Lord, for what a thin line they tread daily, that separates heaven from earth. At least she knows the pain some women go through – if her own births had been easy, how little she would understand, how substandard the care she could give.

The goats are contented now and at once she's aware of her own needs... Oh, where's the pitcher... it must be on the roof, full of warm water! She makes her way up the stairs to retrieve it, only to discover it empty, and evidence of the boys having larked around, with flax seed heads littering the floor. They will at least have to clear that up themselves, once they are home. Now someone is calling from the gate – Halle looks across the courtyard and wonders who it is, but they are standing too close to the gate to be seen. It sounds like her near neighbour – she really hasn't time for this –

'I'm coming – I'm on the roof so bear with me.'

Halle opens the door to her precisely dressed neighbour, and instantly feels shabby and wants to apologize for the chaos. 'You can come in. I'm doing jobs in the courtyard – I'm really behind. I've delivered a baby for a woman living close to your temple today. It was a quick and uncomplicated birth, but it means I have more grain to grind and supper still to prepare.'

'I'll come back another time.'

'No, please come in now.' Oh, she didn't mean to sound unwelcoming. Sometimes she says too much; her husband, a man of few words, says if she only said what's necessary it would be much easier. That must be why he doesn't seem to hear most of what she says. 'As long as you don't mind me working while we talk.'

'Of course,' she replies, though her almond-shaped nails and head of plaited coils suggest to Halle that this woman always has time on her hands, and must have servants to do everything.

'I never set out to be a midwife,' Halle tells her. 'I seem to have gained a good reputation though. I think it's because I pray for the women from the moment I'm called out, asking my God for safe deliverance for both mother and her child. I know he's with me, even in the most difficult scenarios.'

Her neighbour nods, looking all serene and polite, if a little reserved. Can she even begin to understand? Halle looks down at her own hands and tunic – she is clean, having washed at the baths on the way home and changed into a new tunic, but she does feel rather unkempt beside her guest. She pushes away the hair that has fallen over her eyes and winces – she had rubbed the newborn with salt earlier, and though she has scrubbed herself, there must have been salt on her brow, which is now in her eyes.

'Please, sit down with me here, Gilda,' she says, inviting her onto the raised platform situated beneath a canopy. 'Do you mind if I prepare the grain? And I'm sorry, I haven't offered to wash your feet – I –'

Gilda laughs. 'I've only come from a few doors down. My feet are hardly dusty.'

That's true, of course.

'So, what is it?' says Halle, beginning to turn the millstone. 'It's lovely to see you, but I sense something's on your mind.'

'Halle, we'll be coming to your gathering this evening. Our husbands have arranged it.'

'Oh?' Halle looks up at her and stops what she's doing though she's barely begun.

'Uri has had a long chat with Bart. He wants us to be Christians now.'

'Well, you're looking very pleased about it!' She is – she's wearing a modest, contented smile, though she's a little embarrassed and looks away, seemingly afraid to catch Halle's eye. 'I've been wanting him to try your religion for a while – for him to let me try it.'

Halle wonders how much to say here and starts to turn the millstone again, but it's hard to think at the same time, for it requires much of her strength. 'That's interesting,' she says, before pausing again. 'You know, Gilda, I like to think of it as more than a 'religion'. Our God is real, and we don't pack him away if he doesn't respond to us as we would like. The important thing to remember is that he loves us. How many other gods do that?'

'I know,' she says, looking Halle in the eye now. 'Artemis has always been silent in my life. You'd think with a temple as impressive as that you'd be a god who is effective, powerful. I've never felt love in that place. And my prayers have never been answered.'

'I can promise you things will be different as a believer – God's love is real. Jesus –'

'Yes, I know about him,' she replies, adjusting her shawl across her shoulder. 'Uri has told me, and to be honest, it would be hard to live a few doors down from you and not know something of what you believe. All your comings and goings at strange hours, the needy folk who come knocking on your gate. And I know your God is powerful – I think that's what swung it for Uri, seeing the seven sons of Sceva flee like that. I think your God is able to help me; if he can't then no one can.'

'What do you want from him, Gilda?' says Halle, still unable to restart her task, though she's no interest in it now – this is far more important; she'll find *something* to feed everyone when the time comes, and they will understand.

'We want children,' she tells her, looking over Halle's shoulder and into space. 'They are meant to be a blessing from the gods, an affirmation, and an absence of them – well, the shame is too much, the stigma...' Her voice trails off for a moment as she tries to articulate her pain. 'I feel incomplete as a woman and I bear the responsibility of my husband feeling incomplete as a man. I am lucky he hasn't gone and taken another wife, though he has spoken of it.' The vulnerability is evident in her face and her dark eyes have filled up with tears. They'd always looked like the couple who have everything, but now Halle knows this isn't true. I mean, she'd always suspected, for who is married for years without children unless there's a problem?

'I know my God can bring you fulfilment,' Halle replies, 'but I can't promise he'll give you children.' If only this was easier, but it's no use giving her a false hope.

'Then what's the point?' says Gilda, shaking her head, then tilting it on one side. 'All my life all I've ever wanted is to run a home and have children.' Run a home – but she doesn't even have to do that, if we're honest – 'The most basic craving of a woman's heart – and the gods have deprived me of that.'

Don't some people think money can buy them everything? Perhaps the Lord can teach her something through this, but she must show her more compassion, for she does feel sorry for her –

'My God is good, Gilda. He's not against you. He's not one to add to the collection, either. With him, you don't need any other gods, and there's no comparison.'

'Your god! We'll let's see how real he really is – and how good. He'd act if he's real – but then, the sons of Sceva?' She's crying now, though there's a self-consciousness to it, a self-pitying that is hard to stomach. Is this the real Gilda coming out, or is Halle just weary from her day? 'Let's as-'

'Gilda, I really don't think that's the attitude with which you should approach him. What does he owe us? Why should we feel entitled to anything? Aren't we all sinners in need of his grace? I think when we are able to surrender everything to him, to love him and put him first, he is so often merciful in our lives, but we don't approach him with any sense of *him* having to do as *we* ask. We get to know him, to love him, and then sometimes he gives us our heart's desires. Yet that's not why we get to know him. His blessings are perhaps a by-product of our relationship with him; certainly not the reason for it. You know, when Jesus was on earth he said, "Keep on asking, and you will receive what you ask for. Keep on seeking, and you will find. Keep on knocking, and the door will be opened to you." He's not harsh. He doesn't want to withhold good things from us, but we do need to approach him in the right spirit.'

Gilda nods now and seems to understand, or is she just embarrassed that she's said so much, and keen to get away? 'Thank you. I know you are right. I'm sorry if I seem presumptuous and I will do my best to get to know him. You have given me much to think on.'

'We shall see you later. We'll call from the rooftop when we're leaving. You will be very welcome in our community – remember that I am always here for you, too.'

And with that Gilda leaves Halle to her labours, and Halle praises her Lord for unexpected mercies. She mustn't be so suspicious of people – and who is she to judge? God clearly is at work in Gilda and her husband. She should have been praying for her neighbours more, but thankfully the Lord's working is not at all dependent on how much or little she prays. It might be challenging, disciplining Gilda, but they've always felt their neighbours are God-given and not living near them by chance. How hard it must be for Gilda, knowing Halle's work is so bound up in the thing that she longs for, but he is big enough to carry this, and trust him they must.

There are voices outside the gate – 'I've just seen your mother boys – it's a good thing you're home. It might not be customary, but do give her a hand. She's worn out.' How embarrassing! Yet she's clearly regained her composure. 'I've a mind to send one of my staff round to help her.'

With that the boys stumble into the courtyard, one having pushed the other, it seems, faces flushed, hair damp and sticking to their foreheads. They look guilty and Halle has to ask – in fact a raised eyebrow is enough –

'*Boys*, you weren't meant to hear that conversation,' she says, pausing in her task once again. 'Why didn't you cough or something or push on the gate, so we knew you were there?'

'How could we walk in on that?' says Miles.

'She was crying so loudly we were worried, Imma,' joins Phelix. 'We thought it was you who was upset.' They are good boys, and she mustn't be cross with them. How much did they hear? She is in danger of divulging more than she should by assuming...

'He's getting another wife! He's fed up with her – you said something about that – or she did,' says Miles.

'She thinks our God is rubbish,' says Phelix. 'I heard you having to defend him.'

'No boys. Please come and sit down with me and stop leaping about the place. The truth is they've never been able to have children. She seems to think that becoming a believer will solve all that.'

'Well, God can do it, can't he?' says Phelix, pouring grain through the small hole in the top millstone for her and spilling most over the edge.

Halle simply smiles at him, for this conversation is too important to stop. 'Of course. But we don't barter with God – he's real, and just as we don't seek to control each other, allowing people to make their own judgements, or bring their own blessings, so it is with the Lord. Only more so. For he knows what's best for us, even if it doesn't make sense at the time. God owes us nothing and we owe him everything, for his kindness and mercy to us–'

'Yes Imma but back to the point,' says Miles, stretching out his long legs on the matting, as if they need the space to grow. 'I thought Uri didn't like children, the way he reacts to us.'

'It's not that he doesn't like you. It's just complicated. You represent something he's been denied – that's how he sees it. And we've had that blessing not just once but twice. Boys, too. He has no son to continue his line, his business, his reputation – see it from his perspective.'

'His reputation!' says Phelix, looking up for a moment from the grain that he's placing back into the hole, one piece at a time. 'Of being a grumpy old man!'

'A bit harsh, Phelix! But that is perhaps why he always seems a bit hostile to you. They want children of their own and it's preoccupied them for a very long time.'

'You don't see what he's like,' says Miles, coming to his brother's defence. 'Grown-ups always behave differently in front of the parents. To be fair, Imma, you've never witnessed him at his worst.'

'That's as maybe. But when you see her later you must act as if we haven't had this conversation. She'd be mortified.'

'Yes, Imma,' they say in unison.

They are both on their feet now, as if keen to get away from her. Is her company really that tiresome?

'So, where's your father? I thought he was finishing early to-'

'Nowhere,' they say in unison again, as if this has been rehearsed.

'I know when you're not to be trusted – just look at the pair of you!'

'He's... shopping,' says Phelix.

'For one of the old believers, he said,' Miles continues. 'Yes, that's it.'

'Boys!'

But they've run off – 'We're thirsty,' they say, 'and Abba has given us an errand.'

Sometimes these things are not worth pursuing; she'll find out from her husband what he's been up to soon enough.

Yet the afternoon wears on and still there's no sign of Bart. He'd finished a big carpentry job recently – ornate carving for a doorway, lattice windows, all the exquisite extras you might dream of, and it had paid well, and so this afternoon was meant to afford them a little catch up time. The boys seemed to be concealing something, and before long she'd hoped the whole family would be sitting down for the evening meal, and then of course the meeting. What to do? He could have gone to visit someone, but this uneasy feeling won't go away –

The boys are back again, having dashed up to the roof the moment they were home. Halle has swept the courtyard, prepared the stew and generally put the place back into good order, and now there's nothing to preoccupy her but her fears. 'Miles, can you come and join me down here please. I need to speak with you!'

'Coming, Imma!'

Her son joins her in the courtyard and squats down on his haunches beside the bread oven, like he's not stopping long. 'Yes, Imma. Can I help?'

'Please can you tell me where your father has gone?' she says, sitting down next to him and expecting an honest explanation. 'I feel sure you know something.'

'I'll go out and look for him,' he says, ruffling his hair in that distracted way of his. 'I'll run to Paul's workshop and see if he's gone there – he can't have gone far Imma – don't worry, I'll have him back by nightfall.'

'I should hope so!'

Chapter Three

That was a crisis averted, but now there is no choice for Miles but to face his fears. At least he's been able to get away without Phelix noticing... to have him tag along for this errand really would be dangerous. Miles had wanted to avoid going anywhere near the Wildman's house after today, but they've waited long enough, and as the man-of-the-house with his father absent, he has to do the responsible thing. If he's honest with himself, he's actually feeling frightened right now. Very frightened. No wonder Phelix peed himself; you could hardly blame him. Wildman is proper crazy, and their father is proper clueless... There should be a medical term for it – everything is so black and white with him. He has such a trust in Jesus' name – and rightly so – but we are meant to keep our rational minds. The polite word for him is authentic – a word Phelix couldn't understand when he explained their father's behaviour to him earlier, but that is the thing – there is logic in his thinking. It just doesn't allow for the mess of the real world.

Miles will find Paul now – he'll know exactly what to do. Perhaps he'll even come with him to the Wildman's house. Surely Abba isn't still there, though? He's been gone hours and it is concerning. Miles jogs to the agora[57] – it's quite a stretch from home and he's already worn out from his day. If only the way wasn't so crowded! He passes the turning for Jorge and Daria's amazing hillside house where they'll be meeting later, and runs on past the stinky public toilets and then the brothel – those women hanging around outside give even a young lad like him the eye and this time Miles watches his feet as he runs. Soon he reaches the marble pavement – someone has drawn a picture on it – a woman, a left foot and a heart, directions for the sailors, as if they need them – and Miles feels the statues are looking down on it disapprovingly.[58] He slows down now as he begins to gather his thoughts – Paul always has exactly the right words and Miles has always admired his short and precise sentences, a style of speaking

---

[57] https://magical-steps.com/ephesus-map/commercial-agora_th/
[58] Detail on the Marble Street of Ephesus found at http://www.ephesus.ws/the-marble-street-of-ephesus.html

213

he could aim for himself. He's taken the long way, but he prefers the agora gate that's outside the theatre, for there are always less dodgy characters hanging around. Once inside, Miles straightens his tunic and looks all about him to make sure no watchful eyes are on him, then plunges his hands into the fountain here and splashes his face with water. A wizened old man sitting in a doorway gives him a long look – he's a self-appointed guardian of the place – but everyone else seems occupied, going about their shopping and admiring the architecture. There must be a hundred shops here, but it doesn't feel oppressive – there is space all around and the open sky above. The breeze coming in from the harbour helps too; the place feels clean somehow and more alive. Miles loves that Paul has his premises in such a busy place; it means he has an excuse to visit his favourite part of town, with its marble slabbed pavements and mosaics at regular intervals. It's a shady place, with the tall columns and high galleries, but more than anything it's the fact that Paul is so accessible here. You step in from the bustle, a perfect little haven, and there's always a welcome. But today Miles knows he cannot stop for long –

'Shalom!' says Paul as Miles nods his greeting and pushes his hair from his face. 'Have you come to give me a hand? I've a big project going here, and I could use some young, nimble fingers!' Paul is laying out some lengths of rope that he'll need to cut and then sew onto the goat-hair section that he has stretched out on the floor.

'Not today. I'd love to but there's a problem at home.'

'Oh?' Paul looks up from what he's doing and wipes the heel of his hand across his brow.

'It's why I'm here. We can't find Abba and I'm not sure where to search for him.'

'I did see your father earlier,' says Paul. 'He was looking the worse for wear.'

'He'd been to see the Wildman,' says Miles, stepping up closer to the bench. 'He planned to deliver him! Only he hasn't come home – no one has seen him, and I can't tell Imma where he's been.'

'So then, he might have taken himself somewhere to get patched up. It looked like his arm was broken – I offered to make a sling and immobilize it myself but he winced at the thought. I expect the pain has got the better of him.'

'Sounds like he got off lightly,' says Miles. 'What did he say to you?'

'He did tell me what he'd tried to do.' Paul smiles, like he's impressed. He always likes any boldness for the sake of the Lord, though Imma says she's intimidated by him. She says she's not about bold gestures but quiet service of the Lord Jesus, though Miles feels sure Paul appreciates this too.

'And did it work?' questions Miles, knowing the answer already, but feeling compelled to ask.

'Unfortunately not. I had to explain to him that not everyone wants to be set free. We have to respect that. I told him to keep praying for the old man. I explained that it'll happen in the Lord's timing.'

'Has it ever happened to you?' says Miles after a pause, running his fingers over the taut fabric on a loom. 'I mean, have people not been delivered sometimes?'

'Of course! People always think that everyone is delivered by me, but they are not. If the person doesn't want the Lord's touch, nothing can change that. Their family and friends might be willing them to be set free. That is not enough. Deliverance can only take place when the individual *wants* to be released. The Lord is always respectful, you know.'

Miles nods and gives Paul his full attention now, willing him to go on.

'Physical healing is different – we can pray for unbelievers, and their healing may in part lead them to faith. Sometimes believers live with physical ailments – take my awful sight, for instance – and therein lies the paradox. Yet we know the Lord loves us, and it will all make sense one day.'

'Will you help me find my father now? I'm too worried to go to the Wildman's house.'

'I'll pray for you. I'll pray again for this wild man, too. But I need to get this tent finished, Miles – I don't like to keep customers waiting or I lose them. I'll see you later on – I won't make it to the start of the meeting tonight, but I'll be there.'

Well, that was helpful – kind of – and it's always an encouragement to see Paul. He's said to drop in on him any time, so he does. They just talk about stuff and it's easier than with his parents. He hasn't said it to all the boys – he seems to have recognized more faith in him than his own father has. Now, where to look for him? Perhaps he should just go home. At least he has something to tell Imma now, that doesn't sound *so* awful. He will rehearse it in his mind. *He's probably alright, Imma. Paul has seen him since. He thinks he might have sought medical help* – no, that sounds terrible – *he's on his way home…* well, he is, isn't he, strictly speaking? Perhaps he'll be home already. Yes, that's it. *"You've asked Paul – why should I feel reassured by anything he says?"* He knows what she'll say, but what else has he to offer?

Miles runs back along the marble street, dodges the sailors loitering outside the brothel, takes a deep breath and runs faster past the public toilets and at last slows as the turning for his little obscure street comes into view. 'You're back! We've been so worried about you,' says his mother slightly prematurely as he flings open the gate, but Miles quickly realizes that she's talking to his father who must have been moments ahead of him, though coming from a different direction. Miles needn't have gone out searching after all, though he's glad that he did, and a break from Phelix is always welcome. Nobody seems to have registered his own arrival though – 'Bart, we don't have long before we're out and the neighbours ar-'

'No need to be worried about me – ever!' he says, responding to her first comment. 'The Lord was with me. I might not have been successful in delivering him, but I'm fine. I've lived to tell the tale, you might say.'

He sounds a bit drunk, but that can't be the case.

'Let me get you something to eat, to drink,' says Imma. 'Nereus saw where you went –'

'There's no need. Please just let me sit down. There's nothing wrong with me,' he says, holding his slinged arm close to his chest.

Phelix is leaping around at his father's feet and Imma puts out a steadying and calming hand.

'We're very proud of you, brother,' says Nereus, an old family friend who always stops with his family on the way to the gathering, so they can all walk together. 'And no matter that today wasn't the day for the old wild man to come to faith. The Lord has seen off the seven sons of Sceva, for which we are very grateful.' The man slowly shakes his head and closes his eyes a moment, his astonishment at the situation all too evident.

'This is the power of God at work,' says Bart. 'At last we're seeing him flex his might. We've put up with the enemy's ways here long enough.'

'Well, in some ways I'm not surprised,' says Sepphora, a new believer who is tagging along with Tryphena, Nereus's wife. 'When

I saw them this morning, I did pray that the Lord would deal with them. That he might improve our community. A bit of a bold prayer I know, but we're all fed up of the disruption they bring. It was only an 'in-passing' prayer. The speed of the Lord's answer did shock me though!'

Even Miles has been praying for years and never seen the likes of this. These new believers, thinking everything is immediate, that they mention something to the Lord once and it's dealt with! Being young though, no one thinks there's any depth to him – except Paul, of course. The Lord is yet to teach them persistence in prayer, endurance living. Oh, it will come... and will they stick around then? Speaking in tongues already, hearing from God... it's not normal, not natural...

'It won't always be like this,' he says at last, feeling part of the adult believing community and actually quite liking it.

'People are still people,' continues his father, picking up his thread as if it were his own, seamlessly. 'They'll be tempted back again. They'll follow their own hearts and evil desires. It never was this simple, nor will it be.'

'We saw them running,' says Tryphena, 'my husband and I. "What's rattled their cage?" he said to me.'

'Good riddance,' I told him. 'I don't care what it was. They've been giving the real church a bad name for long enough.'

'"Don't they know that's not the right way out of town?" we said to each other,' adds Nereus, continuing the tale. 'Keep running that way, they'll end up in the sea!'

'"That's what I'm hoping," he said to me,' finishes Tryphena, and her husband gives her a long look.

'Honour the Lord at all times, remember?' says Bart, and his boys smile at each other. 'Oh, I can hardly stand,' he says now, his legs buckling beneath him.

'What is it, father? Sit down over here, let me help you,' says Miles, taking his good arm without the sling.

'That man injured you more than you think,' says Halle, coming to his aid and resting a hand on his back, but he shirks it off, objecting to her *fussing,* as he usually calls it.

'It's the glory,' says Bart and his legs begin to give way again, and this time Miles experiences it too, the weight of the Lord's presence touching him deep inside.

'Praise the Lord,' says Bart. 'Well, blow me down.'

'We'll go on ahead,' Nereus tells them; Abba says he always has been overly cautious about the Holy Spirit, but this is a moment when you don't want spectators, to be fair.

'We won't be far behind,' says Halle. 'We're bringing our neighbours anyway. We'll see you there.'

Their friends make their way out of the courtyard, and feeling somewhat relieved, Miles takes himself into the house. His spirit feels an incredible heaviness – in a good way and he knows he needs to settle somewhere. He heads to the back room, leaving his parents in the courtyard and Phelix who knows where, and crouches down as a weighty sense of God's glory overcomes him. He could stay here like this forever – knowing the presence of Jesus, sensing his blessing and affirmation, and he feels sure he belongs to God now as much as his parents do. 'What do you want from me, Lord?' he asks quietly. 'What can I do for you?' He starts to feel embarrassed that his behaviour is so juvenile when he's out with his friends, that he can be so hard on his little brother when –

'Bart, we're ready when you are!' carries across the rooftops and into the house below.

He hears his mother's feet scuffing up the stairs above him. 'We're almost ready!' she calls, sounding flustered. 'Do come round.'

'I thought we'd have left a while ago,' comes the reply.

'Sorry – we got a bit… caught up,' Abba shouts to them.

Miles rubs his face and heads through to the courtyard where his parents look all composed and ready to go. 'You've been gone a long time,' Imma tells him.

'Have I? I thought your friends had only just left.'

'Your father was praying a while and then we had to eat without you. We wondered what you were doing in there.'

'It was the Lord, wasn't it?' Abba asks him. 'He touched you too.'

Miles nods and his father gives him a knowing, perhaps prideful look, but before the conversation can go on there's a rap on the gate and Imma opens it to Uri and Gilda. The man actually smiles at Miles, who is feeling surprisingly alright about this – an hour ago he wouldn't have, but having the Lord close at hand is clearly the way to go.

'Where's Phelix?' asks Imma.

'Here I am,' he shouts, leaping on Miles' back.

'Where did you spring from?' he asks him, ruffling his hair. Now this *is* trying, but one step at a time, he tells himself. He should pray for him more – he knows that. And perhaps take a bit more interest in him, show more kindness? One step at a time, as he said.

'Are we ready?' asks Imma.

Bart leads the way with Uri beside him and the women follow on, with Phelix weaving in and out of them, and Miles bringing up the rear. Everyone is quiet for a few paces which is welcome, but it feels as if someone should say *something*. At last, 'We've missed out on fellowship time,' says Bart with a light shrug of his shoulders but great joy in his eyes. He's turned around so the women catch what he says, and it does raise a question, which is so often his way. Miles can see his mother waiting for him to go on, but clearly his father is expecting her to explain – either that or he hasn't noticed that they are more than just a little intrigued. 'Something special has happened here which delayed us,' she continues, and now Gilda stops walking to look at her, and Uri joins his wife at her side '– the Lord's presence has been here in a profound way, and when he wants to do business with us – well, we drop everything. For what's more important than that?'

They all start to walk again, the men together and the women, with Miles' parents each explaining to their guest what it is to have access to the Lord at all times, to know him as a friend, and to sometimes be taken by surprise by him, as we can be by anyone who is in our close circle. How should Miles explain it to his own friends? He knows they don't share his love of God or even understand it, so it's been much easier to have it as an 'unspoken issue', but this in turn has meant his behaviour has been less than desirable. He's ashamed of it now. He ruffles his hair and drops back a bit from the group. Most of his friends don't come from Christian homes – Imma says that's a good thing, for he may yet win them for the Lord, but Abba always tells him to be careful, and says it's like building a structure with sections of rotting wood – that it won't hold, that it can't… Can he now start to prove him wrong?

Miles can see the houses on the slopes from here but it's not the quiet, secluded place it usually is – it's thronging with people. Perhaps a boat has come in and everyone's lost. Will Paul be at the meeting by now? He said he expected to be late too, which makes him feel a bit better that they'll probably be walking in when things have started. Tonight Miles is actually looking forward to the gathering. His heart feels full and he's excited and proud to be serving his Lord. He feels new. It's hard to explain, but when you encounter the Lord like that and you know him close it does something in your spirit – like it's turning cartwheels, or... those somersaults that Zeb does in the air, running up the side of a wall, leaping, turning and landing on his feet. Yes, it's exactly like that. Now he needs to stay close to the Lord, be disciplined and not led astray.

They reach the heroon monument that honours Androclus[59], the founder of Ephesus, which Imma and Abba always comment on, saying, 'Why should a mere man be so honoured; the people of Ephesus have got it all wrong,' but today they are silent on the matter. It *is* unnecessarily high – thirteen metres, they say, and while it's beautiful, Miles thinks that the more there is to preserve and protect around the place, the more highly strung the neighbourhood can become; not that it's his neighbourhood, but the boys like to explore here, as everywhere. 'Get off my wall,' 'Are you meant to be here?', 'Take your noise and nonsense away with you.'

They enter the terrace now and navigate the narrow alleyways, catching glimpses of their destination, all the while rubbing shoulders with people trying to go the other way, as if they've established something and are on their way home. 'We'll come back later, when the children are asleep,' says one man to his wife. He is carrying a small child on his shoulders, who has to duck beneath the elaborate coving at intervals, and the ornamental trees.

'They are all outside Daria and Jorge's house,' says Imma as they get closer.

'How astonishing,' says Abba.

Uri and Gilda look confused and so Imma explains – 'This house belongs to Jorge and Daria and it's the largest home in our believing community. It has twelve downstairs rooms and one of them is very large! We usually spill out of the hall into the courtyard, but I've never seen anything like this.'

'Your God really does bless his people,' says Gilda. 'I'm beginning to see that.'

---

[59] Useful information is found in 'What Can the Archaeology and History of Ephesus Tell Us About Paul's Ministry There' by Deirdre B. Hough. See fig. 61 in her text. Accessible online here: https://core.ac.uk/download/pdf/234108535.pdf

'He certainly does provide for us, though we don't expect luxury,' Imma explains. There's little point really as their guests' home is luxurious for sure, but once you get his mother going on the Lord's provision she's hard to stop. 'Take our own house. We wouldn't have expected to live there, as Bart wasn't earning much from his business in the early days. But when I was praying and we were needing more than our one cramped room, with Phelix on the way, I felt the Lord say the house he had for us would have flowers over an internal doorway.'

Gilda smiles, looking a little embarrassed at her confession of their earlier lack of means.

'Well, how often do you see that?' his mother asks.

Gilda shakes her head and gives a little nod, her pursed lips almost smiling again.

'We looked at one or two places that for some reason weren't right for us, but then we were taken to see one a short walk away from where we used to live. Miles was happy, of course, as it was close to his best friend's house, but I knew it was the one the moment we walked through the courtyard and into the house. I looked up and there was a small pot of dried flowers on a ridge above the inner doorway. The word 'Imma' was written on it. Then I really knew.'

Imma loves sharing this tale and Gilda does look genuinely pleased now. She needs to know that Jesus is for us – from what they'd overheard, she's felt no god could be on her side – but now she's hearing that the one true God wants to be involved in the lives of his people. Miles is very proud of Imma – the way she just naturally shares what the Lord does for them.

As they walk up the slope towards 'the gathering place', as the believers call it, it's obvious that tonight's meeting cannot go ahead as planned. 'Ahem,' coughs Bart in a very unnatural fashion to a crowd of people all turned in on themselves and talking. Miles doesn't recognize a single one of them, but they have parted for his father. 'Excuse me,' says Bart to a couple of young men now blocking the path, 'I just need to get inside to talk to Jorge. I am one of the elders here.'

The men make a way through for him and Miles looks on aghast as his father makes excuses to everyone in his way before getting through the gate and inside. Phelix is following and was just too quick for Miles and Imma to be able to prevent him. They are more similar than Phelix can realize, and Miles smiles to himself. 'He won't be long,' says Imma to Uri and Gilda. 'There's no stopping him, anyway. Perhaps he'll be able to tell us what's going on.'

Miles would quite like to have followed but it would have been inappropriate, and he's trying to be more adult now. Miles loves this place – it's his second favourite haunt, and the sort of house you could get lost in, given the opportunity. They have no windows, but light floods through from the hall, and actually, the semi-darkness adds to the sense of mystery when exploring it. And explore it they can, for Jorge and Daria seem to encourage it! The houses here have heating and hot water … If you could imagine every conceivable comfort, entertain every outlandish whim, these houses on the slopes have it. They are the most desirable properties in Ephesus[60] and Miles feels glad to be associated with them, though it's the fellowship that really makes this space special – the Lord is here with them when they meet, which really is the important thing. They could meet in a falling down shack and it wouldn't matter – not if the Lord was with them.

His father is back now and about to be embarrassing, by the looks of it. He is looking all around him, waiting for them all to notice him, but, unfortunately, he doesn't have the most commanding presence. Imma says she values his depth and intuition and that most of his gifts would be wasted if he was in leadership, but at times he does speak in public, and here they are again. Something about his intensity and demeanour though causes people to stop talking, and soon he has everyone's attention, as nudges and shushes are given. When the quiet ones speak everyone knows it's going to be worth listening to, though, to be fair, not everyone here knows him!

'Those of you who wish to join me, I have some old religious items to burn, outside the city walls,' he says. 'They have nothing to do with the Lord Jesus and are an insult to his name. His is the real power, the real glory. No other god comes close, and I wish to honour him.'

---

[60] This property is based on a real home among the houses on the slopes: 'One of the largest villas of the Western Complex was a two-storey peristyle house, built in the 1st century AD, and altered in the 2nd century AD. There were 12 rooms on its ground floor, and the total habitable space was 900 square meters. Among the preserved rooms, there is a vestibule, a hall, a kitchen, and a bathroom with a bathtub. In the area of this villa, you can see ornamental floor mosaics and beautiful wall frescoes, depicting Herakles, Ariadne, Eros, a peacock, and floral motives.' These remains can still be explored. See https://turkisharchaeonews.net/object/terrace-houses-ephesus

Abba – with ungodly materials! He'll never live this down. He can't really mean – he doesn't – can he? Miles looks at his mother – she is a little embarrassed – her face is shiny with sweat, yet she pulls her shawl into an elaborate hood over her head.

'Can we go? That will be much more fun to watch,' says Phelix. He's standing in front of their mother and is jumping again, springing high with no lead up, like he's their kid goat. 'Abba's done something naughty for once!'

'You stay here with me,' she tells him, grabbing a handful of his tunic and holding it tight so that he can't go roaming off again.

Miles watches his father take his leave and the crowd make a path for him once more. Some people are already following him, including respectable members of their Christian community. There go the old twin ladies, Margreta and Monika, taking careful yet hasty steps, if that's possible – they look worried they won't be able to keep up, yet they know they are at risk of falling over, so they teeter, bird-like. There's Hestia, the young leader with an excellent singing voice who the young girls all look up to – she's keeping her head down, like she's embarrassed – and a whole family who run a shop in town selling Ephesus nick-nacks – Imma and Abba have often said some of their stuff is dodgy. 'Questionable' is the word they use, and the shop *is* close to the temple, with all of its weird demands and practices. Now the new people are mixing in with the old and Miles watches the movement of this crowd as they walk down the hill, like a river in full flow… All those people from church, though! But better this way – perhaps it shows they have integrity after all. Uri looks like he doesn't know what to do and turns as if to follow, but it's already too late to catch up with his host. 'We'll stay,' says Imma to him. 'I want you to meet Paul, and it looks like lots of people are going with Bart anyway. We'll catch up with him later.'

Miles is glad that his father suggested this but really – what can he possibly have to burn? Is he an old hypocrite? Though what about himself? His job now is to help Uri feel comfortable here. No doubt there will be some interesting discussions to follow later.

At last, there's no one lingering in front of the house at all and Imma leads them inside. Gilda looks impressed by the standard of living here and gives one of her approving nods – like someone's mere worldly possessions should make them more worthy of being known! Daria does have these long, soft woven drapes in the most fantastic of colours, and there are embroidered pictures on the walls, and mosaics on every floor. Gilda has stopped to admire a peacock design before she treads on it with her now bare feet. A servant has even come up to her and offered to wash them – we don't normally get this treatment, but then, we're considered 'family' and there's so many of us. How will church change after today? Will things ever be the same again? But that's a selfish thought! "In my father's house there are many rooms" said Jesus, and our capacity to welcome and love others should be the same on earth.

Daria and Jorge come up and greet Uri and Gilda – they have perhaps heard of each other, or even met before, who knows, but there is a special warmth today and a respect, for they are the Lord's guests and he has drawn them. Have they welcomed everyone like this, though, even the poorer people? Why should Miles doubt them? And to be fair, most of them looked afraid to enter the house and seemed to be waiting outside. They have gone with the crowd, Miles thinks, and now they are led into the hall, which is fuller than he expected, even with the rush of people down the hill.

Jorge welcomes everyone from the front, and on a low table has had prepared the Lord's supper, with a round bread to break and a large wooden goblet of wine. That would have been like the feeding of the five thousand, should everyone have stayed. How will their communal meals work now? Will they have to meet in a few different houses, just to contain everyone? As it is they'd outgrown Priscilla and Aquila's (though their house always stank of leather goods, so no loss there). Who else has a large enough house to take a good number of those who'd come today? Uri and Gilda of course – she'd love that! Perhaps they will use their own?

Uri has been given a space on the floor next to where Jorge was sitting, and Phelix is occupied with twisting Imma's belt. Miles thinks it could be time to make his exit – his mother hasn't looked around for him since they arrived – she knows he's usually with Olaf, Jorge and Daria's grown-up son – so he could leave now and they'd be none the wiser, though his little brother would be sure to notice. Would it be wise to take his own tokens to the bonfire, or should he dispose of them secretly? Wouldn't his father go crazy – or 'ballistic' if he saw? Is that even a word? Well, it is now! For he can be like a ballista, throwing 'rocks' into the air, and everyone has to duck! But then he's in no position to judge him... not this time.

Miles unearths his sandals and steps into the yard with small and steady steps so that no one glances back. Those loitering outside have now gone and he can make his way home unhindered. A fresh breeze catches him and propels him down the hill, so that he is fast catching up with the last few stragglers at the end of the 'procession' as bystanders are calling it. 'They're the Christians,' says one old woman.

'What are they up to now?' asks her friend.

'Off to find some more flesh to feast on,' says the first with a cackle, then a slightly nervous laugh.

'There's too many of them – just look!'

'They have some funny ideas, you know.'

'Go on –'

Miles gives them a hard stare, then rebukes himself and prays 'Lord, would you reach them, and would you stop us being so misunderstood,' before turning onto the street and sprinting home. He knows where they'll build the bonfire, it's obvious. With his father leading, too, if he's wrong the first time he'll have a pretty good idea. Will there be worship there, once everything has been burnt?

Miles makes it home in half the time it usually takes, but then they do amble as a family, chatting with their friends. It really is getting dark now and lamps glow from windows and even from some of the more fancy gateposts in the neighbourhood. Once through his own gate and into the house he fumbles around without a light, but then he knows every familiar turn without looking. He ignores the goats who are reminding him of their presence and heads through to the sleeping chamber, where he takes out the loose stone from the wall that he usually faces when he rests.[61] He's fiddled with it for years, when he's been sent to bed early for some misdemeanour or other. He's taken it right out before and had a good view of the street below, but it was hard to get it back in again properly, without a new chink of light shining through, so now he only pulls it halfway, which is

---

[61] I am imagining my way into first century house construction. We know construction was often less than perfect. In *Manners and Customs of Bible Lands* we learn 'Because the walls of the stone houses were built so that the joints between the stones were wide and irregular, therefore a snake might readily crawl into the crevices and unexpectedly come in contact with an inhabitant'. See also https://www.biblehistory.com/links.php?cat=39&sub=476&cat_name=Manners+%26+Customs&subcat_name=Roofs

enough for him to slip two fingers in and pull out the small silk bag.[62] He lets it dangle at arm's length, as if its physical presence could taint him. He's not wanted its contents for a long while now, but he surveys it and wonders if it's worth going to all the bother of burning it. But it *is*, and so what if there's some explaining to do afterwards? He's doing this for Jesus. Today is going to mark a new start in being responsible, being trustworthy for the Lord. He hesitates no longer and takes giant strides across the room, through the house and courtyard and out onto the street, the door swinging behind him in his wake, and the oldest goat bleating in fright. Miles holds the small bag firmly in his grip now, squeezing it in the palm of his hand. Are its contents the reason why he'd been so disengaged spiritually for such a long time? His moments of enthusiasm for God would come in bursts. He remembers the times they'd enjoyed the contents of this pathetic, superstitious keepsake. The lads had tried out the voices they imagined the dodgy Ephesians using, expelling illness, infertility and shame, but even then Miles had often felt uncomfortable. Now he is going to do away with it once and for all.

He is heading for an area of wasteland just outside the city. This land isn't farmed – people come here to burn their rubbish, to discard all sorts of things. The thought of the place makes Miles feel a bit sick, and he belches and swallows a bitter mouthful. They say that child sacrifice has happened here, though he's heard it happens inside Artemis's temple too. Sacrifice of unwanted babies, left out in the elements to die. Even *wanted* children... sometimes they go missing

---

[62] 'The so-called "Ephesian spells" (*grammata Ephesia*) were small slips of parchment in silk bags, on which were written strange cabalistical words, of little or of lost meaning. The words themselves are given by Clement of Alexandria (*Strom.* v., c. 46), and he interprets them, though they are so obscure as to baffle the conjectures of philology, as meaning Darkness and Light, the Earth and the Year, the Sun and Truth. They were probably a survival of the old Phrygian *cultus* of the powers of Nature which had existed prior to the introduction of the Greek name of Artemis.' **Ellicott**
'The Ephesian letters, by which incantations and charms were supposed to be produced, were much celebrated. They seem to have consisted of certain combinations of letters or words, which, by being pronounced with certain intonations of voice, were believed to be effectual in expelling diseases, or evil spirits; or which, by being written on parchment and worn, were supposed to operate as amulets, or charms, to guard from evil spirits or from danger.' **Barnes**

around here. The believers do all they can to prevent such tragedies, but, as Abba has a habit of saying, 'Ephesus is an evil place.' Though perhaps not for much longer. Perhaps all these people coming to faith really will make a difference. The rubbish dump is the acceptable place to burn things, but the thought of going there is still off-putting. But then isn't our sin to God? Those children whose lives have been taken there – how that must be abhorrent to God. Burning them, like they are worthless...there is often bad-smelling smoke that wafts over the city when the wind blows in from that side, especially on a hot day. Will he see children's bones in the ash from previous fires? Would they be distinguishable from animal bones? Does he even need to go there?

Miles takes the narrow alleyway now – a short cut – and from here can see the ginormous blaze – it's a couple of miles out of the city and he starts to sprint now. Though darkness has fallen he can see where he's going as the fire is just so bright. As he gets closer, so the bonfire gets bigger, until as he gets near enough to see people's faces he realizes that it's as tall as the highest cypress tree... even the highest house on the slopes, and just as impressive. There are sparks flying, and insects, drawn to the fire, are throwing themselves in, burning out. This is massive – there are so many people here! Way more than were waiting outside the gathering – way more! Miles recognizes neighbours, friends, lads his own age, and they haven't come to gawp and spectate, but they seem to be reverent, moved, as if their hearts are really in this. Faces are glowing in the heat, but it's more than just the heat... It's all that sin going up into the air and evaporating as people renounce their former lives and ways.

There is a constant throwing of dodgy scrolls and tokens onto the fire, and each time the flames leap and roar, zealous to consume them.[63] Even the elements want all this stuff gone. Now Miles notices some of the magicians and astrologers who had stalls and shops at the agora – those who antagonized the believers. This is the night to end all nights. How heaven must be celebrating!

Miles can't see his father, but it doesn't matter. All around the fire people are weeping, with others there to counsel them – people from church, yes, but some Miles doesn't even recognize. Could they be

---

[63] Acts 19:19 – 'Burned them up' – 'The imperfect is graphic, describing them as throwing book after book on the pile'. Vincent's Word Studies. These notes can be found on the Bible Hub page for this verse.

angels? Has the Lord deployed them to help in this mammoth task? 'Out with the old, in with the new,'[64] Imma often says, and Miles wonders what this will do to the spiritual atmosphere of this place that's had such a heaviness, such a gloom over it, for so long. Yes, Ephesus is beautiful and not without wealth, but a joy has been lacking that they know as believers, but don't see elsewhere.

Miles steps up to the fire now though the heat makes it hard to walk towards, and it feels like his skin is burning up. It's hard to keep his eyes open, for the smoke is stinging and the heat so overpowering. It's as if his very eyelashes are alight. But he is determined, and he throws the bag with its contents into the flames, which turn green for a moment then fade, before flickering brightly again. Miles feels clean, like the fire has licked him on the inside. He steps back, aware that his toes have been scorched – will blackened sandals betray those who have been here tonight? It will be more than that though, he's sure: lives changed, renewed. Ephesus will be a good place to live, despite Abba's past pronouncement of it as 'the crime capital of the world'.

Miles looks around him – no one seems to have noticed him or what he has done. He feels glad of this; it gives him time to focus on it, to reflect. He will stay a while longer though, as this is just too phenomenal. People will be talking of it for years, and no doubt it's being gossiped down heaven's corridors even now. Miles edges to the back of the crowd so that those in front of him are blackened silhouettes. As he does this, one outline stands out. It is of a small, shrunken figure, doubled over as if in pain. It is a man, Miles thinks, and he watches as he rocks on his haunches whilst apparently wiping tears from his eyes.

Wildman!

If only others could see this.

Miles moves forwards and crouches next to him. Now the man isn't scary at all.

He looks at Miles and it's obvious this is a new thing for him – having kind human interaction. Miles is conscious that the man smells quite bad, but he's careful not to let it show.

---

[64] "The city of Ephesus purged itself of bad literature by burning magic books and became the depository of sacred literature that made up the canon of the New Testament." *Acts* by Simon J. Kistemaker. Revell, 1991. P. 691.

'I encountered the Lord Jesus himself,' the once wild man says, and they sit in the silence, side by side for a while. 'I've nothing to burn but myself, and this city would be good rid of me, but the Lord tells me he values me,' he says crying.

'Of course he does,' says Miles.

'You might know me, or think you know me. You probably don't recognize me, but I'm the one everyone has been frightened of for so long.'

Miles nods at him, then casts his gaze at the floor.

'A man came to see me today. He tried to deliver me like all the rest. I shouted at him, lashed out and sent him on his way, but something he said lodged inside of me. He said I could be free, my life could be different, and all I had to do was invite Jesus in.'

'Oh,' says Miles, speechless really, watching a spark as it turns in a crazy circle, then dives to the floor.

'So I spoke to Jesus. And then it all happened! I don't know where he came from, but he was standing right next to me in my house. "Peace," he said. He explained everything and asked if I'd like to be set free. "Of course," I said. He explained how the man who'd come earlier was a servant of his, sent *by* him, unlike that group of seven men who'd come in recent days, who he didn't know. He asked me to get to know the man who came earlier, said that I owe him an apology. Of course, he's right. He said he's very fond of that family, you know. And I think, very strangely, that he's fond of me.'

Miles is keen to find Paul the next morning and tell him about everything. He'd expected to see him at the bonfire, though so many people were there that it would have been easy to miss him. Abba had seemed quite dismissive when he'd mentioned it to him: 'Oh, he was probably busy at the workshop,' and 'You'll see him later in the week, I am sure.' But he needs to hear Paul's take on what had happened – after all, they'd been praying for revival for so long, it was what they'd been craving for.

School is starting late today and so Miles slips out of the yard while Abba is on the roof with Phelix, helping him with his arithmetic from what he can make out. Good – that'll keep them occupied for quite some time! Abba seems quite distracted this morning, anyway... perhaps a little embarrassed? And with good reason. Imma is already out visiting a woman in labour, and Miles might not get another chance to disappear today, no questions asked.

Last night's bonfire reaches him from the back gate; he could smell it while they ate their bread and figs together this morning, but now he's on the road somehow it's even stronger; Ephesus is known for being a windy place, full of smells blowing in from every direction, but for once there's an aroma of triumph being blown in from the waste dump. Miles feels his stomach turn, like it's still empty, but it's not. The place is different now, for the better, yet he's nervous in a way he can't even begin to explain.

He has much to think on as he makes his way across town, and so it comes as a surprise to him when he finds himself in the agora, and as even more of a surprise when he finds the shop is closed. But on his way out he spots Aquila and hollers at him from across the square, before running up to him and standing by his side. Aquila looks like he wasn't expecting to see him and seems preoccupied –

'Shouldn't you be in your lessons?' he asks him, as he adjusts a heavy bag on his shoulder and looks ready to turn.

'We're starting late today. Where's Paul? Why isn't the shop open?'

'I haven't seen him, but he did say something yesterday about how the Spirit is compelling him again. He was talking about going to Macedonia and Achaia before Jerusalem and Rome. That's all I know. He couldn't have meant he was leaving this soon, though.'

Miles hopes not. Why is he always so restless? Why can't he just settle down and let the Lord use him here? Why do some people think belonging to a community second best?

'Will you tell him I'm looking for him – when you see him?' Miles asks him.

'Of course. Will you tell him that *I'm* looking for him if you see him first!'

The day rumbles on with no news – why should there be? – when at supper time the rumours start. 'He's been arrested,'[65] comes the message. 'You can't trust anything Demetrius says,' Imma tells him, adding 'he always looks smug.' Miles tries not to think about it, but for as many people were delighted by that bonfire, there were twice as many who were angered. As the days pass certainty increases that

---

[65] N. T. Wright, among many other commentators, is adamant that Paul spent time in prison in Ephesus. It is thought this would have been after the bonfire or the riot. Wright believes Paul was 'put on trial for his life' there and that all the prison letters were written from a cell in Ephesus. Read chapter 10 of *Paul: a Biography* for the full discussion.

Paul is in fact still in Ephesus… in prison. Miles is told to stay away from the tower in the wall.[66] He imagines Paul pressing his head flush against the stone wall for a view of the harbour, and planning his next trip away as soon as he's allowed out. What is there to hold him here now? It seems the church is shrinking as fast as it had grown, and a nervousness has crept in, with adult believers wondering if they might 'be next', or if their businesses might be boycotted, or some dreadful rumour will be started about them. Don't they need to get over themselves? Miles' faith isn't dependent on anyone other than Jesus, though. It's disappointing that God has allowed this, but he is God after all, and Paul is big enough to look after himself. It's about time for him to stop looking to heroes, and to become his own best example. When will they notice the change in him at home? That's where it all is to start.

---

[66] Local tradition locates the prison in the wall itself: 'On Bülbül Dağı, the wall follows the natural features of the hill, and runs down toward the west, ending by the so-called Prison St. Paul. The tower, with its double-storied guard stations, played an important role in the defense of the city, the protection of the harbor, and general communications.' https://www.acetestravel.com/Ephesus-City-Walls-andGates.html#:~:text=When%20Lysimachos%2C%20one%20of%20the,erected%20the%20massive%20city%20wall See also https://www.bible-history.com/maps/romanempire/Ephesus.html

Chapter Four

Two years later...
Gilda is at the loom, more as a distraction than anything, for she doesn't have to do this work. But the occasional creak of the wood is rhythmical, as she pushes a new row up with the comb, the weights brushing against her shins. The sound can at least punctuate the discussion, though of course it cannot drown it out. The arguments – for that is what they are – have become tiresome, but Gilda feels glad Bart won't let things go. For he is visiting Uri yet again – he has had more than his fair share of doubts recently – though while he has barely grown in his faith, questioning every tenet and motivation among the believers, she has found Jesus to be trustworthy and only wishes she'd come to faith sooner. She smooths her tunic as she stands, and her still-slim physique reminds her that her new religion hasn't provided her with a child either – but she has learned that God isn't for manipulating, and she can honestly tell you that her life feels fulfilled now, and in ways she wouldn't have expected. She tosses her head and feels the lose curls down her back – so much more freeing than those old intricate plaits that took up so much of her time, along with that prim, ornate appearance that made her feel so constrained.

'Now, Christ as a *shepherd*. Explain this to me again,' says her husband. 'A shepherd of *all* occupations. I don't think I've ever spoken with a shepherd in my life. I certainly haven't sat down and listened to one. Such mysteries and contradictions. Do explain, Bart.'

Uri is more outspoken with her presence obscured by the cloth on the loom, that she peers through, to watch. He is never so expressive of his doubts to her – only in his reluctance to participate fully in the believing community.

'Not your average shepherd,' Bart says with an extended laugh, perhaps to buy himself time to think. 'It's symbolic anyway, for how he tends to his flock: to us.'

'So much shame is associated with your religion,' her husband goes on.

'Think of the order he brings – and the value. There is no lawlessness in Jesus, no chaos, and there is no shame in being a believer,' says Bart. 'It is a chance for us to demonstrate our loyalty to God. Even our boys are experiencing the challenges – no doubt they are facing them even now, for they have set off for their learning already.'

Uri looks into the distance and his eyes lose focus, but Gilda is willing to hear this at least. It doesn't matter anyway, for Bart seems not to have noticed. 'Lads are waving Paul's old scraps of material in their faces, in a mocking way; you know, the bits of material he tied round his head when busy at work making tents in the heat, those offcuts that brought healing.'

'Isn't he back making his tents now?'

'Yes, but people aren't queuing up to see him. Some say it was part of the condition for his release, that he stops evangelizing quite so enthusiastically, but I can't see it. I think he's just wounded, in an emotional sense, and choosing more carefully who he bothers to share with. He's recuperating and no doubt waiting on God for his next instruction – then he'll be off.'

'What was going on back then? Those healings?' says Uri. He always did like to be on the winning side, and these quiet days are a challenge for him.

'They were the Lord's work, for certain. They say it started as an accident. Those were such incredible days, when Ephesus was the place to be, when the Spirit was so at work. But it's God's work, not Paul's – always was. God can put the power into anything he chooses. And it's up to us, his people, to remain faithful when revivals ebb and we don't know what he is doing.' Uri looks unconvinced, and so Bart continues his appeal – 'Isn't life so often more about the slog than the euphoric moments? Isn't it about sustaining our faith – and that of others – when we're not on the mountaintop, but the downward slope, or the uphill climb?'

Uri still looks unsure – what frustration Gilda feels, with him dragging his feet, holding her back from all the radical things she wishes to do. She has had enough, and she can't keep waiting for him to follow as he should. And today she has a plan.

The men don't notice her get up from the loom and head to the upstairs rooms. When she is sure the servants are out of sight, she unwraps a ceramic figurine that she's stored at the bottom of a large trunk in their chamber. Her mother passed it on to her when she married – 'let Artemis bless your home and your womb,' she had said. There is a superstitious part of her that had wanted to keep this, just in case, but what good has it done her in all these years? The great Artemis who had fallen from the skies – *as if*. This is a valuable – a *desirable* – one.[67] She smiles at the irony of that thought, and places it back in its cloth, then brushes the residue from her hands. Uri hadn't noticed it was missing from the alcove – or if he had, he hadn't bothered to mention it – and the urn with dried grasses looks like it has always been there. She *will* dispose of it, she decides, but not without one last visit to the temple.

Gilda makes herself a hood from her woven grey shawl – the least conspicuous one she possesses, and the warmest, for the wind is wild this morning and the sun not yet warm. She is out of the gate at last – the men didn't seem to notice her go – her steps quick and purposeful as she determines to get to the temple as quickly as she can. The ships have only this week started returning to the harbour after the winter months. It has been stormy, unseasonably so, for the port is usually busy again by now. Yet now it is nearly 'The Artemisian', the month in which Artemis is really celebrated… a million people will swell the city in the coming days and weeks, and the bustle is already beginning to build. If she doesn't do this early, she'll be spotted, and no doubt mocked herself. Gilda was once one of the elite group of women who were allowed to prepare the statue, oiling her, cleaning her, draping a garment on her and placing a crown on her head before she was taken through the city on a carriage. At intervals the growing crowd would pause so that sacrifices could happen, and songs and prayers be offered. She had always thought it strange, even as a small child, that there were stones with the words 'Altar of Artemis' along the way. Her mother told her the sacrifices were so that those buried on the route would receive 'immortality'. Now Gilda has Jesus for that, and it feels much better… and real. Even so, in many ways she loved that life – being with the other women, enjoying the sweet-smelling oils that they rubbed into their own hands, experimenting with the drapes on each other – but it was all or nothing with that religion; you were out or you were in.

---

[67] 'The large volume of statues, terracotta lamps and figurines to Aphrodite found by archaeologists is evidence for extensive cultic involvement by people with limited resources, especially women. Women may have created these artifacts on their own or purchased them by craftspeople.' From: https://www.wisdomwordsppf.org/2018/02/23/ancient-corinth-ii-women-st-pauls-time/

Gilda is leaving the city behind now, her gaze drawn to the two streams that supply the temple, banked by high hedges, her feet feeling the wetness seeping through her sandals. In many ways she feels glad the temple sits well outside of the city walls on this marshy ground[68] but it still dominates life – there's no getting away from it. It's why they are 'on the map', why there's so much investment here, so much prosperity, so many visitors. Their lives had been bound up in it from childhood – it's no wonder she's finding it hard to let go of it entirely and feeling the need for this one last visit.

She adjusts the strap of the bag that is cutting into her shoulder. It has been a while... a couple of years, in fact, since she last came out all this way. Word quickly got around the community that she'd become *'one of them'* – no longer was she allowed to prepare the statue, but that was helpful, because she didn't want to. For she saw what the women were really like, and how could she proclaim Jesus if she still partook in all of that 'nonsense', as she now knows it? But putting yourself on the outside of a group is hard, as is letting go of all that you have ever known. Well, most of it – she had never liked the fact that as women they were not allowed entry to the temple. *Criminals* are allowed in, for goodness sake – so much so that their city is the crime capital of the region – but women are not. Why are they even allowed asylum there? It *is* outrageous. Such an inferior religion to Christianity, where women lead when they are the most appropriate person present; she'd heard of them leading house churches in other communities, and Priscilla herself demonstrates strong leadership, heading up the church with her husband when it began here, before it outgrew their home and other demands crept in.[69]

So why is she doing this? She'd rather not ask herself the question, but coming out here, the distinctions between what she has now and what she's left behind are stark. Of course, she wants children. She always has. She had expected that to change – or at least, that her desire would have been fulfilled, when she came to

---

[68] A fact given by Pliny the Elder in XXXVI
[69] It is widely understood that women took active leadership roles in the early church. 'As householders, women, too, could perform leadership roles and possibly even conduct Christian gatherings, serving as patrons or hosts' – See Valeriy A. Alikin's *The Earliest History of the Christian Gathering*, p.70 (2010).

faith, but she owes it to herself to consult Artemis one last time – doesn't she?

She decides to stop thinking now, for the temple is properly in view. Those vast doors – which she's never been allowed through – over ten metres high, those gleaming marble pillars, all one hundred and twenty-seven of them, glowing in the weak winter sunshine. At least not many people are around yet, and she walks right up to the outer walls – no one stops her – to begin her prayer. She can't help but notice the names etched into the walls, the work of new dwellers here, hoping for her protection. At least they don't have to merely hope in Jesus's protection – it is a living, daily reality. But what of Paul? He always was a man of extremes, after all. God has still been looking after him, but he does put himself in the most ridiculous situations. She must talk to Halle about her boys, about how to encourage them to be sensible in their faith. Paul's influence worries her – he is radical and doesn't seem to know how to live quietly. It has been asked of him, but can he do it? It's very unlikely, and only makes being a believer more challenging for the rest of them. No wonder he appears not to have a wife.

The believing lifestyle is radical enough without stirring up trouble.

She has reached the back end of the temple now – she can hear bustle and movement already at the front of the building, where most of the 'worship' takes place. And no doubt she'll be accosted when she emerges into view again…. It will be considered a scandal. A stamping of feet sounds behind her – 'Watch where you are going!' she calls out to the man running past. This always has been an unpleasant aspect of the temple; it is supposedly a 'safe space' for everyone – soldiers en route, refugees, slaves, debtors and worse – she shouldn't judge like this, but there isn't the feeling of a safe haven really, not the sense of peace that she gets from their own meetings, and drawing close to her Lord on her own.

Still, she is here and needs to finish what she has come for. She'd come to talk to Artemis, but she knows now the god is defunct in her life – there's little point. In fact, there is *no* point. 'Artemis, you are a useless waste of space; you've done nothing for me, and I surrender any belief I that I ever had in you.' She blushes – did she really just say that? It doesn't matter, she's not real anyway. 'Lord Jesus, I want to surrender my fertility to you. All this time I've been clinging on to a useless idol and it's brought me no good… perhaps it's even brought me harm. Lord Jesus, you *are* real and I want whatever you have for me. You are worthy of everything – I just want you in my life, to be around you, to talk to you. Lord, I give you my longings and ask that you take them away as you have not fulfilled them. Give me a purpose, something to do for you, something more than just instructing servants, running the home and serving my doubting husband. Thank you that you're not disappointed in me. That my value to you doesn't depend on whether I am physically able to bear children. That you simply love me for who I am.'

The bag on her shoulder feels especially heavy now – she would like to toss the figurine it carries, toss it so far that it shatters on the marble path, but perhaps it wouldn't break. Perhaps someone would find it and piece it back together. But what else can she do? She's not about to go out to the refuse heap, is she? She looks about her – no one is coming – and throws it on the path at her feet, jumping on it to ensure it shatters completely. And it has! Heat rises to her cheeks again and she adjusts her shawl, stopping for a moment just to take in what lies at her feet. She has done it, and she kicks it off the path, feeling a burden lifted from her soul and quite light-headed – she didn't know the feeling of release would be this great. She stops to look back and make sure no aspect of it remains – no hand, no foot, no head – but it is all crushed and she is free to go on.

'Great is Artemis!' comes a shout and she shrinks her head further into her shawl and speeds up now. The moody god seems to have noticed... Could that be it? It's so hard when your culture tells you one thing, but you know you have experienced something else! Then what to believe? She kicks the remaining grit from her sandals and breaks into a run. But this is foolish – no one is shouting at her for what she's done – the voices sound like they are coming from the city, not the temple compound, and no one is on her trail. How can you anger a dead, non-existent god? The important thing is she has pleased the living one, after all. Still, she must get on home now, for it sounds like trouble is brewing and she doesn't want to be caught up in it. Ephesus can be a dangerous place when tempers are running high.

Gilda quickens her pace now, returning at twice the pace she arrived. She is tiring quickly, but there's nothing else for it – as she nears the city it's obvious the place is in turmoil. A group of young men run her off the path, heading to the temple and shouting slogans, like some revolution is underway. She's struggling to catch her breath, as much from the shock as the brisk pace she's adopted. There is smoke rising… it looks like it's coming from the agora… what's been set alight? What on earth is going on? She hopes Priscilla is safe, and her husband, and Paul of course, who is no doubt involved in all this chaos somehow.

She pulls a deeper hood from her scarf, even though she's overheating, and lets her feet carry her along the city streets, which are so crowded that she dare not look up. Where have all these people come from? It's like they've arrived en masse, especially for the purpose, but then the festival is due to start, and perhaps they have brought some antagonism with them. If only she could understand what this is all about. It doesn't take long to form a picture though – she's catching snippets of conversations as people rush past her on either side, shouting, breathing their toxic breath at her –

'Look at this scar,' says one man, waving an arm that knocks Gilda in the face. 'I got this in Ephesus before. I blamed the Christians then. We were doing quite well until Paul was on the scene. My six brothers say they'll never come back here. The youngest is still traumatized.'

'Our economy will never be the same again.'

'Don't you believe it! It's the end for the Way now. Those people've done enough damage to our livelihoods. Now it's our turn…'

'Our city is losing its status, its reputation. Great is Artemis of the Ephesians!'

'Great is Artemis!'

Uri won't be happy when she's home – her getting caught up in this, the further decline in respect for the believers. His approach is so increasingly different from her own. He is so negative about everything imaginable – she used to think they had so much in common, but now she's finding herself at odds with him on everything. *Lord Jesus, would you bless my marriage*, she prays. *Would you reach Uri again* – he won't be pleased when he sees her. How sad it is that he so undervalues her opinion and thinks his own worth so much more than hers! *Show him that you're real, Lord*, she prays. *Show him* –

Gilda stops in her tracks, her sight arrested by the skinny young legs of a lad slumped in a doorway. She looks up and up, to discover a familiar face, and his eyes are wild and wide.

'Miles? Whatever's happened to you?'

'It's just a limp, it's nothing,' he says, getting to his feet. He seems euphoric, as if this thing is actually exciting and he wants to be here. 'I got a bit caught up in the crowd that was surging towards the ampitheatre. I pulled back to stop in a doorway to catch my breath. Why are you out here in this, though? It's not safe for women to be in this environment. Your husband will be worried.' Such a strange mix of maturity and irresponsibility in this lad. And who is he to criticize her and take the lead?

'It was fine when I set out. All this trouble has flared in no time. We both need to get home, Miles. You must walk with me.'

'But I want to go to the ampitheatre now, it's where it's all happening. They've taken Gaius and Aristarchus, dragged them like they are to be fed to the lions. I need to....'

'I don't think so. Your parents would never forgive me if anything more happens to you – not now that I've seen you.'

Miles stands where he is, rooted to the pavement. 'Paul's been locked in the shop! They won't let him out as they say he'll be skinned alive. Can you imagine that? I was almost locked in there with him, but he said to let me go. That it was dangerous for me. Now there's smoke com–'

'Well, I think it's even more dangerous out here. Where are you meant to be? Why aren't you in your lessons?'

'We'd been sent home early. We were told that trouble was afoot and we would be safest at home today.'

'Where's Phelix?'

'Oh, I don't know. He went on home without me. I came here as soon as I'd heard. Followed the noise. What else was there to do?'

'What about your friends?'

'What friends? I'm less popular now I'm outspoken about my faith. It's how it is.'

'Come on then,' says Gilda. 'Let's have no more nonsense. We're going home.'

'I'll come, if only to protect you. I'm coming out again later, you see if I don't.'

And so they walk on in companionable silence, Miles still energized, though his limp seems to be worsening, and she can see that a gash on his forehead is bleeding. 'How did you get that?' she asks, pointing.

'Oh, this? It's nothing – just a graze. There was a bit of a stampede but I'm okay – it's when I hurt my leg. It's Paul I'm worried about, and Gaius and Aristarchus, perhaps more to the point.'

'You know, it doesn't make you any more of a hero, to be out in this, risking your life, getting wounded. Jesus won't think any more of you, and your mother certainly won't.'

'You really don't get it, do you? I'm not trying to be anybody. I'm just out here, living my faith. We're not meant to huddle behind closed doors.'

'On a day like today, there's no shame in it.'

'Oh, really?'

Motherhood is really not just about having babies, ponders Gilda. They grow and have a life and intent of their own... She'd never really thought this far down the line. Surely her own children would be more respectful of her, wouldn't they? Of course they would. There is no question.

Gilda hovers at her neighbours' gate when they reach home. Miles opens it with a steady hand to lessen the drama of their entrance – he looks skilled at this, as if he could open it without it making a sound. She is sweating profusely but feels she must speak to Bart and Halle, assuming they're inside ... But heated debate is going on. Of course it is – why did she even think their discussion would have finished?

As she enters the courtyard her eyes confirm what her ears have already told her – her husband and Bart are still conversing and have not yet acknowledged their arrival. 'This isn't what we prayed for,' says Uri, 'this, this... chaos outside our gates. If that was a move of God a couple of years back, why did he not sustain it?'

'Moves of God are never comfortable.'

'And what is this? A move of God. I hope not.'

'It is true, this upheaval is because our Lord has been at work,' replies Bart. 'There is less interest in the dark 'arts'. But the livelihoods that are struggling are evil ones. So many have heard our message and they have listened. Jesus said that while we are on this earth, we can expect trouble. And even when the spiritual forces are not rattled, we must remember we live on a fallen planet. There was an earthquake here of course, when we were young men.[70] Are we going to take every twist and turn in life and hold God accountable? It is not our place.'

Uri is silent for a moment, then turns his head. 'Gilda, where have you been?' he asks her. 'I didn't know that you'd gone.'

'And you are back too,' says Bart to his son. 'Why are you not in school? And what's happened to you? You're injured!'

'Oh this? It's nothing,' he says, touching just above his brow and trying not to wince. 'I'm fine. School was cancelled because of all the trouble.'

'Well, that was a good decision,' mutters Uri, giving the lad a hard stare.

'I see that you came straight home,' says Bart, with a raised eyebrow. 'And where's Phelix?'

'I thought he'd be home already,' Miles tells him. 'Phelix!' he calls. 'You home?'

'Well, it doesn't look like it. Do you realize what's going on out there? Has it occurred to you just how much danger he's in?'

'It's not that bad – not really, not when you're out in it. And he knows his way home.'

'Under normal circumstances, yes. Miles, can you not see this is terribly irresponsible. This is *Ephesus*, crime capital of the known world! You know how the low life take opportunities like this to surface! You know th–'

'I'll go and look for him now.'

'We'll all go,' says Gilda.

'You stay at home,' Uri tells her. 'We'll find him. Lord Jesus, would you prove yourself today,' he prays out loud and with emphasis, so that everyone hears. Then turning to Gilda, 'It's decision day for us. If the Lord comes good here, we will belong to the believers. But if he can't resolve this – then he's redundant, like you say all the other gods are around here.'

Gilda nods her acceptance, though in her heart she knows no one can ever separate her from her Lord.

---

[70] AD 23 'An earthquake shook the city and caused much damage; reconstruction partly with imperial help.'
https://www.ephesus.us/ephesus/ephesus_chronology.htm

***

'And just where do you think you're going?' says an ugly man with matted hair who lunges at him and grabs a hold of his tunic.

'I'm going home. Right now, home,' says Phelix. 'I know the way, I –'

'That's where you are wrong boy,' he tells him. 'Today the meaning of *home* has changed for you.'

The creature laughs – for that's what he is – and shows a mouthful of broken teeth and a face of unkind wrinkles, like he's been pulling unkind faces for a very long time. He tightens his grip on Phelix, circling his upper arm with his thumb and forefinger, and holding a fistful of his tunic with his other hand. He knees him in the bottom to get him to walk in the direction he has chosen.

Should he shrug his way out of his tunic and run home naked? It seems to be the only option, and Phelix squats then squirms but it does no good, and now the man squeezes his arm with an iron grasp. Surely he'll see someone who recognizes him? He can't do this, can he! Miles would know what to do. 'Help!' he cries, but now the man covers his mouth with his hand. Phelix bites down on it – it tastes of bitter herbs – which is what you'd expect – and of how faeces smell.

'Get off you little bastard,' he shouts, kicking him in the shin from behind. Phelix falls to the ground, and now he's kicking him all over, laying into him like he's a punch bag. 'Get off!' he tells him.

The man drags Phelix across the ground to a horse that's tied to a tree and throws him over its back. Then it all goes dark – he's put something over his face and is tying it at the back of his head. 'I don't want to damage you too much or no one will want to part with much money,' he says. 'That's the point.'

When Abba gets a hold of him he's going to be in so much trouble. What would *he* do now? 'Lord Jesus, help me,' he prays to himself, under his breath.

'Eat this,' he says, stuffing something into Phelix's mouth and holding his jaw shut so he cannot spit it out. 'Now chew. Now swallow. Again,' he says, forcing more of the nasty tasting leaves into his mouth. 'Swallow, boy, swallow. I'm watching!'

Phelix does as he's told. He'll find a way out of this, but now isn't the right moment. At least he'll have an adventure to tell Miles later! Miles has never been abducted. What would Miles do though? What would be his plan? He's going to be brave, just like him. He'll find a way out of this... you see... if he doesn't.

***

The hours pass slowly for Helle and Gilda, each with their own anxiety for the future. Of course, the men wouldn't dare come home without him, but now the light is fading, and the only sounds are of gates slamming in the neighbourhood, of wives shouting that supper is ready, of hungry animals braying and bleating, and of laughter too. They haven't all heard, though perhaps they'd be out hunting for Phelix if they knew. 'Should we tell the neighbours?' Gilda says to Halle. 'I'm sure they'd help search for him. I'll ask Yo-'

'And look where?' says Halle. 'They must have been everywhere by now.'

'Of course, the city is still busy. It's festival time, isn't it? It takes longer to get anywhere with all the tourists slowing down to look at every statue and monument, read every inscription. He'll be home, you see.'

But darkness falls and still the men don't return home. Halle has taken to hysterical crying as she paces the courtyard. Gilda is praying out loud and interceding with the power of heaven and the will of God behind her. Yet time continues to drag on. Neighbours hear the crying and knock on the gate – 'We know something's the matter. Can we help?' Shouts are heard across rooftops, torches are lit and more feet stamp out into the night.

***

No one is going to be able to find Phelix where he is – he feels sure of that. The man has uncovered his face now, and at last he feels able to breathe, though he tries not to take deep breaths – it smells funny – like something is rotting in here. The room they are in is damp and dark. The ground is hard, and Phelix knows he has bruises forming over his entire body, though he can't see them in this light. It hurts to move, so he stays in one position and hopes that if he's very still the man won't notice him again. Some hope. The man has a frightening way about him – jerky movements, and Phelix flinches in the fear he's going to be hit, even though he's sitting on the other side of the room. 'Why would I hit you again, now that I've captured you?' he asks. 'I'm a good man, and only doing my job. We've all got to make a living,' he says. 'You're my property now.'

Phelix says nothing, which seems to rial the man. He can't help it though. No words will come, even when he tries. Instead, he drops his head onto his knees and shuts his eyes.

'Boy,' the man shouts at him. 'Are you listening?'

Phelix nods.

'Then look up.'

Phelix does as he is told and waits for the man to speak.

He says that tomorrow they are going on a long journey, far away from Ephesus. He says that he won't remember this place, and that he won't be coming back. He strikes a stone and sparks fly from the first moment, and then he lights a lamp. He looks even uglier in this light, even more menacing, and Phelix has to turn away.

The tears are coming now, and Phelix finds they are impossible to stop. The man throws an old, dry piece of bread at him that resembles leather. Phelix can't eat. He can't even swallow; he's too frightened now. Why hadn't he stuck close to Miles?

And so the evening wears on. The man leaves the room and shouts occasionally, but not at him anymore. He puts his head around the door at times, and his footsteps are never far away. Now is not the time to run for it, and he can't run anyway, his body hurts too much.

It must be dark outside now – it is inside as the man has blown out the lamp – and just to be sure his property won't be running away, the man ties the cloth back over his eyes. It's damp from the first time, but perhaps at least this means he will be left alone. If he won't be able to sleep, he will have time to think. But more importantly, time to pray, for what good is thinking at a time like this? Abba always used to say, 'worry is meditation on the wrong thing'. He never could understand it before, but now he can. He knows Jesus is here with him in the dark, and, pretending he's at home and settling down to sleep, begins to talk to him. He'll focus on Jesus and his power. He's the same all the time, and right now he really needs him.

***

How bright it is in here, thinks Phelix – it must be morning, but that light is brighter than morning – it's like the sun at midday, and the room is feeling just as warm. There is a movement of air, perhaps like there's an open window – but yesterday there was no window – and

Phelix can sense a gentle flapping movement, as if a giant bird has come to land in the room. Phelix reminds himself of where he is. He's captured and he must be dreaming right now. He bites down on his tongue and that feels real, but so does the light and warmth. Then someone scoops him up – but gently, lovingly, as if aware of his bruises – and takes him out into the cool night air.

'What ar–'

'Shush,' says a voice. 'You don't want to wake anyone!' He can feel a tugging at the cloth on his face, and now he can see again. The kindest face is looking at him, whilst holding a finger to his lips. 'Please don't speak. There's no time for that. Here, climb on my back.'

Phelix does, although he doesn't so much climb as find himself already in place, seated between two giant wings that part envelop him, part flap, and soon they are away. He's not sure if his rescuer is flying or simply taking giant strides, but the wings are definitely helping.

The city ahead of them is dark but the brightness continues to shine, meaning Phelix can see the road in front of them and way off into the distance. Ephesus will be sleeping. There are no lights shining ahead – but then he catches a glimmer through the trees as they draw closer – that must be one of the manned entrances to the city. Won't the gates be locked? Will they simply fly over the top of the city walls? If only Miles could see him now!

A feather brushes against his face and Phelix starts to relax at last. God was watching over him all along, and he had a plan to get him out of there. Imma didn't talk so much about God's protection as Abba, because she said she didn't want her boys 'taking foolish risks' – he'd heard them talking in the courtyard one night when she'd thought they were asleep. 'They're reckless enough as it is!' But she had told him some special words from a Psalm when he was ill once and they were all worried, and he was frightened too. She said 'He will cover you with his feathers. He will shelter you with his wings.' At the time he'd smiled to himself and thought, *trust Imma to like that, she's like a hen herself,* but now it all makes sense. So, are these feathers the Lord's? The motion is soothing and he is very tired. No words have been spoken since the instructions were given, and being quiet in itself is tiring, and soon Phelix rests his head in the downy feathers and is fast asleep.

***

'Phelix! How did you get here? And on the right side of the gate, too, though we hadn't locked it in the hope that you'd be home.'

Phelix looks around for his rescuer but discovers he has gone. He can't remember the last part of the journey – he wanted to savour entering the city like that, see the astonished faces of guards, view his neighbourhood from on high, all safe and protected. It was wild!

'I've been brought home by the kindest being,' he lisps. 'I think he was an angel – or perhaps he was Jesus himself! But then does Jesus have wings? Imma, do you know?'

She doesn't answer but hugs him like he'd been away forever. She seems to enjoy the moment and want him all to herself, before calling out to the household, 'He's home!'

Phelix hugs her back with all his might. Then he's leaping up and down in his usual way, that Miles always tells him off for.

'I thought you'd be red-eyed and snivelling,' she says, 'not excitable like this, as if nothing had happened. Where did you go? Did someone take you? Remember, you've been very fortunate this time,' she goes on. 'It probably has something to do with the fact I've been up praying all night, checking the courtyard repeatedly. I know Uri and Gilda have stayed up to pray through the night too.'

'Uri?' he replies. 'Old Uri!', and he pulls his best Uri face, cheeks puffed out, eyes unblinking in a stern expression.

'You need to know that he's one of your rescuers, even as much as that angel, who was only carrying out the Lord's demands.'

Abba has arrived now, and Miles. They hug him too and take him up to the rooftop with armfuls of blankets, for it's where the best family stories are always told. 'Now, tell us what happened under the stars,' says Miles. 'I don't care if it takes until the sun rises and the stars disappear.'

For once everyone wants to listen to him, and Phelix begins – 'I didn't think it would end this way,' and he stops to pull out a feather that's causing an itch behind his ear.

***

There is an angel watching on who smooths the place from which the feather fell, and though he'd love to watch this little family group, he knows he's late for a meeting that has been called.

'Mission accomplished?' asks their commander as he lands himself at the back of the assembly, discreetly, he'd thought, though apparently not.

'Safely delivered,' he replies before falling in line.

'Good. Sometimes, in extreme circumstances, we need to blow our cover. That child will be bold for the Lord now – almost as bold as his brother. They are both going to need just as much cover as Paul, especially as the years go by. Not quite yet, but just wait. Indeed, life is never going to be dull if you are shielding them.'

Excitement ruffles its way through the ranks as they think about how this pleases the Lord, and of how it's good to be given charges like them.

'Yes, engaging projects the pair of them. Sem, I want you to stay with the young boy, and Markos, stay with Miles. There will be back up for you both when needed.'

They both look up into the night sky, then catch each other's eye.

'Now, Merob, we want you to remain in Ephesus, too. Shortly there'll be a new child in the womb to protect and stay with.'

Merob knows some of the others would despair of an easy project like this, but she loves the little ones and is glad the Lord understands what brings her joy. Her grin is now almost as blinding as her sword.

'What's the bigger picture here, Chief?' asks Barak. 'Is the upheaval going to continue? Is Ephesus slipping back into its old ways?'

'Yes, so why *are* we gathering now?' adds Noe, his wings trembling. 'The boy has been found, we've returned him to his parents.'

'The Lord is deploying more of us around Ephesus. The believers need help. There are many who are new to the faith here and some of the more outspoken ones need special protection, for their time has not yet come… We await the Lord's instruction, any moment, for there will be some regrouping. Paul is entering an even more dangerous phase – he thinks he's getting away from the trouble by leaving, but he's heading straight into the path of more. The doctor will be joining him, but he needs more than human help.[71] A host will be going with him – some are still on their way. Paul and his men will be heavily protected at all times – not just when doing the work itself, but when travelling, sleeping – there's to be no let up.'

---

[71] Luke brings himself back into the Acts narrative in chapter 20, verse 5.

A tall angel with a thoughtful face and long beard steps forward to speak. 'I'm not surprised we've been called on to help from Macedonia.' So that's where he's from. 'The Lord had me talk to Paul once before when he and the brothers were in Troas and we directed them to our location. The believers are expecting him back in Troas. We'd be glad of some extra help there too, whether or not Paul is present.'

'You'll have the help you need, but go on.'

'I've got to look after that dozy Eutychus, and sometimes I could just do with a break – share the load with one or two – you know, his name means "fortunate" but it should really mean is 'rescued from stupidity, on every occasion. ...'. The angels are smiling. 'That's the trouble... these believers can't stop themselves right now. Of course, the message is amazing, the presence of God with them so profound that you can't blame them for their enthusiasm. Why would you? The Lord loves it... It just means we're extra busy. Very little time for reflection,' he says, his fingers smoothing his beard now.

'You could always have a quieter task – some time out? Only things are about to get turbulent wherever you look, and I think you'd regret missing out of the action.'

'Point agreed. I'll stay with him.'

'If you haven't quite worked it out from what I've already said, there are those plotting to kill Paul – not just here in Ephesus but throughout the region. We must be extra vigilant, for it's not his time. The Lord has more purposes for him yet.'

'Well, yes, I'd heard that there's more trouble ahead for Paul,' says Joe. 'I'd anticipated a lull after what he's just been through. Believe me, and he has *no idea* of the demands he places on us. To think that our forces were pitched against him once, and the demons that clung to him. I remember our discussions with the Lord – *You want me to shadow Paul? Are you sure he's one of ours now?*'

The gathering listen to the experienced angels intently, for they are in awe of their service. 'The Lord explained how he really was, and that my duties started before the scales were to fall from his eyes... We'd been protecting people *from* him, and now we were to *guard* him!'

'Yes,' the commander replies, 'I've seen more than a handful welcomed into heaven, banished from earth because of him. But he's got it together now. That's the thing. He knows how unworthy he was – how unworthy he *is*. As do we all of our own selves.'

'They think all this is about Paul, some of them,' says Barak, waving his arm across the ranks. 'They don't realize it's about Jesus. Those sons of Sceva for instance – they want the power but not the source. That really doesn't work.'

'Will they ever be as challenging as Paul, keep us on our toes quite so much?' asks the Macedonian angel. 'He's never one to be put off through fear, whatever the pending consequences.'

'You don't find many like him – not in Ephesus anyway,' says their commander. 'In some ways we should be more grateful, but the kingdom would advance much more quickly if the remaining believers could be a little bolder. If only they knew how we protect them!'

'Of course, right until the Lord deems it their final breath on this earth and calls them home,' says Noe. 'It really would help them if they could view life on our terms.'

'Indeed. Now, Ephesus. When your name is called, you will be the ones remaining here, and, as I'm sure you are aware, others are coming here too to support you. Not everyone will be leaving with Paul. If you are selected to remain here, you will not be disappointed, for this city will be very different before long. Indeed, it will be transformed.' There is a shivering of feathers at this and he waits for them to compose themselves. 'The Lord has permitted me to see what his plans are, and really, you would not believe it is the same place. What happened today – it's the beginning of something... Or a continuation, for you remember that bonfire?'

There is a nodding of angelic heads.

'The Lord doesn't walk away from his plans, he doesn't forget the promises people make, or, of course, that he makes, either. Only sometimes there can be a lull. We know he is never defeated.'

'Tell us how it will look. How will things be different!'

'The temple will be demolished.' He pauses again to allow them to gasp, for they are predictable. 'Future generations looking for evidence will struggle to find it. Their evil practices will cease. They will lose interest in their false gods... frescoes depicting them will be painted over. There will be the trend of marking buildings with crosses – they will be everywhere – on the foreheads of their religious statues.[72] In some ways hardly necessary, but it makes me smile.'

---

[72] New laws "required pagan monuments to be 'cleansed' by carving on them the sign of the cross" (Ladstatter & Pulz, 2007, p 415.).

This smile is infectious and soon everyone is smiling and uttering praise to God.

'You want to know my favourite part?' He doesn't need their affirmation for he's on a roll. 'That statue of Artemis near the library – they will take that down and replace it with a large empty cross. What could be clearer?'[73]

The throng cannot contain their excitement now, despite the formality of the occasion, and the celebrations begin, with somersaults and shouts of praise. They look down on the commander from their lofty heights – he looks exasperated – mildly – but he's never one to stop exuberant worship. It's what they're designed for, after all – that and warfare, of course.

He waits for them to land and catch their breath before going on. 'Now, how we get to that point is going to take serious commitment on your part. I don't need to remind you that the humans would struggle without you. The work here and beyond will continue way beyond Paul's presence on earth. Indeed, it's an unfinished story until the Lord returns.'

Note for the reader: Ephesus as a location perhaps holds more relevance to our own 21st century world than any of the others found in the book of Acts. Believers are in the minority and are aware that their faith is, in many ways, counter-cultural. The strong interest in the occult found in this community results in spiritual clashes, and the Christian community need grace and wisdom as they relate to those around them.

---

[73] *See What Can the Archaeology and History of Ephesus Tell Us About Paul's Ministry There* Deirdre B. Hough p171.

Resources

Alikin, Valeriy A, *The Earliest History of the Christian Gathering*, Brill, 2010.

Bareither, Levi. 'Orphan Care and the Early Church', January 2019.

https://www.storyintl.org/blog/orphan-care-and-the-early-church

Bruce, F. F. *The Church of Jerusalem in the Acts of the Apostles*, *Bulletin of the John Rylands Library* 67 (2):641-661 (1985).

https://www.escholar.manchester.ac.uk/api/datastream?publicationPid=uk-ac-man-scw:1m1650&datastreamId=POST-PEER-REVIEW-PUBLISHERS-DOCUMENT.PDF

Gobry, Pascal-Emmanuel. 'How Christianity Invented Children', The Week.

https://theweek.com/articles/551027/how-christianity-invented-children

Gosbell, Louise. "As long as it's healthy": What can we learn from early Christianity's resistance to infanticide and exposure? https://www.abc.net.au/religion/early-christianitys-resistance-to-infanticide-and-exposure/10898016

Hough, Deidre B. *What Can the Archaeology and History of Ephesus Tell Us About Paul's Ministry There*, Avondale, 2013.

https://core.ac.uk/download/pdf/234108535.pdf

Josephus, Flavius. *The War of the Jews or History of the Destruction of Jerusalem*.

Minucius Felix, Marcus, The Octavius of Minutius Felix. Gale Ecco, Print Editions, 2010.

Vincent, M.R. Vincent's Word Studies on the New Testament. Hendrickson Publishers Inc.,1984

Wight, Fred H. *Manners and Customs of Bible Lands*. Moody Press, 1953.

Wright, Tom. *Paul: A Biography*. SPCK Publishing, 2020.

Inspiration for Lydia: See painting of Miss Eveleen Tennant by Sir John Everrett Millais, 1874. She wears a red dress, several strands of beads, and has a basket on her arm. Though painted in an entirely different era, there was something about her poise and presence that spoke of Lydia to me.

From Minucius Felix, Marcus, The Octavius of Minutius Felix. Gale Ecco, Print Editions, 2010. First published 197AD. This book champions the work of early Christians, touching on the allegations and misunderstandings that abounded then. A fascinating resource from when Christianity was yet young. A few quotes from the book:

'He is invincible, for he is too bright for us to look upon. He is impalpable, for he is too pure for us to touch. He is incomprehensible, for he is beyond our ken, infinite, immense, and his greatness is known to himself alone. Our mind is too limited to understand him; therefore we can only form a just estimate of him, calling him 'inestimable.'

On the gossip about Christians: 'so that they may begin to hate us before they know us.'

'The story of our incestuous banquet is a monstrous lie, invented …to injure us, in order that our reputation for chastity might be sullied by charges of infamous and disgusting practices, and that, before they had learnt the truth, men might be driven to shun us owing to the terror inspired by unutterable suggestions… such practices rather originated amongst people like yourselves.'